'Artless and bootless.' She angrily picked up each branch and leaf and tucked them into the crook of her arm. 'That's what you are. In more ways than one.'

She slid backwards until the slope became flat and then she whirled around. Robert stood a hand's breadth from her. Startled, she stumbled, branches flew, and her body slid against his.

Her world was instantly, aggressively, the smell of hot male and cedar and the feel of sweat-covered skin. Her fingers clawed down the shoulder muscles she'd stared at all day. Her breasts burned…her legs tangled. She teetered and pressed harder for support.

Robert inhaled sharply, as if he'd been dropped into an icy lake. He ripped himself away.

AUTHOR NOTE

There are times in your life when you think you're going to have one experience and you have a completely different one. This is what happened to me when I toured castles in Wales.

Now, I knew I'd be excited and awed, and that my imagination would run wild. They *are* castles, after all. What I didn't plan on was the unerring sense of story, of the people who lived during that time. I didn't have to close my eyes and pretend, and I didn't have to squint to force my eyes to see. They were all simply *there*.

Robert, an English knight, was there. Hunched and grieving under a tree. His broad back and bared arms were a testament to the times and to his training—and to a man used to war. But his grief came from something else…from loss, from hope forsaken.

I could do nothing for him. But I knew he couldn't stay where he was and I knew there had to be someone for him.

And there *is* someone…in Scotland…in 1296… on the cusp of the greatest conflict. But Gaira of Clan Colquhoun laughs at conflict—in fact she curses at it all the time. And when she meets Robert she curses at him, too.

THE KNIGHT'S
BROKEN PROMISE

Nicole Locke

First published in Great Britain 2015
by Mills & Boon, an imprint of Harlequin (UK) Limited,
Large Print edition 2015
Harlequin (UK) Limited, Eton House, 18-24 Paradise Road,
Richmond, Surrey TW9 1SR

© 2015 Nicole Locke

ISBN: 978-0-263-25551-5

Nicole Locke discovered her first romance novels in her grandmother's closet, where they were secretly hidden. Convinced that books hidden must be better than those that weren't, Nicole greedily read them. It was only natural for her to start writing them (but now not so secretly). She lives in London with her two children and her husband—her happily-ever-after.

THE KNIGHT'S BROKEN PROMISE is Nicole Locke's dramatic debut novel for Mills & Boon® Historical Romance

To Mom.

Chapter One

Scotland—April 1296

'Faster, you courageous, knock-kneed, light-footed bag of bones!' Gaira of Clan Colquhoun hugged lower on the stolen horse.

How much time did she have before her betrothed or her brothers realised in which direction she had fled? Two days, maybe three? Barely enough time to get to the safety of her sister's home.

She couldn't push the horse any faster. Already its flanks held a film of sweat and its breath came in heavy pants with each rapid pound of its hooves. Each breath she took matched the same frantic rhythm.

There it was! Just up the last hill and she would be safe. Safe. And there would be food, rest and the vast warmth of her sister's comfort and counsel.

She turned her head. There was no sign of pursuit. Her heart released its fierce grip and she eased up on the reins.

'We made it. Just a bit more and you can eat every last grain I can beg from Irvette.'

She smelled the fire before she crested the hill. The stench was a mixture of blackened smoke, heat, dried grass and rotting cow. The horse sidestepped and flicked its head, but she kept its nose forward until she reached the top.

Then she saw the horror in the valley below. Reeling, she fell upon the horse's neck and slid down the saddle. Her left ankle twisted underneath her as it took the brunt of her descent. She didn't feel the pain as she heaved her breakfast of oatcakes and water.

When she was emptied, she felt dry dirt under her hands, crunching grass under her knees. Her horse was no longer by her side.

She stood, took a deep breath and coughed. It wasn't rotting cow she smelled, but burnt hair and charred human flesh.

The stench was all that remained of her sister's village. The many crofters' huts resembled giant empty and blackened ribcages. There were no roofs, no sides, just burnt frames glowing with the fire still consuming them.

The entire valley looked as if a huge flaming boulder had crashed through the kindling-like huts.

Large twisted and gnarled swirls of black heat and smoke rose and faded into the morning sky.

She could no longer hear anything. There were no birds chirping, no rustling of tall grass or trees and no buzzing insects. All of Scotland's sounds were sucked out of the air.

Her heart and lungs collapsed. Irvette. Her sister. Maybe she wasn't down there. She wouldn't think. Pushing herself forward, she stumbled as her ankle gave way. It would be useless for the sloped descent.

She looked over her shoulder. Her horse skittered at the base of the hill. He was spooked by the heat and smells; she could call, but he would not come.

Bending to her hands and knees, she crawled backward down to the meandering valley. Blasts of heat carried by the wind ruffled up her tunic and hose. She coughed as the smoke curled around her face. When she reached the bottom, she straightened and took off the brown hat upon her head to cover her mouth.

Her eyes scanned the area as she tried to comprehend, tried to understand what she saw. Thatch, planks of wood and furniture were strewn across the path between the huts and so were the villagers: men, women, dogs and children.

Nothing moved.

They were freshly made kills of hacked and

charred bodies. The path was pounded by many horses' hooves, but there weren't any horses or pigs or even chickens.

Dragging her left foot through the ashes behind her, she stumbled through the burning village, which curved with the valley.

At the dead end of the devastation, the last of the crofters' huts stood. More intact than the others, it was still badly scarred by the flames and its roof hung limply with pieces falling to the ground.

Near the doorway, she looked at the two burned and face down bodies of a man and a woman. The man was no more than a husk of burnt flesh with his head severed from his body.

But it was the woman's she recognised: the flame-coloured hair burnt at the tips and the cream-coloured gown smeared with dirt. Blood spread along the gown in varying flows from the two deep sword-thrusts in the stomach. Irvette.

Her world twisted, sharpened. She suddenly heard the popping and hiss of water, the crash of brittle wood splintering into ashy dust and a high keening sound, which increased in volume until she realised the sound came from her.

She stopped, gathered her breath and then she heard it: a whisper, a cry, fragile and high-pitched.

She quickly limped into the hut and weaved before crashing to her knees.

'Snakes and boars,' she whispered. 'Thank God, you're alive.'

Chapter Two

Scotland, on the border with England

Sheets of rain drove down on the battlefield, making mud out of dirt and streams in the dips and cracks of the earth.

Robert of Dent fought on foot. His black surcoat and hose were plastered to his body. His quilted black gambeson, saturated with mud, no longer protected him from the chainmail of his hauberk and chausses. Long hair streamed over his face and shoulders impairing his sight, but it did not matter. The rain provided no visibility. He could no longer see his men, whether they stood or had fallen; he could no longer call out, for the downpour drowned out sounds. All he could hear was the harshness of his own breath.

Rain fell, but blood sprayed the air. It was everywhere: on his clothes, in his hair, streaming through his mouth and beard. His sword from tip to hilt was slick with it and it flowed from his wrists to his shoulders.

He knew his enemy only by the swing of a sword towards him and he thrust upward, sinking his own sword deep through the man's neck. The blade stuck fast and he wrenched it free.

Shoved off balance, he had just enough time to block the fall of an axe. The reverberation of the strike pushed him to his knees and he quickly rolled over spikes of broken arrows to miss his enemy's killing blow. The Scotsman's axe sunk deep into the mud. Still rolling, he sliced his sword across the man's shins. The man fell. He stood and plunged his sword into the Scotsman's chest.

Spitting the mud and blood out of his mouth, he fought, moving forward, trying to keep his balance as he stepped over the dead covering the ground. His boots slipped as he continued to parry and thrust, block and kill.

He emptied himself of everything but the battle. He did not think of glory or survival. He did not count the enemies he felled. He did not think at all. He was muscle and training and sword.

When this battle was done, there would be the removal of the wounded and dead. Then there would be food, drink, sleep and another battle. He knew nothing else, breathed nothing else. His past was forgotten by his will alone.

* * *

Robert stepped through the mud and tangled grass of the battlefield. He could hear the screams of his men, their cries of pain and, worse, the gaping silence from those who could no longer make a sound.

He swallowed his anger. Too much haste had cost them dearly. He was tired, but his men were worse. Since King Edward had rallied more soldiers, the battles were more frequent, more driven. The men had not had enough time to rest between the fights and as a result, he saw men fall today who had no place on the battlefield.

He looked up. Hugh of Shoebury slowly walked an abandoned destrier towards him. Hugh was tall and lean like King Edward, but there the similarities stopped. Hugh was no seasoned ruler, but young with blond hair, blue eyes and skin so white, a touch of the sun burned it red.

'How many?' he asked when Hugh was close enough.

'Too many to count,' Hugh replied, his hand on the shredded bridle of the destrier. 'What are the instructions now?'

'We pull camp and wait for the king's reports from the east.'

'At least we get to rest.'

Robert stopped surveying the field and turned to walk to camp. 'Let us hope for a long reprieve.

There are too many complications with this war we wage.'

'Hardly a war. Balliol hasn't the troops to defend against King Edward's fleet.'

'Since Balliol was crowned, it made sense for us to strengthen the northern defences. I have too many questions why a fleet of our countrymen was sent north as well.'

Hugh shrugged. 'It is not for us to know. And since we followed orders, the king could hardly fault the infamous "Black Robert".'

He ignored Hugh's use of his title. He did not welcome the description of him on even the most favourable of days. This day was not favourable. 'It will take several weeks to recover.'

'Aye, but he will be pleased at what we accomplished today. Even what happened up north could not weaken his resolve.'

'What do you mean, "what happened up north"?'

'You did not hear? There's a small village, Doonhill, tucked into a valley just northwest of Dumfries. A faction of men, under Sir Howe, went there when it appeared we would not be victorious.'

'Howe purposefully pulled his troops when the battle was not yet over?' He quickened his stride. 'That could have cost us victory!'

'Aye, but Sir Howe said he had to retreat or all of them would have died.'

The story was sounding familiar. 'Howe? Is he the one who commanded and pulled the destriers at Lockerbie?'

'The very same.' Hugh coughed into his hand.

'So the bastard thought he could do it twice?' His jaw tightened. 'What happened at Doonhill?'

'It was a small village, but apparently had many women.'

He did not need to hear any more. He was not naive and knew rapine happened as a result of war. Indeed, many men thought it was their due.

'What did the king do for the women?'

'Nothing.'

He stopped and turned his entire focus on Hugh. They had almost reached the camp and he wanted to finish this conversation in private. 'What do you mean, "nothing"?'

'There could be no repairs. The king said he'd be sending a message to Balliol about the incident in case there were repercussions.'

'Why would there be consequences? Why does he not pay the men of Doonhill as he has done in the past?'

'There are no men, Robert, or women, or children to pay,' Hugh spoke slowly. 'Our men destroyed the entire village.'

His head and body filled with anger and disbelief.

Even to his own ears, when he spoke, he sounded distant. 'How is that possible?'

'It is the risk of war.' Hugh's horse yanked impatiently at his bit. 'Pray excuse, I need to get this horse to rest and food.'

He shook off the hesitation he felt in following Hugh. Long ago he had stopped looking to correct the past and the destruction of the village could not be undone. Dismissing his thoughts, he patted Hugh on the back. 'I will come. I find I must be more hungry and tired than I thought.'

Robert crested the hill. He still did not know what had compelled him to come. Hugh hadn't been pleased he travelled alone in enemy territory. But it wasn't logical for others to make the journey. Now that he saw the valley, it seemed meaningless.

The day ended, but the impending darkness did not dim the devastation. It was worse than his dream. Howe would have to pay for what he'd done.

His horse impatiently tossed his head and he tightened the hold on the reins. It would never make a good war horse. What good was a horse if a few smells made it shy? And there were smells. The valley was steeped in death.

Dismounting, he walked down. The stench of decaying bodies and burnt wood accosted his nose. He breathed through his mouth and stopped.

There were no bodies. He could smell them, he had been in Edward's wars too long to mistake the smell, but they were not strewn along with the furniture or broken pots. He quickened his pace.

Close to the lake, he came across a large plot of freshly tilled land. It was a garden. The stench was so strong now he wished he didn't have to breathe at all.

There were fresh, shallow graves mixed with patches of burnt vegetable stalks. The bodies were laid close together and there was a long scrape made in the dirt between the bodies and the garden. The bodies had been dragged to their resting place.

It was a gravesite and a gravesite meant survivors burying their dead. There were footprints, too, but it looked as if they were the same size and at least one foot dragged.

He scanned the surrounding area again, but he could hear nothing. Everything was still.

Was one man trying to bury many? He wondered why anyone would bother. There was nothing left in the village to save, no way of healing and rebuilding after the destruction Howe's men had caused.

Knowing he was not alone, he unsheathed his sword. Keeping his weapon low and at his side, he carefully walked towards the lake.

Then he heard it: a scrape, quick and loud, coming from one of the partially burnt huts.

Wanting to make sure his words were heard, he waited until he was closer. 'I come in peace!' he said in English and again in Gaelic. 'Please, I mean you no harm.'

Another scrape—it sounded like metal. There was someone definitely inside the hut.

'I offer help.' He tried to make his words as convincing as he could. Whoever was in there, they could not have warm hospitality on their minds.

Approaching the open doorway, he raised his sword to hip level. He would rather have waited until whoever was in the hut had come out, but the person inside could be injured and needing his help.

Setting his shoulder in first, he entered the hut. The moon's light slashed through the burnt roof. The one room was small, square, but he could see little else. There was no time to avoid the small iron cauldron swinging towards his head.

Chapter Three

'Oh, cat's whiskers around a mouse's throat, I've killed him!'

Gaira stopped the still-swinging cauldron and swallowed the sharp bile rising in her throat. With shaking knees, she knelt beside the man. Slowly, so slowly, she lowered her hand to his mouth and felt hot breath against the back of her hand. He breathed!

Her heart swiftly rose. Dizzy, she closed her eyes and drew in a steadying breath. When she was sure she could, she opened her eyes to inspect him.

He was a large man, not taller than any Scotsman, but maybe thicker, and his chest was so broad it was surely carved from the side of mountains. She could not discern his face in the moonlight, but she could see his hair was long, wild and he had let his beard grow unkempt.

His hair and beard puzzled her, for it was very un-English and this man grew his as if he were the lowliest of serfs with no comb. But an English serf would not be this far north and all alone.

Carefully, she felt along his sides for a pouch or weapons. He smelled of cedar, leather and open air. Only the fine, soft weave of his clothing gave beneath her fingers. His body, warm through his tunic, was hard, unforgiving. She frowned at the fanciful word. A body could not be unforgiving.

Feeling along his front, her palms suddenly dampened, tingled, and she stopped at his hips. She wanted to continue her exploring, but she realised it wasn't to find weapons.

What was wrong with her? She had three older brothers. This man could be no different. *But he feels different.* She squashed that thought. Foolishness again. If her hands felt strange or hot, it was because she was scared he'd awaken. Aye. Plain nervousness was all she felt.

Willing her hands to obey, she moved them around his waist. Did his breathing change? No. His eyes were still closed. Taking a steadying breath, she felt the flat ripples of his waist, the knot of his hip bones. She stilled her breathing as she slid her hands down each bulging cord of his legs. At a strap near his boots she felt the hard hilt of a dagger. Pulling it out, she felt the weight and heavily carved decoration on the handle.

'Nae a peasant, are you?' Setting the dagger aside, she felt along his broad arms and immediately felt the cold steel of an unsheathed sword at his side. Her skin prickled with anger.

'Even if you hadn't spoken, I'd know you're English for the liar you are. Peace! Hah! What man comes in peace when his sword is drawn?'

With trembling fingers she unwrapped his fingers from his sword. Wobbling at its weight, she set it on the other side of the room and grabbed the rope hanging at her waist. It wasn't long enough to tie his hands and feet, but it was mostly his hands she was worried about.

Her heart thumped hard against her chest. She was worried about other parts of him, too. She was not so naive to think this man was safe. His muscled body, his ability to speak English and Gaelic, were testament to a soldier's training.

Without a doubt, he would have a foul temper when he woke. But what choice did she have? She had hid in the hut. It wasn't her fault the brastling man had entered. She'd had to swing the cauldron and protect herself.

But now what? He was sure to awaken soon. He was English, but she didn't know if he'd burned the village. She couldn't take any chances. It wasn't just her own life she had to worry about.

'Think, Gaira, think!' She had his weapons. They

might give her some control. Quickly finishing the knot, she scrambled back into the scant shadows to wait.

'What do you mean she's not at her brother's?' Busby of Ayrshire spat on the ground. The glob hit square in the centre of the old leather shoe worn by his messenger.

'She's not on Colquhoun lands, my laird,' the messenger stuttered. 'Her brothers were most surprised to see me.'

Busby rubbed his meaty hands down the front of his rough brown tunic. The only satisfaction in this bit of news? His cowering messenger was afraid. He liked it when they were afraid.

'Did you explain to that whoreson Bram if he dinna produce his sister to me within a sennight, our bargain was off?'

'Aye. We were given leave to search the castle.'

Busby took a step forward. 'Did you tell them for this bit of inconvenience, I demand the further compensation of five sheep? And I wouldn't have taken her had I known she was so bothersome? And if they want war between our clans they'll have it?'

'Aye, my laird.' The messenger bent his body to look up. 'I told them all, every bit of it. It dinna make nae difference. We searched everywhere and there was nae sign of her.'

The wench had been missing for three days while he waited for the messenger to bring her back or bring him news. The fact he had neither fuelled his fury.

'Tell me their response,' Busby demanded.

The messenger shifted his feet and almost imperceptibly took a step back. 'They were not pleased.'

'What. Do. You. Mean?'

The messenger took a full step back. Busby let him. It did not matter. The messenger was still within his reach.

'They were most displeased. I, er, feared for my life. They said something about losing their sister and, if anything should happen to her, it's on your head.'

'*What*?' he roared, and clenched one hand around the man's thin neck.

A croaking sound escaped the man's mouth and Busby eased his grip. 'They told me they'd search the area from here to Campbell land first, but you should go south.'

He released the man, who scrambled back. 'Go south? What for?'

'There's a younger sister,' the messenger wheezed. 'Married and living in Doonhill.'

'That is days south of here! Prepare my horse. I'll not be wasting any more time.'

The messenger started to shake. 'Which horse for you, my laird?'

'What do you mean which one? *My* horse, you knapweed. 'T is the only good horse in this wreck of a land!'

The messenger gnawed the inside of his cheek. 'She took it.'

'She *what*!'

'Took it,' he stuttered. ''Tis also missing.'

Busby took a ferocious step forward. He desperately wanted to wrap his hands again on the messenger's throat and squeeze until he could release some of the raging frustration he felt, but instead, he turned his anger inward, let it cool. Only one person deserved his full wrath and he had every intention of delivering it to Gaira of Clan Colquhoun.

Pain throbbing through his temple woke Robert from blackness. He opened his eyes and saw shafts of moonlight through wisps of a burnt roof. He started to sit up.

'Move too fast, English dede-doer, and I'll throw this dagger at your loopie nobill part!'

He stilled. The voice came from the corner of the hut. A woman took a step forward.

Highlighted from the moon above her, she stood dressed in a tunic and leggings too large even for her tall and thin frame. Her hair was plaited in sections and swung like tiny ropes over her breasts. Her stance was wide-legged and crouched and she waved a dagger in front of her. He peered closer. His dagger.

'You threw a cauldron at me,' he accused in Gaelic.

'Swung it, more like, and I reckon you deserve a lot more than that! You had your sword drawn and you stink like an English knight.'

Moving his arms, he felt the ties of rope around his wrists, but his legs were free and, using them as leverage, he sat up. The grip on her dagger tightened and he moved slower. He knew from his battles that those afraid were just as dangerous as those angry. From the pain ringing in his head, he knew she was both.

'The hut was dark. It would have been foolish not to have my sword drawn.'

'That's supposed to make me feel better?' she scoffed.

The conversation was not going well.

She was angry, a Scot and a woman. He was English and in a Scottish village that Englishmen had massacred. She held a dagger and his wrists were tied. The odds were not in his favour.

As far as he could tell, it was only she and he, and she could not make him stay on the floor for ever. But if she was a villager, how had she survived?

'I mean you nae harm,' he continued in Gaelic. 'What do you do here?'

'Now, that should be a question I should be asking you.'

'I am but a traveller.'

'An English one despite your trying to use our language you're mangling,' she pointed out. 'What is your name?' she asked in English.

She spoke the King's English. If she was a villager, she was no simple one. 'I'm called Robert of Dent and there's hardly a crime to being English.'

'There is when we stand in a village where my kin were killed.'

She straightened; the dagger did not waver. His hands were still tied, although he was fast loosening the rope. 'I have just recently come. I had no play in this. What do they call you?'

She ignored his question. 'How am I to know you had nae hand in their deaths?'

He was surprised by her response. 'So are you not one of the villagers?'

Even in the dim light, he could see her features pale, then darken with anger. 'Nae, you weedy outwale! How'm I to be a villager? I'm alive, I am.' She stopped. Tears sparkled, when she continued, 'You must have seen what happened to the villagers when you passed this way.'

He didn't understand. 'You escaped.'

'Nae, I'm a traveller, too, and came too late.'

Her reply was too careful and his wrists were now free. 'You are more than a traveller, you said you had kin here,' he replied. 'Did your kin perish?'

Her body jerked at his question. 'You just be passing by?' she asked.

She ignored his question. Given their surroundings she had a right to be suspicious of him.

'Aye,' he lied.

'Hah! You with a sword drawn and a fine dagger, I'm to believe you?'

He could tell this wouldn't be easy. 'Pray—'

Running footsteps behind them!

'Auntie Gaira, there's a horse at the top of the hill. Auntie Gaira, it smells and I can't see anything. Are you all right? I've come to warn you!'

The woman's attention flew to the door. It was all the diversion he needed. Dropping the rope, he sprang to his feet and caught the boy entering the hut.

'Put him down!' she shouted. 'He's done nothing to you! Put him down, I say!'

The boy, absorbing the woman's panic, wriggled and fought in earnest. Robert grunted when sharp teeth chomped into his side. Yanking the boy free, he held him out in front of him. 'Seems I've got something of yours.'

'He's innocent, I tell you.'

'He may be, but it seems we're even now. You've got the dagger, but I've got your boy. I'll guess you'll not throw that dagger any time now.'

The woman looked defiant and he tensed, ready to dodge if the dagger flew. Regardless of what he said, he had no intention of the boy getting hurt.

She threw the dagger at his feet. 'You may do what you wish of me, but I beg you to leave the boy be. He has seen enough.'

He took the dagger and the boy flew into the woman's arms. The darkness would not allow him to discern her features, but he sensed her relief and something else.

'Can the boy leave the hut before we begin?' she asked.

Her voice was uneasy. It was so different from before that he didn't comprehend her words, but then he understood. She thought he'd rape her. What horrors had she known before he arrived? He'd been here only moments, but seen charred ruins and shallow graves.

It had been two days since the attack. From the rancid smell, he knew some had died of sword wounds, but many more had been burned. She'd been here longer than him and seen too many horrors.

'I'll not be harming you or the boy. I may be English, but I meant it when I said I came in peace.'

'We are beyond your peace.'

Guilt. An inconvenient feeling along with his need to protect, but he suddenly felt both. It had to be the woman.

Her arms were around the child. She was vulnerable, yet she still challenged him. She was brave, but through the filtered moonlight, he could see the exhaustion in her limbs and hear the grief in her voice.

He lowered his eyes. Her ankle was crudely wrapped and didn't hide the swelling. It was her feet he had seen in the tracks. Only hers.

'I passed by your...garden. Are you the one doing the bedding for the spring?'

Instead of answering, she fell to a crouch and tried to turn the boy to face her. 'Alec, please go up to the camp.'

The boy wrenched his head to keep his wary eyes on him. 'Doona want to.'

'Alec, you be listening to me on this. You know I forbade you from coming to the valley. You disobeyed me. But I'll be letting any punishment go if you leave now.'

The boy didn't move.

Her tone softened. 'Alec, if you go right now I'll give you my last honeycomb.'

The boy looked at her, his face scrunched up. She nodded vigorously at him. With barely a glance back, he ran out of the hut.

As the boy's footsteps faded, the woman slowly straightened.

'My life for a sweet. Ah, to be five again,' she said wistfully. She smiled and grasped her hands in front of her. 'I fear we had a misunderstanding. I'm Gaira of Clan Colquhoun.'

He wondered where her anger and defiance had gone. Her stance, the very air around her, had changed. He was suddenly suspicious. 'Your manner has changed.'

'Aye, you may be English, but you are different than the men who burned Doonhill.'

This woman made no sense. 'Aye, I am, but how do you suddenly know?'

'Gardening?' she said, looking at him in exasperation.

He was thoroughly confused. Did she want to speak of plants?

'You did not ask if it was I burying the dead. You asked whether I had been gardening. Any man not wishing to hurt the feelings of a child cannot be the same as the monsters who destroyed this village.' As she turned her back to him and bent down, the large tunic fell forward and exposed her stretched backside under the tight leggings.

All thoughts left his head. He knew the moonlight played tricks on him; knew his thoughts were filling in what his eyes couldn't possibly be seeing. But still his mouth turned dry. The fine strong curve of her legs seemed to stretch to heaven and her derrière was round, full, lush and entirely too... there.

All these years without a woman and he had never been tempted. They had pressed against him, flashed their breasts, licked their lips and he hadn't felt a flicker of emotion except annoyance. But this woman's backside, wrapped tight in a man's leggings, struck him across the loins with heat. He felt the rush, the quickening, and forcibly focused at the object in her hands.

It was a sword and pointed towards him.

'I thank you,' she said, her tone still polite. 'I have been trying to protect him from what really happened to the people here.'

She cleared her throat. Paused. She was waiting for his response.

It wasn't just any sword. It was his sword. Embarrassment doused his lust. What would Edward think of his soldier now? The sword flexed slightly as she wiggled the hilt.

It would be so easy to take the blade from her. Her balance was off and the sword was too heavy for her. She was no threat.

But he was a threat to her. 'What are you doing?'

'I'm pointing a weapon at you, that's what I'm doing.'

'I thought you said I wasn't a monster.'

'Aye, I said you weren't the same as the monsters who burnt this village. But you're still English. I can't trust you.' She nodded her head. 'Kick that rope and dagger to me. I'll be using them again.'

Concentrating on his movements, rather than his thoughts on what she looked like, Robert slowly kicked the dagger and rope to her.

'I'm awake this time and you're all alone,' he said. 'Why would I hold still so I can't protect myself?'

She didn't take her eyes off him. 'To prove you aren't one of the monsters.'

He paused. He knew there was a woman and a boy. He didn't know if there were any other survivors.

'It didn't hold me before,' he pointed out.

'I'll not be making that same mistake twice.'

'And my sword?'

'I'll be keeping it, as well as your dagger.'

He fought the instinct to fight back. She was Scottish, but a woman and she had Alec to protect. She was vulnerable enough without him adding to her fears. Still, too, he needed more answers and she wouldn't be talking if he was a threat. But if she tied him more tightly, he would be defenceless.

He held his clasped hands in front.

She shook her head. 'Behind you and turn around.'

'I'll need to relieve myself.'

He could feel her weighing his words before she nodded and placed the sword down.

'For an Englishman, you're right, you know.' She slowly walked to him.

He didn't feel right as he held still for her to bind him again. 'About what?'

With more twists around his hands, she wrapped the rope around his wrists. She tied more securely this time, but he didn't clasp his hands tightly and would still be able to loosen the rope. It was dark and she didn't notice.

'I've been burying the dead,' she said, stepping away from him. 'But only at night and my ankle slows me too much.'

He turned around and saw her picking up his sword and dagger. The angle wasn't the same as before, but his memory was still too fresh and her legs were still too long...and shapely.

'Why at night?' He cleared his hoarse voice.

'I'm trying to hide what I do,' she answered.

He thought of the boy running past the gravesite. Even at such a tender age, he had to have known what she was doing. 'You have more to bury.'

'Aye. I'm afraid the smell is getting so bad I can hardly do it any more.' Her eyes filled with tears. 'But I won't leave Doonhill till it's done.'

He ignored the conviction in her voice. He had

come only to get some answers and report to Edward. Not help her bury her kin.

She pointed towards the door and he turned to leave the hut. Keeping her distance and his sword, she followed afterwards. She held it over her shoulder to support the weight. Robert honed his blade so it could slice full-grown trees. Her neck was no barrier and her ankle made her clumsy.

'Take my scabbard,' he offered.

'It won't fit around my waist.'

He stopped. 'Hold the sword like you are, just put it in my scabbard.'

She gave him a look he did not understand, but she did as he asked. After placing the sheathed sword back on her shoulder, they continued walking.

Why he wanted to save her neck, he did not know. 'Your name's Gaira?' he asked instead.

She stiffened. 'Why do you ask?'

'I thought *Gaira* meant—'

'Short,' she interrupted. The tension in her shoulders eased. 'It does. I think my ma had hopes I wouldn't end up like my brothers.'

She had brothers. Were they the ones killed here or were they camped nearby? He had no intention of being strung up by some Scotsmen.

'Is the boy safe where he is?' he asked.

'Aye, we have seen nae one for almost a week and the camp is somewhat hidden by the forest. He'll

stay there till I return. He has been too frightened
to disobey.' She stopped, shrugged her shoulders.
'Or maybe too busy eating honeycomb. Do you have
a camp?'

'No, I just arrived.'

'Will there be other Englishmen?'

'Shouldn't you have asked that question before
you kidnapped me and walked me to your camp?'

She laughed, but it was the sound of panic and
she quickly silenced it.

Not for the first time, he wondered at his acqui-
escence, but for the first time, he was apprehensive.

She had not revealed if there were others, but he
was fairly sure there were not. It had been only her
footsteps in the dirt. Still, he could not be certain.

He knew he could protect himself from one Scots-
woman, albeit one mercurial in nature. But he could
not control the consequences if there were others.
He would not shed any more blood here. She might
have tied him up and taken his sword, but he still
knew how to fight. If there were more, he needed
to leave. 'Give pardon, but I fear—'

'Ach, I won't have you afeared. You'll stay where
I stay. And I'll not be biting you. You're too hairy
for that.'

He blinked, not understanding the direction of

her thoughts, until he remembered his overgrown beard and long hair. Hairy. Something rumbled inside him. Laughter. She had almost made him laugh.

Chapter Four

Gaira kept glancing over her shoulder at the stranger who quietly followed her. No, not quiet. Contemplative. Dark. He was dark like the bottom of a turbulent river. This man, though seemingly tranquil, was as forceful and powerful under his surface as any Scottish river. It made her nervous that he hid it.

He hadn't said a word since he'd retrieved his horse. Now he walked behind her with the huge horse in tow. She had his dagger and sword, but the horse was laden with a larger sword, blankets and two pouches, one she was sure jangled with coins. He was quiet, but she could almost feel his thoughts. She tried to stop biting her lip.

She had invited a stranger to the camp. An English soldier, who talked of peace but walked with his sword drawn and carried more weapons on his horse. But she had to invite him. What else could she do?

If he truly meant her harm, all he had to do was follow her to camp and catch her unawares. It was best to keep him tied and close. But close did not mean stupid and she had some talking to do first.

She whirled around to face him. He stopped just as suddenly and looked at her expectantly.

Robert watched the woman staring at him. In less than an hour she had displayed several emotions: bravery, fear, gentleness, affection and humour. Now a myriad of expressions were crossing her face, the dominant one being determination. She clearly wanted to tell him something, but didn't know how to say it. He felt the heady rush of anticipation. It had been a long time since anyone had intrigued him.

But then he saw them.

Behind her was a crude camp. A fire blazed around a steaming cauldron. The fire was strong and the moon was full. Both provided enough illumination. The night's light was not playing tricks with his sight.

'Who are they?' he asked.

Her eyes, so expressive before, became shuttered. Her only movement was the almost imperceptible tensing of her shoulders, the slight raising of her chin. 'You'll not be harming them, you ken?' She kept her voice low. 'If you do, I'll be taking away more than one sword of yours.'

'Who are they?' he repeated.

She did not answer him, but kept her eyes unwaveringly on him.

As if pulled forward, he walked past Gaira to face four children who emerged out of the trees. They lined up like soldiers for battle. Gaira hurriedly passed him and stood behind the tallest girl.

The image hit him. These children were not lined up like soldiers for battle, but for inspection. His inspection. Gaira did not stand between them to protect them, but behind them as if to point out their merit.

He couldn't speak.

She brought the children close to her, whispered low, but she did not take her eyes off him.

'Children, this is Robert from Dent and he is English.' She stood and raised her voice. 'I do not believe he means us harm so I asked him to our camp this eve.'

He could sense their wariness turn to fear, but they did not make a sound, nor did they break ranks. Ridiculous as it was, he could not get soldiering terminology out of his mind.

Pressing her hands on the girl's shoulders and briefly pointing to the boy of equal height to her left, she said, 'These are Flora and Creighton, they're nine and, well, twins.'

Flora and Creighton shared the same dark brown hair and, although he could not be certain, their eyes appeared bright blue.

But where their colouring and height were the same, the way they acted towards him was not. Flora's nose was jammed into her chest, her lips trembling.

Creighton's eyes were a flat stare and he held his hands fisted at his sides.

Gaira took a quick sidestep and waved her hand briefly over the head of a boy whose hair looked as if it were trying to escape. 'You met Alec.' She roughed the boy's brown hair and it barely moved. Alec smiled, obviously pleased to be introduced.

'The little one there is Maisie.' Gaira pointed to the girl hanging on Alec's left arm. 'She's not two, but learning words.'

Maisie's hair was so blond it was practically transparent in the firelight, but her eyes were round, green and took up half her face. He could not discern much more of her features because it looked as though she were trying to swallow her free hand and arm whole. Spit glistened.

He forced the words from his mouth. 'Are these yours?'

'Aye.' She jutted out her chin.

None of the children resembled each other and certainly not the tall woman in front of him. The camp itself was a single blanket attached to a rope tied to a tree, making a crude tent too small to fit them all. She had a single horse, with a single satchel.

This woman was not their mother, maybe not even their relation. Yet she claimed them. He didn't know who she was, or even if she was from Clan Colquhoun, but she had been taking care of four children who had survived the massacre. By herself.

And she was burying their decaying parents' bodies at night. By herself.

It looked, too, as if she had no protection, no companion and was camping in a godforsaken land on the brink of the most bloodthirsty war he'd ever known in his lifetime.

Her eyes were challenging him, her hair coming loose from the many plaits resembling Medusa's snakes. In the full fire's light he could make out the roughness and largeness of the tunic she wore. It was not a woman's garment, but a man's. Had she been wearing that before or after she arrived here? There were too many questions.

Whatever he was expecting by coming to this small farming village, this was not it. By coming here, he had wanted to see if the rumour was true— if his English brethren could have the capacity for such horror. He hadn't expected survivors. Yet here they were: four children and a woman.

And he didn't know what to do with any of them.

Chapter Five

He was going to leave. Gaira could see it in his eyes. She felt a moment of panic before she relaxed again. His hands were tied. How was he supposed to go?

She glanced at the children. Creighton looked as though he might murder Robert. Flora looked as though she might cry from fear. Alec, bless him, looked happy just to be there. Maisie's big eyes absorbed everything around her. At such a tender age, she had seen too much.

She couldn't soothe the children's feelings, which had to be just as confused as her own. She had just brought an Englishman to the camp and the English had slaughtered their families. Had killed her sister. She choked on the grief clogging her throat.

She couldn't risk letting him out of her sight. 'You must be hungry. Would you like some food?' she asked.

He looked to the children as if they had some say, but they were quiet. They knew something was held in the balance.

He nodded and she released her held breath.

Sobbing.

Gaira woke. The sun was just cresting the hills and it cast the morning mist a milky white. When had she fallen asleep? Late, but it should not have happened.

She moved slowly, careful not to wake Maisie and Alec, who were snuggled against her.

Broken words. Nightmares again.

With the crisp wind biting her cheeks, she tucked her shawl around the children and turned to Flora and Creighton, who slept closer to the fire.

Flora was awake, crying, frantically patting her brother's shoulders.

Creighton made not a sound, but his entire body keened of the demons trapped inside. This nightmare was worse than the last.

She gently laid her hand on Flora, who jumped. 'Let me,' she asked.

Flora shifted away from her brother, her hands locked tight in her lap.

Singing very low, Gaira gently brushed Creighton's brow until his breathing eased and his body slumped. Singing helped. She had startled him awake before and wouldn't do it again.

Slowly, Creighton's body eased and when he woke, he looked surprised that Gaira was there.

Smiling, she stood. The cold wind whipped around her and she wrapped her arms around her waist. Then froze.

Robert was sitting and staring at her. She became aware of the arch of his brow, the shape of his nose, the colour of his deep brown eyes.

She was no longer aware of the children or the biting wind. All she could feel were his eyes. She thought he hid himself just under the surface, but now everything she ever wanted to know about the world, about him, was right there. Without blinking, his eyes became opaque, the brown turning flat.

She felt as though she had been pushed from a summer brook to the cold sand of shore with no chance of submerging back to the warmth.

Acutely self-conscious, she looked to Maisie and Alec, wrapped tightly in her only shawl. She glanced again.

He looked angry and more than frightening.

His hair was a beautiful shade of brown, but it was long, unkempt and fell in deep waves to his shoulders. It looked soft and wild at the same time. She followed each strand, each curve of each wave. A

strange tingling in her palms occurred. Nervousness again?

Trying to calm her suddenly heightened nerves,
she unwrapped her arms and raised her chin against
him. Without her arms, the wind plastered her tunic
and leggings tight against her body. 'Twasn't de-
cent, but it couldn't be helped. She wouldn't show
her nervousness.

His eyes flickered; his frown deepened. Aye, he
was frightening. She couldn't believe she'd invited
him to their camp.

His entire appearance indicated he couldn't be
bothered with a comb, frippery or anything to make
him pleasing to the eye. He wore a beard, like a
Scot, but his did not have pretty plaits to keep it
tidy—his was full, waving and long. If it wasn't
the same beautiful colour, she'd have thought him
an old man.

'We'll need food,' he said.

The timbre of his voice was clipped, abrupt, the
tenor still too pleasing.

Stray curls swept across her face, blinding and
stinging her eyes, but she did not push them away.
'I've set some traps.' She waved her hand in the direction of the trees. 'We haven't had much luck. Our
baits have been—'

He interrupted her and gestured with his tied
arms. 'I can get food if you untie me.'

Arrogant. She looked at his hands, which she had tied in the front so he could relieve himself. He must think her small bit of kindness meant weakness. He would soon learn otherwise.

'You need to eat,' he continued.

She took several steps closer to him. He continued to sit and was forced to look up at her. He should have looked diminished to her. But his eyes remained too steady and the tilt of his chin too proud.

Who was he? An English solider—a nobleman, too, she suspected.

His clothes were fine, rich, but he wore all black. Not a bit of ornamentation or colour. Except for a gold ring, he dressed plainly as if he had no money. But he travelled with a jewelled dagger, two swords and a pouch weighted with coins. Such costly items spoke of great wealth. She had never known a wealthy man to go without ornamentation on his clothing. Even her brothers wore a bit of this, a bit of that.

'You think me gluttonous enough to risk our lives by releasing you?' she retorted.

'Your taking my weapons and tying my hands is but a false sense of security,' he answered. 'If I wanted to harm any of you, I would have.'

'I haven't given you the chance, Englishman.' She pushed her hair behind her ears. 'And I won't. Ever.'

'Aye?' he answered, his voice gone softer. 'And

the times you closed your eyes last night? Those moments weren't enough for me to strike?'

Oh, aye, he was arrogant and just a bit too frightening. He was sitting, he was tied and yet he was still intimidating. Worse, she feared, he also spoke the truth. She had fallen asleep a time or two last night.

She was these children's only guardian and she was all too aware of how little protection she was. Even more so for bringing this man to their camp. He might not have slaughtered their kin, but she knew he'd killed others. There was no other reason an Englishman would be here. It was not safe to release him.

'You need to eat, Gaira,' he continued. 'And so do the children.'

The fight, if there was any, went out of her. They did need to eat. Desperately and in great quantity. Their traps did not work and the fires had scared most of the animals away.

He seemed to sense the change in her and stood.

'What promise do I have?' she asked.

'None that you'd believe,' he said, his lips curling at the corners. 'But I have to eat, too, and maybe that is enough.'

She searched every nuance of his face. What she saw wasn't quite a smile, but it wanted to be. 'Maybe that is enough.' She untied his knots. 'But the moment you take your sword and dagger, leave this camp. I won't let the children see a weapon in your hands.'

She didn't wait to see him go, but grabbed the kindling to rearrange the fire. She sensed his departure and she let out the breath she'd been holding.

He was gone and there was no reason he should return. She trusted him, which made her all the more nervous because he had done nothing to deserve that trust.

He was a nobleman that kept his hair like a peasant and hid the wealth from his clothes. He was an enigma, obscure, as if trying to hide something of himself and personify another.

There was something he hid just under the surface like a river. She pushed her hair behind her ear again. And one she had no time to contemplate. Maisie would need feeding, changing, and the leather skein would need filling for water to boil.

And she would have to explain to the children that they were on their own again.

Busby threw together the few supplies needed and walked down the narrow stone stairs of his keep.

The rushes in his hall squished under him and even in the dim lighting the grease-splattered walls and thrown bones from previous meals were visible. He breathed in the smell of damp wood and rotting meat and couldn't wait to get outside. But his three youngest were crawling on the ground and prodding the rushes with sticks.

'What do you three do inside on a fine day as this? You should be outside.'

Delight widened their eyes before they rushed to their feet and surrounded his arms and legs. Wiping away his impatience for the delay, he roared, 'What do we have here?' They giggled and gripped him even tighter.

Familiar with this game, he crouched down and they immediately climbed on top of him. He lifted all three and clumsily walked outside, where he shook them off.

'What were you doing on your hands and knees?' he asked.

The oldest of the three stepped forward eagerly. His heart swelled as he realised it was his daughter Fyfa. She was a brave lass.

'Papa, we're removing vermin, just like you wanted!' she exclaimed.

'Vermin?'

'Aye, we heard you wanted to remove the vermin from Scotland, so we thought we'd help you.'

Busby snorted and blinked his eyes. 'You're good children, you are, and do your papa proud, but I doona want you crawling. 'Tis not becoming of your station.'

'But, Papa—'

'I'll be obeyed in this. Where is Lioslath? She is to be taking care of you.'

Fyfa pulled a face. 'She's cleaning the stables.'

'Hmmm,' he growled. His wilful oldest daughter had run the keep since his second wife had died. But she never took care of the softer things, like clean rushes or good food. Always with the horses or in the fields, she was unfit for any marriage although she was of marriageable age.

If only he had a wife!

'Get along now. I doona want to see you cleaning again.' He shoved them all towards the fields and waited until they were away before he headed to the stables.

He kicked the rocks at his feet. Blast his betrothed for running! She acted as if she didn't want to be wed. But wed her he must. He had made a deal with her no-good lying brothers and he would make sure she kept it.

When he had received the invitation from the Colquhouns to meet their sister for a possible betrothal, he had thought they were joking. Everyone in the region knew his second wife had died years ago and had left him with children and a poor keep. No one had ever approached him as a suitor and he had long ago stopped his own fruitless pursuits.

It all should have made him suspicious, but when

he had seen their clean profitable castle, tasted well-spiced fare and had been offered twenty sheep, he was eager to get the deal done. Fool that he was.

When his intended had finally been presented to him, her face was puffy and splotched red. Despite this, he assured himself he had made a fine deal and had packed her up along with her belongings.

Now she had run away and before he could even show her the keep or his children!

His keep needed order and a wife could do it. Aye, a wife could order clean rushes and have bread made without stones.

And his children needed a mother. His children had good Scottish blood on the inside, but even to him their outsides needed some polishing. It was too late for his eldest daughter, Lioslath, to be made into a lady. Yet Fyfa, only seven, still had a chance.

And what of his clan? They expected him to return with a rich bride and twenty sheep. He had the sheep, but without the bride, he'd have to return them.

There were only two places she could be. She was only a woman, after all. Weak-hearted and a Colquhoun at that. She wouldn't last on her own, which meant she was either on her way north and his snivelling messenger had missed her, or on her way south as her brothers had suggested.

He was confident if she returned to her brothers, they would bring her to heel. In these turbulent times, they would not want a feud between their clans.

But if she was south it would be he alone who would capture her. He allowed the pleasure of revenge to course through him.

Aye, he would catch her. At the least, the ride south would give him time to think of the punishment that would not hamper her use to him.

Chapter Six

'Paddocks and spiders!' Gaira exclaimed. 'Not again!'

She grabbed at her loosening hair, but the swirling wind wreaked havoc with her attempts to replait it and she tugged at the strays until her head hurt.

'Alec!' she called high and sharp, her agitation growing with the pain in her head. 'Alec! Where are you?'

She heard no reply and she could see no movement. The hills around her dipped and rose as they saw fit. All she saw were the sparse, thin trees to her right and the wide steep valley that dipped to a small lake on her left. She turned her back on the valley.

She limped towards the trees and away from the camp. It was a sparse affair meant for her lone survival. It wasn't enough for her and four children. Especially since one of the children included a five-year-old with a penchant for stealing.

'Alec!' she shouted. 'So help me, dearest God, if you doona return that leather skein, you won't get a drop of water for a week!'

Giggles.

Gaira whirled around on her right foot and spotted a blur deeper in the trees. She limped, trying to catch the boy who ran as fast as his legs could run. She admired his spirit, even though she had to lunge to tackle him as gently as she could. The boy struggled in her arms before becoming still and looking at her solemnly.

Laughing, she grabbed the skein. 'You've got to stop stealing, 'tis taking me too long to get the chores done and I still have to find food.'

The boy's eyes widened. 'Will that man return, Auntie Gaira?'

Frowns. Arrogance. English. But they were all still alive. She hoped she was right to trust the man. He hadn't returned and it was already late morning.

'I think not,' she answered. Knowing her concerns could be read in her eyes, she poked him in the belly. 'Now get, so I can prepare food for your fat belly.'

The boy stood. 'Won't there be food where we're going?'

There should be food, but whether her back-stabbing brothers would give him any, she didn't know. 'Aye, child. There's food a-plenty back at my home.

Why, my brother is the biggest, strongest laird in all of Scotland, and his larder is so full he'll be grateful for you just showing up to help him empty it.'

'But if there's so much food for you there, why were you fleeing down here?'

Her heart flipped. 'Who says I was fleeing?'

'When we were in the trees, we could see you flying up the hill on your horse. Flora said you were running away from something bad.'

'Oh, Flora said that, did she?'

'Aye, we figured you couldn't be running from Doonhill because you hadn't seen...' He stopped. His eyes started to tear. 'Hadna seen...' he started to say again.

Gaira knelt down and gave him a fierce hug. 'Aye, Flora's right. I hadn't seen what had happened to your home yet. But I was anxious to get to Doonhill all the same. Nae reason to think I was fleeing.'

The boy leaned into her. 'Are we going to be safe again?'

Dear God, she didn't know. She wasn't sure of anything since her brother had forcefully handfasted her to the cruellest laird in all Scotland. But her brother's land was the only safe place she knew where to take the children.

Gaira tightened her embrace. 'Nae matter what it takes, I swear I will keep you safe.'

Quickly, she grabbed and tickled him. 'Except

from me!' Alec squirmed and giggled again, all worry leaving his face.

'Now get your fat belly back to the camp and doona let me be catching you stealing again.'

Laughing, he ran towards the camp.

She walked after him. His belly wasn't as fat as it was just a few days ago. Still, if they didn't leave Doonhill soon, they'd be in a worse predicament than starving to death.

When she reached the camp, Robert sat hunched over the fire pit. He was poking several large pieces of meat that sizzled and flared over the open flame. Her stomach growled in response.

But it wasn't Robert's returning or the fact he was cooking that surprised her. It was the children peaceably nibbling on oatcakes. Each sat, perfect as could be, in a semicircle around the campfire and Robert.

Except for Creighton, who sat the furthest away, his eyes never leaving the Englishman's back. She so wanted to soothe Creighton, to help him release his anger, but despite wishing otherwise, he still would not speak.

Creighton and Flora were the ones she had most been worried about with Robert's presence. They were the oldest and the most aware of who had killed their parents.

Robert suddenly met her gaze and she stumbled.

'The meat will be ready soon.'

The timbre of his voice, rather than his words, broke her thoughts. She breathed air into her starved lungs and straightened herself. What was wrong with her? She felt as if nothing would be normal again and all he was doing was making them break-fast.

'You're here,' she said, not hiding her confusion from her voice.

'Aye, the food is far into the wood line. No wonder your traps weren't working.'

She wanted to ask him why he'd returned. Why bother, when he so clearly did not belong here? But she was all too aware of the children watching her and all too worried about his answer.

And now he had brought them food, shared his own oatcakes.

'Do you have any more oatcakes?' she asked. Maisie would need them.

'Plenty.' He glanced at Flora. 'But I've already promised I'd save the remainder for Maisie.'

Flora's cheeks were rosy. No doubt, it was protective Flora who had braved asking Robert for the cakes.

'I dinna know men cooked,' she said.

He shrugged and poked at the meat. 'I like to eat.'

So did her brothers, but that did not mean they had

bothered to learn. She wondered what other skills he was hiding behind his appearance.

It was too much thought this early in the morning and too much thought when she had troubles of her own. She didn't need to be wondering about the workings of one lone Englishman. She lifted Maisie from Flora's lap.

'She'll be needing changing again,' she said to no one in particular.

She went to her satchel hanging in a small tree and grabbed the squares of cloth she'd cut.

How many days had she been here now? Two? Three? Alec thought she had been fleeing when she had raced up the hill towards Doonhill. She'd never tell him how close to the truth he spoke.

They were too close to the borderlands and too close to the skirmishes beginning there. That alone would be bad enough since she had nothing to protect herself and four very dependent children.

She laid Maisie down, unwrapped her dirty linens and quickly wrapped her in the clean ones.

No, her proximity to the borderlands and one confusing Englishman were not her trouble. Her trouble was an angry Scotsman, who thought she was his wife. And worse, far, far worse, was that she'd have to return to and beg for protection from her brother. A brother who had tricked her into marriage and leaving Colquhoun land.

If she had just herself, she'd never return to her land again, but she had the children now. She had to return to keep them safe.

Her entire plan for escape, to find sanctuary within her sister's village, was gone. Scorched. Her only means of survival now was nothing more than burnt timbers, dead bodies and conflicting vows. All of which she meant to keep.

But her vow to bury the dead had slowed her down. And if Busby caught up with them, she'd never get the children to the safety of her clan.

Squealing, Maisie grabbed the tall grass around her and Gaira stood to scrape the dirty linen against a trunk. It would have to be washed later.

She quickly pivoted and stumbled. Gingerly, she lifted her left ankle and tried to flex it within the splint she'd made. Her ankle was still swollen and she could barely wear her boot. She sighed. There was no hope for things to be different, no chance that things weren't worse than they were just days ago and no use wishing otherwise.

But, she reminded herself, she still had some supplies, a strong horse and she was smart enough to get them out of this mess. What she didn't have was time. She scooped Maisie back to her hip. She wouldn't worry over something she couldn't control. There was simply no one to come and help her.

She gripped Maisie tight against her.

What of Robert? No. He wouldn't want to help them.

But she couldn't help her sudden thought. Somewhere between her clobbering him on the head and his cooking breakfast, something had changed.

He hadn't killed them, had even cooked them breakfast.

Maybe he was the answer to her prayers. He was an English soldier, but he was here. He was here. And that's what counted.

Sending this Englishman appeared to be God's will or His joke. Either way, this Robert of Dent would help her bury the dead.

Shifting Maisie to her other hip, she cleared the trees. If her ankle wasn't hurting, she'd be skipping.

'Aye, you're getting to be a big girl, you are.' She snuggled her closer and snorted loudly into her neck.

'Big!' Maisie grabbed one of her plaits and yanked.

'Oh, it's going to be like that, is it?' Gaira, limping, swung her around.

Alec bounded over. 'Can I play?'

Alec's face was covered in oat crumbs and charred meat. Just as it should be. She feigned resignation. 'Ach, I suppose so.'

She dislodged Maisie and picked up Alec, who squirmed until he was safely on her back. Bracing her weight on her good foot, she swung Alec back and forth, making sure her plaits whipped along so he'd squeal louder.

Dizzy and stumbling, she dropped Alec and sprawled on the grass to look at the spinning sky.

Sighing and giggling at the same time, she closed her eyes. Suddenly, a darkness covered her. Robert was standing over her, his thick body blocking out the sun.

She couldn't determine if she was dizzy from whipping her head around or because warm brown eyes stared at her.

'We need to talk,' Robert said.

Aye, they did. She patted Alec's stomach and got up. Maisie had walked around a tree. Brushing the dirt from her little fingers, she placed her in Flora's lap and grabbed her shawl.

She gave Flora a smile. 'Please check the traps and set them again. See that Alec picks up some kindling sticks. We're awfully low. I'll be right back.'

She turned to Robert. 'We'll walk to the valley.'

Since her arrival, she hadn't dared go to the valley in the full light of day. However, it would afford them some privacy and maybe in the light of the devastation he would offer his help.

Robert followed. He tried to pretend to himself it was curiosity that made him watch the way she walked or how she nervously bit her bottom lip.

Her shawl was a deep hue of green and it high-lighted her colouring, framed the length of her curves. Her hair was not a dark brown as he had supposed, but a flaming red. Not the soft red of English beauties, but a deep poppy-coloured hair, almost unreal in its intensity. Her eyes were the colour of whisky in bright sunlight. Her skin was covered by so many freckles they darkened her skin. Her mouth was wide and her lips were the colour of peaches.

Her limping was more pronounced the further they walked and he slowed his pace to walk beside her.

In all his years, he had never seen a woman look as she did. It was as if she were sent down from the sun. Her colouring alone would have made her unusual, her height something to gawk at. She was not beautiful. Indeed, her nose was almost crooked and her chin too pointed. But it didn't matter.

He wanted her. He was too experienced not to recognise the first talons of lust. But that, too, did not matter. There were other matters needing his attention.

'When you came here, you didn't come with four children, did you?' he asked.

'Nae. They are the only ones who survived.'

'Is the boy mute?'

Her brow furrowed and she gave a quick shake to her head. 'Creighton refuses to speak.'

He suspected as much. All morning, the boy had glared with silent unflinching hatred. Fortunately, Alec's chatter had filled any awkward silences.

There had been plenty of awkward silences, too. He did not know what to do with the children. So he had fixed breakfast for himself and for them. He was glad he wouldn't have to worry about their care much longer.

They reached the crest of the hill and Gaira turned around to begin her descent.

'Here, let me help you.' He moved closer and gestured with his arms.

She waved him away. 'I've been doing it fine.'

He pointed to her ankle. 'Is it broken?'

'I doona think so.'

She didn't say any more, though the ankle was swollen. What woman didn't complain about an ailment?

'You said you were travelling to Doonhill when it occurred?' he asked. They passed the valley's curve and he could see the lake.

'Aye, I think I arrived only a few hours later. I was coming to visit my kin.'

'Alone?'

'Of course alone.' Wariness entered her eyes. 'What does it matter?'

It didn't. He didn't know why he asked. But he didn't know why he was here, either.

'What woman travels alone and dressed in a man's clothes?' he asked.

She stumbled, but he pretended not to notice.

'What kind of English soldier travels alone in Scottish lands to inspect a village his men massacred?' she retorted.

He didn't have an answer for that. What would she think when she knew that he was no mere solider, but 'Black Robert', the most feared of English knights?

His squire had started the rumours and songs of Black Robert. The more deeds he did, the more the rumours and songs spread. He couldn't enter a new camp or battlefield without the name being whispered. He was lucky she did not recognise him. If she had, his sword would be through his own gut.

They reached the bottom of the hill and walked to where she'd been digging. As they neared the bodies, she made a clearing sound in her throat.

He waited. Although it was he who had wanted to talk, he knew why she wanted the conversation here. In the light of day, there were unflinching views of the horror. Children with their plump arms ripped off, women sliced and men face down were all lined up. Waiting to be buried with the potatoes.

'Will you help me?' she asked.

After battles, dead bodies had simply been landscapes of war. He and his soldiers had buried many.

But she was no hardened soldier. She could not have seen such atrocities before. Why would she endure such hardship?

'Why do you not just leave?'

'I won't.' She paused. 'So, will you do it? I need to bury them and quickly.'

'It would be more expedient if you burned them on a pyre,' he said.

She gasped. 'They've seen too much fire.'

He was not prepared for the weight of grief hovering over him. He was not prepared for any feelings. But this woman, bringing him here, was causing all the emotions of the world to stab and slice at him.

There was no logical reason for him to be here. He had had a bad dream and suddenly he was making the journey. He massaged the back of his neck and tried to distance himself from the gnawing gripping his chest.

But it hadn't been a bad dream compelling him to come here. It had been a memory and one he had tried to forget.

It had been a long time since he'd felt anger and even longer than that since he had thought of the fire. But he had done both. It was the village that troubled him.

An entire village destroyed and his fellow Englishmen had done it. He could not shake the feeling he was responsible. If he had not been fighting a battle so near Doonhill, then all those people would be alive. They were innocent and shouldn't have died.

'So, will you bury them? Put them at peace?' she repeated. 'Quickly?'

To answer her would be to commit to something he did not want. But he could not mistake the urgency in her voice. Alone and only working a couple of hours a night, she would have to be here the better part of a sennight to get all of them buried. It would make her vulnerable to more danger.

'You risk much staying here as long as you have.'

''Tis their kin. I felt... Nae, I needed to let the children know their families rest peacefully.'

It was practically a death wish for her to persist. 'I am sure they are grateful for the efforts you have been making, but it is foolishness to remain here. The Englishmen who did this could have returned and slaughtered you all.'

She stopped biting her lip. 'Like you?'

'I told you it was not me.'

The haunted look in her eyes vanished. 'Aye, but I'm not so sure I believe you. You're obviously an English soldier and couldn't have just been passing by.'

He did not answer her. He didn't need her to believe him.

She folded her arms across her chest. 'It is irrelevant to discuss this. They did not return and all I ask is for your help.'

She wasn't leaving him alone. He added stubborn to her personality. 'Aye, but there are other dangers here. The children informed me your supplies ran out. How are you able to gather food enough to feed five?'

'We've been surviving.'

'But for how long?'

She whirled to face him, anger bringing her to her full height. 'I had hoped to have been done by now. I hadn't planned on being injured. Will you help me? Because I know how precious little time I have to survive out here. I doona need you telling me. What kind of man won't help a woman bury her kin?'

She pushed herself forward and grabbed a spade lying on the ground. He could see it was a crude tool, hardly sufficient to do the task before them. The blade was black, the handle nothing but a roughened stick. The original handle had probably burned in the fire.

Aye, she was stubborn, her chin was sticking out and there was a challenge to her eyes, but her lips were trembling and she was pale under her freckles.

Cursing, he covered the distance between them and grabbed the spade from her hands. She stumbled a bit from his force and he put his hand at her elbow until she got her balance.

'Your dead will be buried today,' he growled.

He could see her anger was quickly crumbling. She was struggling, choking on emotions and words he didn't want to hear.

'Why now? Why now are you being kind?' Grief filled her voice.

An image of a slender body wrapped in white and lying against green leaves flashed before him. He abruptly let go of her elbow. She lost her balance, but this time he did not touch her.

'I will bury your dead,' he repeated, his voice cold. 'But do not mistake what I do for kindness.'

He drove the weak spade through the tilled earth. The blade wobbled, but did not break. He could feel her standing behind him, but this time she did not interrupt him.

Chapter Seven

It was late in the day when Gaira stood on the crest of the valley's hill. It was her third time to do so, but this time she had a purpose. She clenched the greenery she had gathered for the graves.

Where she stood, she could see the garden of graves and the lake just beyond. Her eyes did not linger on the landscape, but on the man working below.

In the heat of the day, he had taken off his clothes and wore just his braies as she had seen the English peasants do in the fields. But this man was no peasant.

He dug with a spade and toiled at her request, but he held himself as a man used to commanding. Maybe it was the tilt of his head, his shoulders thrown back, or his sword gleaming by his feet.

He dug deep into the dirt and threw it off to the side. Each rugged cord of his muscles was defined by each movement he made. There wasn't an ounce of waste on him and he was thick from his neck to his calves. A woman could trace his sinews with ease.

She felt a curious pull and her fingers were tingling again. She didn't understand the tingling now, but she knew it wasn't nervousness.

She focused on his more disagreeable features: the unruly length of his hair, the scruffiness of his beard, the flat scars peppering his body from his neck down and along his arms. But it was no use. His body pleased her.

'Nothing but a ragabash loun you are, Gaira of Colquhoun.' She had more important matters than noticing Robert of Dent was a fine-looking man.

Irritated, she took her eyes off Robert and saw new graves were dug and filled. He had even worked on the few graves she'd started. They were deeper now, the bodies more protected. In less than a day, he was done.

He was a contrary man. She had begged him, pleaded with him, but he hadn't taken the spade until she had given up. He'd agreed to help and she still didn't understand why.

And he had done it far more quickly than she would have been able to. She could only hope it was quick enough; that she had time to make it to her brothers before they were caught by her betrothed. There was a chance of making it. But she still needed Robert's help.

She tried not to think about his reluctance to bury her dead. Surely he would stay now and help them the rest of the way.

Shifting the greenery in her arms, she carefully sidestepped down the steep hill. Slipping, her foot hit a rock and she stumbled, scattering branches everywhere.

'Artless and bootless.' She angrily picked up each branch and leaf and tucked them into the crook of her arm. 'That's what you are. In more ways than one.'

She slid backward until the slope became flat and then she whirled around. Robert stood a hand's breadth from her. Startled, she stumbled again, branches flew and her body slid against his.

Her world was instantly, aggressively the smell of hot male and cedar and the feel of sweat-covered skin. Her fingers clawed down shoulder muscles she'd gawked at all day. Her breasts burned, her legs tangled. She teetered and pressed harder for support.

Robert inhaled, sharp, as if he'd been dropped into an icy lake. He ripped himself away.

She lost her balance. Strong arms yanked around her waist before her face hit the ground.

Greatly irritated and embarrassed, she flexed her foot. 'Ach! 'Tis not further damaged. Nae thanks to—'

She couldn't finish as she met his gaze.

Gaze was too tame a word. She felt pinned by brown eyes moving over her face as though she were a feast laid out before a starving man. She felt him taking in each and every one of her considerable freckles, her too-wide mouth and her unfeminine chin.

She was consciously aware of her raw-boned frame, her small breasts, the gangly length of her legs. The tingling in her fingers was spreading to the rest of her body. Rapidly. And back again.

His arms, arms she had been admiring only moments before, wrapped more tightly around her, cradled her, began to lift her.

She soaked up the thickness of his eyelashes as they shadowed the hard planes of his cheekbones, the cluster of tiny scars disappearing into his beard along the right of his jaw, the fullness of his lower lip.

He was going to kiss her; she knew it. She parted her lips to take in air.

Then he put her down and took a huge step away.

Humiliation swept through her. She stared at the pebbles around her feet. Braving the year-long seconds between them, she finally thought of something to say.

'You're done?' she asked.

'Almost.' He picked up the spade and started to flatten some of graves.

She glanced at him. He wasn't looking at her. Which was good. She was feeling too raw from his rejection.

'What do you do with those branches?' he asked.

The greenery from birch branches, twigs and fern leaves lay as scattered as her thoughts.

Frowning, she concentrated hard before she remembered. 'They're to honour the graves. I wanted to give them more than just dirt.' He didn't help her as she picked up the scattered branches. 'Let them know they were—'

She couldn't finish the thought. It hurt too much to think of her sister. Pained too much to remember how the children had lost their parents. She tiptoed over the graves and placed the branches and greenery over them. She was glad she could hide her face while she arranged the branches. But it didn't take long. She didn't have much.

Now she only had the living to worry about. And that included herself. At least until her body stopped feeling this longing for a stranger and her heart stopped feeling this foolish hurt.

She brushed the back of her hands across her cheeks. She didn't know what to say to him.

'I prepared the food,' she said when she could bear the silence no more.

He didn't answer and she looked up. He was looking at her decorated graves, his brow furrowed, his cheeks hollowed out. He stuck the spade into the ground with unnecessary force, his eyes not meeting hers.

She hesitated before walking back to the camp. He followed her, but when she stumbled at the top of the hill, he did not help her.

Grief, anger and lust coursed through Robert's body as he followed Gaira to the camp. The decorated graves were a painful reminder of his past. His grief crashed into his lust. The feelings could not be more different. Hot, cold, pain, pleasure. His anger at feeling anything at all underlined everything.

Worse, his years of abstinence mocked him as he followed Gaira up the hill. He tried to look at the countryside around him, but the slope of the green hills were weak substitutes for the fire of Gaira's multiple-plaited hair.

He watched as each plait's swing pointed to every female detail of her: the tapering of her waist, the flare of her hips, the curvature of her buttocks, the lean strength of her long, long legs.

His desire for the woman was too complicated and the situation was difficult enough. He had let Hugh know where he was going, but he was late to return to camp. It was good her dead were buried because so were his obligations to her.

'It is getting late,' he said. 'If you don't mind, I'll keep camp again tonight.'

She didn't break her stride. 'Aye.'

'I'll try not to wake the children when I leave in the morning.'

She stopped so suddenly, he almost walked into her back. When she whirled, her plaits slashed like tiny ropes against his arms and hands.

'What do you mean when you leave in the morning?' she asked, one eyebrow raised.

'I told my men I would be gone for no more than one day. I have been gone for almost two. If I do not return soon, they will come to check on me.'

A crease began in the middle of her brow. 'Tomorrow I was taking the children and returning to my brothers on Colquhoun land. It is north up the Firth of Clyde.'

He did not see how this pertained to him leaving in the morning, but he knew well where the Firth of Clyde was.

'That is miles north and across cold water,' he pointed out. 'You and the children couldn't possibly make it that far.'

She did not question why an Englishman would have such accurate knowledge of Scottish territory. 'That is the plan.'

He turned more fully towards her, waiting for her to finish, to comment their next of kin would be here soon and it would be best if he left as soon as possible.

But all she did was look pointedly at him, as though she was waiting for him to say something. He did want to say something. A blind man could see the danger in her plan.

'You'll never make it with one horse,' he said. 'Flora is so slender and slight in body and spirit, you can practically see through her. Alec and Maisie are too young for such a trek on horseback.' He took a step closer to her. 'What if you run out of oatcakes for Maisie—what will she eat? Creighton will not speak—what if he spies danger, but will not warn?'

She opened and closed her mouth a couple of times. She looked as though she had no idea how to reply to him. He started to walk past her.

She did not move. 'You are so good at telling me what cannot and should not be done. You have nae say here. Alec may be small, but his determination is strong.' Her fists clenched at her sides. 'Maisie's teeth may still be coming in, but she has some and if we run out of oatcakes, we can grind the meat we have and mix it with water. I'll make sure she doesn't starve.'

She took a couple of steps away as if to distance herself from him and released her fists. 'As for Flora and Creighton, I suspect they were nae always mute and weak. I believe your soldiers had something to do with that, but they survived; they were smart and quick enough to protect Alec, too.'

The sun was setting behind her, making her hair look licked with fire. The whisky colour of her eyes was shaded a golden tawny. She was all flared anger and determination and she was magnificent. He could not keep from wondering what her hair would look like unbound, what shade her eyes would go when she was feeling emotions other than anger. He could not help feeling a fool for noticing.

'They'll make it,' she confirmed. 'They've grown up despite my trying to protect them.'

She took another step closer to him and he could smell the fragrance of her hair, a mixture of greenery and something sweet, like some berry he'd never tasted.

He tried to focus his thoughts on the children. 'You've come to care for them,' he said.

'Aye!'

'Surely they have kin who would come for them.'

'Do you think I haven't thought of that?' She waved her arms at him. 'Flora says she has some, but she doesn't know where. Alec's too young to know otherwise.'

'And Maisie?'

'I know whose kin she belongs to,' she said. 'This conversation doesn't matter. I need to get them to my brothers. It is the only place where I know they will be taken care of.'

He could hardly argue with her on where the children would be safe. It wasn't as if he could take her back to the English camp, even if she and the children wanted to. The distance to her brother's land might be dangerous, but he knew of no other place for them, far or near. Still, he repeated himself.

'You'll never make it.'

She stepped closer to him, until she was right under his nose, and punched him in the chest. 'Oh, aye, we will and you're going to help.'

Chapter Eight

All sound was suddenly suctioned out of the air. No, that wasn't right, because she heard the sound of a bee buzzing past them, the rustle of the wind through the grass. It was just Robert who was quiet.

His eyes never wavered from her; his arms hung almost unnaturally by his sides. Had he heard her?

'No…' he breathed.

She clamped down on her quick anger. He had heard her. And his unwillingness shouldn't have surprised her. 'Aye, you are. Why did you come if not to do something for a village your fellow soldiers massacred?'

He didn't say anything. She took a step away from him. Guilt for his country wasn't motivating him. She would have to try another tactic.

'The children aren't safe. They must get to my brothers to receive the care they need. You're right, we'll never make it alone. But with your help, your supplies, your horse, we will.'

He still said nothing.

Her anger was quickly drowning in her panic. What if he didn't help? Could this man, could *any* man, really just walk away?

'Where are your feelings?' she accused.

Something moved in his eyes, a dark shadow that left a strange ache in her chest. She suddenly wanted to soothe him and that didn't make any sense.

She pressed her fingers under her eyes. It could not be his feelings, but her own making her heart ache. It had to be. He had no feelings, while she was rapidly losing control of hers—losing control of her pride, too. But she'd gladly beg if it would get him to *move*.

'You inding shirrow weevil, can't you see I wouldn't ask if I dinna have to? You're our only hope!'

To think she had been glad when he arrived. He had barely helped her before and now he wasn't even answering her request.

'Auntie Gaira! I saved you some rabbit!'

Alec, his wild hair flying behind him, bounded towards her. Her heart lifted at the sight of his skips and jumps. Despite everything, children were resilient. And in that, she knew they'd make it. If only the children had a chance.

Stepping away from Robert, she crouched in readiness for Alec to join her. It was so natural, so easy. And there was her answer. They did have a chance. They had her. And with that, she stopped her doubting. Feeling as wild as his hair, she grabbed Alec's loose hand. Alec squealed and tried to get away.

'Oh, you saved me some rabbit, did you? Is this the rabbit you saved me? It looks so succulent.'

'Nae, not me, Auntie Gaira. I'm not the rabbit!'

She poked at him, pretending she was testing his fatness. 'Oh, you're a tasty morsel, you are.'

She began to smack her lips and Alec screamed louder. His eyes widened with delight and mock fear.

She could feel Robert watching her, but didn't spare him a glance. Instead she tossed her plaits and pulled Alec behind her as they ran towards the camp.

The camp was quiet, except for the slight crackle of the fire and the few insects and nocturnal creatures that scattered and rustled the leaves and twigs around them.

Gaira wrapped her arms tighter around her and watched as the fire's flames dimmed. She could not sleep. Her thoughts wouldn't let her alone. And they, just like the fire, dimmed and scattered in different directions.

She thought of the children, now fast asleep, and how she was getting them to her clan. She thought of what was to become of them and her if they were caught by her betrothed.

She thought of Robert, who hadn't said a word since Alec had interrupted them. But she had been aware of him watching her, watching the children. Watching her.

She had no idea what his thoughts were when she returned to camp and had played with Maisie, combed Flora's hair and made sure Creighton ate enough rabbit to fill his growing body.

She tried not to care about his thoughts as she cleaned up dinner, banked the fire and wrapped the children in her shawl to keep them warm in the night's chill.

She no longer felt frustrated at him or even hurt. She just felt confused. He acted and behaved like no man she had ever known.

He had seemed almost angry at her asking. Not angry because her request was an inconvenience, but angry because her request had brought him pain. But instead of giving her reasons, he had watched her all evening.

Even though he was on the other side of the fire, she still felt Robert watching her, which meant, he, too, was not asleep. That knowledge, probably more than anything, was why she still couldn't get to sleep.

Restless, she sat and began to unplait her hair. It had been cleaned before she had carefully plaited it, but the plaits pulled at her head and she wanted to be free from their confinement.

She had not heard him move, but rather she felt him move. It was as if he had sat up, his watchful eyes now intent, focused.

On her.

Suddenly uncoordinated, she unwound her hair with uneven tugs until it was loose enough to comb.

With trembling fingers she massaged her scalp to relieve the sharp prickles. But Robert was watching her and the prickles spread, tingled across her sensitive shoulders and lower through her body and legs.

Shaking, she grabbed her comb. Raising it, she stroked the comb through her thick hair to unravel the coils.

She heard Robert stand and move behind her. But he did not speak and neither did she.

The air around her grew warm, thick, and her heart began to beat in an unfamiliar rhythm. She stroked the comb through her hair again, letting the teeth bite from her scalp through the ends and out.

He inhaled sharply.

For a moment, she held the comb suspended, then, lowering it, she whispered, 'I'm sorry I woke you.'

'I have questions.'

His response was such a direct contrast to what she was feeling. She waited, but he didn't say anything more and he didn't return to his side of the fire.

Unsure what else to do, she slid the comb through the rest of her hair, setting the coils free. But it wasn't enough to loosen the tension and she massaged her scalp, fingering her way through the heavy curls. Her hair felt wilder somehow, her fingers noticing textures she'd never felt before. Just as she'd never felt a man's gaze as she felt Robert's gaze. Just as she'd never felt her breath quicken as if she'd burned herself and kept her hand in the fire nonetheless. She felt like her hair, freed but still coiled.

'How did you find the children?' Robert's voice was hoarse, unfocused.

Unbalanced, it took all her concentration to understand the question. He wanted to know about the children. Not this…unknown breathlessness.

She could talk about the children. He had helped her bury the dead and hunt more food. Her breath returned to normal. He deserved some of the truth.

'I arrived maybe only a few hours after the English left,' she replied.

He sat down beside her, his legs bent, his arms and hands hanging loosely between his knees. He was not touching or facing her, but it did not matter. She felt him beside her.

'In my hurry down the hill, I hurt my ankle, but I still walked through the valley.' She did not want to describe what she had seen. He had been to the valley, he knew what was there.

'I heard Maisie before I saw her. She was in the last hut and under some torn blankets and an upturned chest. They were unwashed horse blankets. I guess the English dinna want to bother with them.'

Even though she had not seen them, she had no doubt it was the English who had destroyed Doonhill. She clenched the comb and let the sharp points press into her palm.

'I grabbed her, held her. She had been my only hope. There was nothing else…salvageable.' She breathed in raggedly. 'I went back up the hill to get my spooked horse. He was near a small copse of trees. By then my ankle hurt and I was grateful he had not gone any further.'

'That was when I saw movement in the trees. I was scared—I knew the English had just left. But it was the children. Flora holding Alec's hand and Creighton standing with his fists at his sides.'

'You did not mention your kin.'

She shoved the comb back into her satchel. 'Aye, I was coming to visit my sister, Irvette, her husband and their daughter.'

'Maisie,' he said, no question in his voice. 'Maisie is their daughter.'

'Aye.' There was no need to hide the truth.

'You buried your sister and her husband.'

She nodded. At night she had buried them and so many others. It was at night she had felt the heavy weight of both the living and the dead depending on her. Only then did she allow herself to feel her grief and her anger.

'I couldn't leave Irvette like that and I wouldn't leave her husband, either.'

'You stayed to bury the rest because of the children?'

'Partly, but that's not all.' She tried to close out the vision of the night and her long trek down the hill, where the wind did not blow so hard and the moonlight obscured the remains of the village.

'I have nightmares now. Not just because of what I saw, but—' She stopped. It had been long, gruesome work moving the bodies to the garden. 'I could hear the dead urging me to dig, you ken? I dug so hard the blisters on my hands broke, but the pain was sharp and dulled the ache in my ankle, allowing me to work faster.

'Yet I couldn't dig fast enough. Even in the cool of the night, I could smell the bodies and the flies swarmed. I moved, but the flies stayed on me as if they were waiting for me, as well.'

She shook her head. 'But that wasn't the worst. The worst was the sound the bodies made when they thudded into the grave I made.'

His gaze remained on the fire and she saw only his profile. She didn't know what he was thinking.

'I couldn't make the graves deep enough to silence the sound,' she said. 'And it wasn't the only sound they made.'

His brow furrowed, but he did not stop her speech.

'I know you'll think me mad, but I heard their voices, faint, coming from some other place, but loud enough for me to hear.'

She had to say it. 'They thanked me,' she confided. These were her most private thoughts, so personal she hadn't thought she'd tell anyone, but somehow she knew he would understand what she spoke. 'Thanked me for taking care of their children when they nae longer could.'

Robert's hands jerked, but he remained silent. If he wasn't sitting next to her, she would swear he wasn't listening. How could he not hear what she was saying? Were her fears so easily dismissed?

'But to what end?' She gave a sort of hiccupped sob. 'You're not even going to help us.'

She was not mortified that her voice broke. She was beyond any pride. She *was* desperate. And afraid. And grieving. And he was going to leave her like this.

He breathed in raggedly. 'This afternoon, I told you I was not helping you.'

She did not need reminders of the afternoon's conversation.

'But Alec came and you played with him,' he continued. 'Then you played with Maisie, too, and cared for Creighton and Flora. You smiled at them, gave them affection and yet, I knew you were distressed.'

'Ach, there's nae sense in self-pity.' She batted at her cheeks and wished the tell-tale sign of any weakness would go away. 'I've never shirked a chore in my life. And the children mean more than that to me. Much more. I made them a promise and I'm keeping it, with or without your help.'

'I'll take you to the nearest village.' His voice was rushed with the release of his breath. It was as if the words escaped before he could stop them. 'No further,' he said more firmly. 'It'll be enough to get you an extra horse and further supplies.'

Instead of relief, her heart stabbed and tingled. He had given her some reprieve from her hardship ahead of her, but she knew it had been reluctant. It just added guilt to her already heavy heart. But she was in no position to refuse. She nodded and wiped her eyes with the back of her hands.

'Aye,' she whispered. 'Only to the nearest village.'

He stood and moved as if he would leave, but then he stopped.

'Gaira?'

She craned her neck to look up at him. His back was almost to her and he was looking over his shoulder. His body was fine and broad. She could see how his tunic stretched taut over the blades of his arm muscles, how his waist tapered to hose that were wrapped around legs sculpted from endurance and strength. The dim flickering fire did not allow her to see all the features of his face, but it did not matter. She felt his eyes, felt the return of the heat in them.

She felt her own body respond. She felt the sluggish heat of her blood, the shallow breath fill her lungs. Her clothing felt tight and confining.

It had to be her grief that left her feeing this raw, this open. She felt vulnerable to him, to thoughts he would not say.

'Aye?' she finally answered.

He did not touch her, but he might as well have been caressing her as the fire did. His eyes moved as if they were his hands. Not soft caresses of sight, but rough, consuming strokes of heat.

'While I am with you,' he spoke, his voice firm, 'do not unbind your hair again.'

She hoped the dim fire hid her blush.

Chapter Nine

Busby did not quench his feeling of satisfaction. No, in fact, he let his pleasure be known as he flashed the crofter a menacing grin. He couldn't help it. It was his nature. It was that exact nature that made the crofter give him the information he needed to find his fleeing betrothed.

It wasn't as though she could hide from him anyway, even with her wearing lad's clothing. She was tall and scrawny, but her long red hair was sure to catch someone's attention, as was her riding a fine horse. A fine horse that was his.

Busby puffed out his chest and walked to his horse. He knew he cut a strapping figure wherever he went. He was a big man, bigger than most.

He loved the fear on people's faces. The few crofter houses along the way were hardly a barrier to his questioning. In fact, the very first hut he knocked on, the resident had let him know a lass had ridden through less than two days ago.

Foolish wench to run in broad daylight where there could be witnesses. All he had to do was follow her, ask questions and eventually he would retrieve her.

Because running to her sister's home and hiding would not dissolve her obligation to marrying him. His keep needed her. His children needed her.

He swung up on his horse, his lips thinning in disapproval. He probably would have already caught her if he didn't have such a poor specimen of horse-flesh to ride. He swallowed his anger.

He'd still get her. When he did, he would show her no leniency. If she wanted mercy, she wouldn't have escaped, wouldn't have jeopardised his twenty sheep and wouldn't have taken his good horse.

Gaira woke the next day to no one trying to be quiet. Alec was crying, Flora was choking back sobs, Creighton was taking a log and banging it against a fallen one.

The racket woke Maisie, who was tightly wrapped in Gaira's shawl. Loosening it, Gaira picked the young girl up. Maisie's piercing scream went right into her ear and it took all her will not to add to the din herself.

It was not hard to spy Robert saddling the horses.

'What are you doing?' she shouted over the children.

He did not turn around. 'Packing our things for the journey.'

'You told them.' She rocked Maisie back and forth until she quieted.

'Aye, I did. It seemed necessary.'

Creighton stopped banging on the log, Alec stopped crying and even Flora's sobs lessened in frequency. She was glad for the temporary quiet, but she didn't want to have this conversation in front of them. 'You had nae right. They are my responsibility.'

Every fibre of her being reverberated with the frustration she was feeling. She wanted to grab Creighton's log, wanted to scream until her face turned as red as Maisie's. Instead she took a few quick breaths to calm her heart.

Even before she had fallen asleep she'd had second thoughts about asking him to accompany them. She did not know him, did not know if he posed an even greater danger to them than the unknown.

But now he had told the children and there was no going back. By telling the children, he had subtly changed the leadership of their little group. She had asked him to help her on the trip, not to take over. She was still in charge. She didn't want to be bullied again. She had had enough of overbearing men to last a lifetime.

'Wait! Just wait. I need to take care of Maisie and I'd like to talk to the children myself.'

He did not seem surprised by her request. He just patted his horse's neck and walked down towards the lake. She waited to address the children until she couldn't see him.

Creighton was looking at her expectantly, Flora was looking at her hands folded in her lap and Alec seemed content to look for things in the grass.

She hoped that what she was about to tell them was the truth. There was too much left to chance. It was chance that her brothers would take the children, when they had done everything they could to get rid of their own sister. It was chance that Robert, despite being English, despite being a soldier, was a good man.

'I've already told you of my home up north. My brothers are good and they'll gladly take each of you in.' She adjusted Maisie and could smell she was more than just wet. There was no time for a full change just yet. 'But it's far and there are dangers. I have asked Robert to take us part of the way there.'

Creighton grabbed the stick again.

Flora, anguish and surprise all over her face, said, 'But, Auntie Gaira, he's...he's English. You said you'd protect us.'

Gaira knew that was coming, but to hear gentle Flora say the words still hurt. 'I'd protect you with my life if necessary, Flora, all of you.'

'But how can we trust him?' Flora asked. 'How do we not know if something bad will happen again?'

She had no answer to that. She didn't know if something bad would happen again, didn't know if Robert brought danger with him. But he had helped bury their kin and he had tamed his words for a little boy. It would have to be enough.

She had known these children for less than a week, but she knew she would do anything she could to take care of them. Anything. Including trusting a man she didn't know.

'I think the only way we are to trust him is how we've trusted each other already—on faith.'

Creighton banged once on the log. His eyes blazed, his lips thinned. It was not hard to see the man he'd look like with his eyes so full of anger. Her heart went to him. He was too young to be an adult.

'Nae doona be thinking I'm taking this lightly, Creighton, because I'm not. Another horse will get us to shelter faster and having a man who knows how to trap and wield a sword are benefits I cannot just ignore.'

She went to a nearby tree and got down dry linen to change Maisie.

'He may be English, but we'll probably meet more

along the way. I'd rather have one, who says he'll help and has already proven himself, then someone who—'

She stopped. Flora had started crying again. She suddenly felt like crying, too. 'I'm so sorry, Flora. To all of you, but I think this is something we have to do.'

She reached into her satchel, but didn't feel anything. She yanked her arm out of the satchel, adjusted Maisie on her hip, flipped the satchel upside down and shook it. Empty and Alec was nowhere in sight.

'Alec, where did you hide Maisie's oatcakes?'

She left Maisie with Flora and walked down to the lake. She was done feeding Maisie, but Robert had not returned. She could wait no longer. Now that she had come to a decision, she was anxious to move.

She found him by the shore. His arms were stretched above his head as he pulled on his tunic. She glimpsed sun-bronzed skin before he tugged the tunic over his abdomen. His hair and beard were wet, but his clothing dry. Her heart skipped as she realised he had been naked mere moments before she reached the top of the hill.

She refused to think why her heart skipped. Or why her mouth went dry at the barest glimpse of his bare skin.

'You bathe?' she asked when she was close enough.

'I swim.' He shrugged. 'It helps me think.'

She had never known of a man to swim before. While her brothers Caird and Malcolm were taken to rushing into the Firth of Clyde, her older brother, Bram, unless he was courting, could hardly be bothered.

No, this man was like no other she had ever known. Her reaction to him was testament to that. She'd seen her brothers undressed too many times to count. Yet she was curious about Robert, in a way she didn't completely understand.

'I did some thinking, too,' she said. 'The children agreed you can take us to the village.'

He started to walk past her.

She raised her hand to stop him. 'Wait. I have some ideas how this trip is to go.'

He was silent, except she thought she saw his eyebrows rise.

'I do nae want you thinking you can dictate how this journey should go.'

His eyebrows rose a bit more, but he said nothing. Which was good. If he so much as smirked or got any twinkle in his eyes, she'd tell him to jump into the lake he had just left.

'I do not like to be bullied, bossed, ordered, directed, or given strong suggestions by any kae-witted arrogant man.' She counted each point on her fingers. 'I expect to be treated fairly and with respect in this venture. If you deserve it, I will treat you with respect.'

His mouth curved at the corner. 'This trip is for respect, is it? I thought you asked me for your safety.'

She ignored his sarcasm and the curve to his mouth. 'As to that, I'm nae certain. I hardly know you or what your motivations are.'

'You asked me to help you. Are you changing your mind?'

She thought she saw his eyebrows rise even more, but she couldn't be sure now because they were so far up to his hairline she couldn't see them.

'Aye, I asked you,' she answered. 'But I wonder now in the broad light of day why you accepted.'

He shrugged. 'Maybe it is guilt.'

It wasn't guilt. She'd tried to use that before to make him feel remorse and he hadn't budged. 'If it is, that story goes so far as to burying the dead. It does not apply to your taking one woman and four children into enemy country.'

'We are not declared enemies.'

'But we are and you know it. Doona go thinking I have nae noticed your fancy warhorse and numerous weapons. You are one of King Edward's soldiers and you've probably spilt Scottish blood.'

Seeing his eyebrows again, she knew she'd

guessed correctly. Again, she was reminded he was like a river with unfathomable depths. She had to remember no matter if he helped, she did not know who he was or where his loyalties lay.

'I did not think it mattered who I was,' he said.

She couldn't believe she was thinking of travelling with such a man, but what choice did she have? This Englishman was God's answer to her wish for help. She was no fool to refuse it.

'Aye, maybe so,' she said. 'Whatever your story is I do not want to know. I just want your word you'll keep us safe from others and yourself.'

His eyes were unreadable. 'You have my word.'

She picked up a clod of dirt and held it out to him. He stared at it. 'Aren't you taking it?' she asked, exasperated.

'Isn't taking of the earth meant to seal a change of land ownership?'

'Aye, it is. But you're on Scottish land now, Robert of Dent. Once you start travelling these hills and see the green forests, the bonny bluebells, the play of sun against the dark blue waters, you'll be wanting ownership of Scots land. I'm just giving you a bit as a gift. To show some trust.'

He continued to stare at it. She stepped closer to him, moving her hand closer to him. ''Tis a goodwill gesture, you spongy, rude, neep-heided—'

He stepped forward and roughly pushed the dirt

out of her hands. 'We need no trust between us and I want no gift. I do what is necessary and that is all. Once we reach the nearest village and purchase the supplies, I will be gone. It is best you remember that.'

Stunned at his sudden change of demeanour, she watched him walk away. He had gone as cold as the Clyde in winter. She tried to breathe through what his rejection had done to her heart.

His rejection should not have been anywhere near her heart. But everything seemed to be too close to that delicate region lately. It was the only explanation why this man, who was English and angry and hairy, held any fascination for her.

She had honestly meant some token of goodwill towards him when she'd offered him the Scottish dirt. Then he'd rejected her. Again.

So he didn't trust her. Fair enough. But that didn't mean she couldn't trust him. She was a Colquhoun and their motto was 'If I can'.

She already trusted him by allowing him anywhere near her and the children. And she'd go on doing it despite what he wanted.

Chapter Ten

By day, the morning mist was denser and the clouds weighed heavily on Robert. He was used to his English rain and even Wales had heavy mist. But he would have sworn Scottish clouds were evil spirits soaking his clothes.

Yet it was not the mist demanding his attention. It was the woman who had not stopped talking since they broke camp.

'I doona see the point of this martyrdom you assume. Despite your opinions, I will not ride the entire way there. You can't intend to walk the entire way to the next village, either. If you do, you'll collapse of fatigue before we are halfway there. Then what use would you be?'

'Then you'll have my horse, which will not be tired because I did not ride it.'

He could not see past the white birch trees with their tender green leaves. The forest they walked through was well spaced and allowed the horses to walk side by side, but he couldn't see beyond the trees and every instinct in his body was on alert, tense, trying to allow his hearing to see what his eyes could not. But it was impossible.

'Your horse!' Gaira exclaimed. 'You nae fool me. This horse of yours could be carrying me, Maisie, Alec and you in a full suit of armour and still not be the slightest winded.'

'He is too young and ill trained.' Although he had noticed Gaira was not having any difficulty handling the temperamental creature. Having Alec and Maisie in the saddle with her did not even trouble her.

'Hmmph.'

'Perhaps he'd be fine,' he conceded. 'But your ankle needs to heal.' He walked around a cluster of trees and emerged in front of the horses again. 'My intention is not to walk the entire way there. I am sure this route you insist we take is the quickest route to a village. As soon as we are there, we'll buy supplies and a horse.'

'And how exactly are we to be purchasing these? We have nothing to barter.'

'I have silver coin, Gaira,' Robert replied. She had to have heard it around his waist.

'Scottish, too?'

Robert almost stumbled. Bartering and English

silver were more common. But he did have Scottish. In a separate pouch too heavy for him to carry; too much a burden to be reminded of. Enough to pay for a destroyed village. 'Some,' he answered.

'Can I keep him?' Alec interrupted excitedly.

Gaira turned her attention to the boy holding on behind her. 'Can you keep what?'

'The horse he's buying. Can it be mine? I've always wanted a horse.'

Creighton's horse snorted abruptly. Robert looked to see Creighton's tight grip on the reins. Flora put a hand on her brother's shoulder.

'I...I do nae think Sir Robert means for us to keep the horse, Alec.' Flora's soft voice carried on the mist. 'I believe his intention is to procure it so that we may ride easier to Gaira's home.'

'Our home now, Flora, doona forget that,' Gaira interjected. 'It'll be home for all of us very soon. But you're quite right. 'Tis Robert's horse and his decision what to do with it.'

'I don't see why the new horse cannot be for the children's use,' Robert said, 'providing we can find a horse. I'll have no use for it once I return to England.'

He slowed his pace so he could now see Gaira's surprise, anger, irritation and frustration all at once. He didn't think anyone could actually feel, let alone express, so much emotion at the same time.

'Ach, now, we doona need any more of your generosity,' she retorted.

'It is hardly generous,' Robert pointed out. 'You will be bringing four mouths to feed—they should come with their own horse. It is a gift for them.'

Gaira made a sound of utter disbelief.

'Think of my convenience. The horse will probably be too tame and more suited for children than soldiers. What need have I for such a creature?'

She didn't say anything.

'So you accept?' he prodded, although he already knew the answer.

'Ach, now, I can hardly refuse such a gift since you seem to be giving it to the children and not to me.'

'We get to keep it! We get to keep it!' shouted Alec.

'Alec, sit still or you'll fall off,' Gaira ordered.

Robert stopped and turned, allowing the horses to pass him. He could not see anything except the trail they left in the thick blades of grass and bluebells. Every instinct in him told him to get to the edge of the forest, but Gaira had instructed the way to the nearest village was through the trees, not around them. Not knowing the way himself, he could only agree, but he didn't like it. If this was the trail north, it was the least travelled trail he'd ever seen.

'Where are we going?' Alec asked.

'Eventually, we'll be at Auntie Gaira's home,' Flora said, patience lacing each word.

Robert was surprised she had any. He had lost count how many times the boy had asked the same question. He walked to the head of the horses again.

'Why?' Alec asked.

'Because I want you to meet my brothers,' Gaira said, her voice cheerful. 'You remember my telling of my brothers. There's Bram, the red, and there's Caird, the not so red, and Malcolm, the dark.'

Gaira launched into further description, but having heard the story, Robert let Gaira's voice fade into the background. She kept a running commentary to the children all morning long and they seemed to enjoy it.

If he reported he had travelled with a woman who talked of one subject, then another and was never quiet, his men would have been horrified. But he didn't mind. Her accent was musical and he found it almost peaceful, as if by her voice alone she kept his troubled thoughts at bay.

It was just another reason why he wanted to get her to the village and leave her as soon as possible.

She interrupted her own dialogue. 'Robert, we need to rest.'

'We just left.' He didn't look back.

'That was hours ago and the children have needs.'

He did not stop walking, but glanced over his

shoulder. The children avoided his eyes. 'They look fine to me. We keep going.'

She stopped his horse. 'They are children, not soldiers, and they need to rest.'

This trip was taking too long. He had told Hugh he would return within a day or two, not weeks. 'We will rest at midday.'

'They will never make it.'

He grabbed her bridle and gave it a slight pull. The horse shied. He never had trouble with horses. The fact this one gave him even the slightest grief and none to her irritated him. He pulled harder on the reins and the horse stepped forward.

He ignored Gaira's set expression. Satisfied, he turned his back. He would brook no more delays. He'd help her, but on his own terms. Not hers.

He took only two steps before Gaira called, 'Do you want Maisie to wet your horse?'

'Horse!' shouted Maisie.

Gaira tried not to laugh at Robert's sudden stopping and she tried equally as hard not to let her triumph show as he released her reins and walked to Flora and Creighton. Creighton refused his help, but Flora, her hand trembling violently, laid one hand in his.

When he got Flora down safely, he returned to her. She could now see his face, his lips pressed, his shoulders set.

She gently dislodged Maisie as Robert reached up. He held Maisie out from him, her entire weight suspended by his arms alone.

Maisie didn't seem to mind. Her large eyes were absorbing him and drool escaped down her four fingers and across her chin.

Robert glanced to his left and right, trying to find a safe place to put her.

Gaira's laughed escaped before she could clamp her lips together. 'You doona hold her that way.'

He took a couple of steps away from the horse and set Maisie down. Then he patted her shoulders as if that would keep her feet firmly entrenched. He turned back to Gaira, but she watched as Maisie, her steps unsure, followed Robert.

Gaira pointed at Maisie. 'You've got to give her to Flora or Creighton. She'll just keep following you.'

He frowned. 'It's not safe for her to be so near the horse,' he said.

'She doesn't know that. She just sees you and probably thinks nae more of the horses. Their legs are nothing but tall sticks to her now.'

'She should be instructed otherwise.'

'Not much around children, are you?'

'I've seen them before.' He picked up Maisie, who had clumsily grabbed the back of his legs.

'Seeing them and taking care of them is not quite the same thing,' she pointed out.

He handed Maisie to Flora and returned to dislodge Alec, who still clutched Gaira's waist.

Once free of the horse, he held Alec out so that the boy's weight dangled in mid-air. Alec's giggles erupted as he started to kick and swing his legs before he even hit the ground. When he did, he scampered out into the trees, doing circles around them like a bee in a rose bush.

'You doona hold them like that, either.' Gaira dismounted and took Maisie from Flora.

'I'm not concerned about how to hold them. My duty was to get them to the ground.'

Gaira walked away from the children and began to undress and clean Maisie.

'Aye, but there's a world of difference between just getting them from point to point.' She raised her voice to be heard. ''Tis how you get them there that's the good part.'

Finished, Gaira straightened Maisie's clothes before picking her up and placing her on her hip. Gaira relished the warm chubby body pressed into her side.

Robert was rubbing down the horses. The horses weren't winded, but she suspected it was part of his training and his care was very telling of the kind of man he was.

'You could be good with them, you know. It just takes practice.'

He didn't look at her. 'What takes practice?'

'Caring for the children.'

'I'm not caring for the children.'

'Ach, now. 'Tis not much different from your taking care of the horses. They need food, drink, rest, a tender hand.'

He stopped rubbing and looked at her across the horse's back. 'I'm not caring for the children. My duty is to get you to the next village. I'll help you there and I'll help with the food, but nothing else.'

She stopped moving towards him. 'Why are you here?'

'What do you mean?'

'You agreed to help us.'

'Aye,' he said.

She noted he hesitated. Good, he should be wary. She was tired, scared, angry and grieving. She didn't want to add frustrated to the list.

'If you're going to help us, you need to help us in every way. None of this reluctant churlish wan-witty behaviour.'

His mouth curved. 'Does every Scottish lass talk as you do?'

She noticed how his partial smile softened his eyes. 'Ach, now, doona be changing the subject. I'll have you helping with the children or you can just hightail it back to your weedy England.'

He glanced at Maisie still in her arms. 'I am a soldier, not a father, and as soon as we reach the next village, I will be gone.'

She walked around the horse. When she was near enough, she moved Maisie from her hip and pressed her against Robert's chest. His arms remained at his side.

She grabbed his arm, placed it under Maisie's bottom and adjusted her. She quickly stepped away and gave a swift silent prayer when he held her.

'Aye, but until then, this will do,' she said.

She watched his stiff body adjust and gave another prayer at Maisie's cooperation. Walking quickly to her satchel, she pulled out an oatcake and handed it to him.

'She's mostly finished her teething, but there are still some growing in.'

He looked at the oatcake and at Maisie. Maisie looked at the oatcake and at Robert.

'Her teeth are breaking through her gums,' she explained.

He looked blankly at her.

She tried not to grin again. It would take a lot of instruction to get Robert of Dent worthy of childcare. 'Chewing on fingers and on oatcakes relieves children until the teeth break through the gums.'

Nodding, Robert lifted the oatcake to Maisie's mouth.

Maisie looked at the oatcake, then with a slurping

pop, released her fingers and grabbed the oatcake with her clean hand, while her now-sopping hand gripped the front of Robert's tunic.

Robert looked down at the front of his tunic. 'I think she won,' he said.

Gaira laughed. 'I dinna think you had a sense of humour.'

'I don't,' he said. His eyes never left Maisie.

Gaira watched the changing emotions cross Robert's face. It was like seeing further into the river he reminded her of. He said he didn't have a sense of humour, but she suspected at one time he had.

She quickly lowered her gaze before turning. 'I'll see if the others need me.'

Feeling him watching her, she tried not to trip on her own legs. She knew her departure was abrupt, but she couldn't help it; just as she couldn't seem to curb her fascination with Robert.

She knew he hadn't meant to reveal anything about himself, had in fact been rather quiet the entire morning, but it was his very nature that fascinated her.

He was patient, kind, reluctantly honourable and generous despite not wanting to be. But those traits weren't revealed to her while he held Maisie. No, something deeper than that. She had seen some pain there, but some tenderness, too. He was a man of marriageable age, but he didn't talk of a wife and she realised she had never asked. She didn't know anything of his life, other than he soldiered with the English King Edward and she had just guessed that little fact.

She suddenly felt guilty for her wayward longing for him. What if he was married?

Chapter Eleven

When she returned from the trees, she saw Creighton playing quietly with Alec and, despite the damp, Flora had fallen asleep against a large tree. Maisie was slumped in her lap.

Gaira's heart tightened to see the children unguarded. When they were like this, she saw weariness shadowed beneath their eyes and their own burdens weighing and drooping their shoulders. She had lost her sister, but they had lost their families and home.

The children were exhausted and they had only just begun their journey. She felt like joining them.

Just getting a few miles away from the valley was a reprieve. She couldn't smell anything since Robert had buried the bodies, but the wind had carried the smell of burnt wood and that was a painful reminder. If she could smell it, so could the children.

Creighton caught her staring at him and he did not return her smile. She walked towards him, fully intending to rough his hair and tease him out of his seriousness. She had done it many times since she had known him. He never laughed, but he did express annoyance and she'd rather have that than the empty look in his eyes.

'We should leave.'

Gaira stopped. Robert stood between the trees, his arms crossed, his shoulder braced against a tree trunk. She wondered how long he'd been there.

'We will once the children have rested,' she answered. 'The weather's holding, perhaps it won't even rain.'

'And if it does? Do you know of a shelter nearby?'

She didn't know. When she had escaped, she hadn't travelled this way. But she hadn't told him those details. To do so would open up too many questions.

'I doona know,' she answered. 'I travelled fast and wasn't paying attention.'

The trees' shadows dimmed his features, but she felt his gaze sharpen.

'They need to rest.' She tried to change his focus.

'At this rate, it'll be winter by the time we reach any village,' he argued.

Robert's words were ridiculous, he had probably

made a weak attempt at humour, but an icy flush swept Gaira's body.

How could she be so foolish? She knew the children needed to rest, but it wasn't safe. Her betrothed could catch up to them and then she'd be in no position to help them. They needed rest, but not at that cost.

'More wanwitty I,' she said. 'How long do you think we've tarried?'

He uncrossed his arms and took a step out of the trees' shadows. His eyes were narrowed. 'At least an hour.'

She turned away from his assessing eyes and clapped her hands. 'All right, children, let us leave, we've dawdled enough.'

'But I'm hungry,' Alec said.

She felt a twinge of guilt. She should have made sure he ate. 'We will just have to eat as we go.'

Robert watched and she knew her abrupt change of demeanour had made him suspicious, but she didn't care. They had to keep moving.

She picked up Maisie from Flora's lap and swung her up on her hip. She stayed asleep. She reached for Alec, but the boy suddenly bounded over to Robert and grabbed his hand.

'Come on, Ame Robert!' Alec tugged at his hand.

Robert's jaw dropped. 'Er...'

Alec tugged even harder and Robert's right foot shifted.

Gaira decided to come to his rescue. 'He's not your blood relation, Alec, so he can't be your ame.'

Alec measured her words and shrugged. 'That's all right, I still like you.' He reached up to Robert.

His arms woodenly at his sides, Robert stared at Alec. His face was as blank of colour and expression as she had ever seen it. She could see he was floundering on multiple levels and the boy was barely five. She smiled.

'He wants to be picked up,' she instructed. 'To be put on the horse.'

Looking only somewhat relieved, Robert lifted Alec on to the horse. To stop from laughing, she quickly turned to Creighton and Flora.

'Come, let's go, you two.'

Flora rubbed her eyes and Creighton helped pull her up. When they followed her to their horse, the enormity of the responsibility hit her. In less than a sennight, these children trusted her to take care of them. Trusted her enough to follow her to a land they had never been. Trusted her enough to allow an unknown *English* soldier to travel with them. It was a trust she could barely comprehend.

She helped Creighton mount first, and then Flora. They looked at her expectantly.

Maybe it went a bit beyond trust. Maybe they had started caring for her.

Handing Creighton the reins, she knew she would not fail them.

The weather did not hold. In less than an hour, the air chilled, the mist turned heavier and within moments the wind was hurtling rain sideways.

Robert bent forward and used his arms to shield his eyes. The trees provided no buffer and the horses trailed behind him. He did not need to raise his head to see the huddled forms of the children and Gaira leaning low on the horses.

Still Maisie's cries were heard above the wind and rain. He was glad the child was enclosed in Gaira's arms and near her ears and not his own.

Something was amiss. Gaira's manner disturbed him. One moment she was determined to stay and rest and in the next she hurried the children on the horses as if there were a rushing river about to drown them all.

And she looked to be just as fearful. It wasn't the first time he had seen fear cross her face or even the first time he'd seen her hurry. She had asked several times if he could bury the dead quickly. He had thought at first her fear and urgency were results of what had happened at Doonhill, but now he wondered if it was something else. But why would a woman with four children need to hurry?

He had no answers and nothing about her made sense.

She wore a man's tunic and hose and she travelled alone. She might have told the truth of her sister and her coming to Doonhill, but she had not told him why she was going there in the first place.

A blast of wind forced him to sidestep. When he righted himself, the rain suddenly stopped as if someone had put a stopper in the sky. Maisie stopped crying right along with it. After the roaring sound of wind and rain, the heavy silence, interrupted by only drips of water from the trees and the snort of the horses, seemed otherworldly.

Blue sky and bright rays of sun scattered through the trees and the rain-covered grass and bluebells sparkled in the bright light. He supposed it would have been beautiful, except he was drenched and heavy cold drops of rain fell on top of him from the trees.

'We have to get out of the trees,' he called back. 'We'll never dry.'

'We might lose the trail,' Gaira answered.

'We'll follow the treeline until the ground dries.'

'But I'm not sure—'

'I'm getting out of the wet trees. You can follow me or not. But I'm for getting dry.'

He began to walk to the east, but he heard her reply before he heard the horses behind him.

'I've heard the English were soft, but I had nae idea a few drops of rain would have you running for fairer weather.'

He did not deem her taunt worthy of a reply.

'I am not surprised, you know,' she continued.

She wouldn't leave it alone and he was rising to the bait. 'Wanting to be dry is practical. Getting ill or chafing the skin so it is open for infection is not soft, but pig-headed.'

'Is it also pig-headedness prompting you to have a beautifully carved saddle with padding so thick, it is like riding on air? Or is it just practicality causing you to wear a weave of clothing so fine its softness rivals flower petals?'

He sluiced the water out of his hair. 'I do not lack for coin. It provides me such things.'

'Aye, and I suppose you'd argue it is nae a sin to want things of comfort.'

'I like comfort.'

'Aye, that's because you're soft.'

Tired of defending himself, he turned around. He was expecting derision on her face or the familiar humour, but neither emotion was there. Instead of a flash in her eyes or a curve to her lips, there was paleness behind her freckles and whiteness around her mouth.

'What game do you play?'

Even with her arms around Maisie, he saw her hands jerked on the reins.

'Do not play me for a fool, woman. You think pricking at my pride will keep me within this treeline, which means you don't want me outside the cover of these trees. Why?'

'I doona know what you're talking about.'

'Or is it you who should stay within hiding?' he questioned, the thought taking root. 'Is this even the trail to the nearest village?'

She pulled roughly on the reins, forcing the horse past him and heading east out of the trees.

'I just want to get us there and be safe again,' she retorted. 'If you want to risk our safety just so you can be dry, so be it, Englishman.'

He let her get a few yards in front of him. 'What would be unsafe outside this treeline?' he asked.

She did not raise her voice, but he still heard her. 'Why, your comrades who burned Doonhill. Who else?'

For the first time in their acquaintance, he did not believe her.

Because even if she forgot, he hadn't. She had already argued she no longer feared the English who'd attacked Doonhill.

She seemed without guile and he had believed her

about Doonhill and her sister. But observation told him there was more to her story.

It was the man's tunic and leggings she wore. Nothing survived from Doonhill, so she must have been wearing the clothing on her way there.

She had also travelled alone. No woman travelled alone. Maybe that was why she had disguised herself in man's clothing, but it was a weak disguise.

Then there were her fear and urgency, which added to the story. And all of it confirmed Gaira was running. But with four children and only two horses, she wasn't running anywhere fast. Without some truths from her, he couldn't protect himself and couldn't protect them.

He was a fool to be stuck in whatever mess she had made and an even greater fool for not knowing the reason.

Because whatever she was running from was going to catch up to them.

Chapter Twelve

When they exited the shade of the trees, Gaira blinked against the sunlight and Alec sneezed into her back. Since his little hands were clutched around her waist, she did not have to imagine where the sneeze landed.

'Cover your mouth next time, Alec.'

Giggles.

They were like an instantaneous balm to her increasing worry.

Robert walked in front again. Except this time, they were on the true trail north to home. The exact road she had travelled before. In plain sight. Where her brothers or Busby of Ayrshire could find them.

She didn't know what she feared more. Her traitorous brothers or her murdering betrothed. Or was it her murdering brothers and her traitorous betrothed?

She hoped she was making the right decision by returning to Colquhoun land. Though her brother had betrayed her, he could not be unkind to four orphaned children. She was also hoping he'd allow her to stay. After all, someone had to take care of the children.

Returning to her betrothed wasn't an option. She didn't know much about Busby of Ayrshire except his wives had died and his home and clan were poorly kept. At the time she'd ridden with him, she'd been too shocked at her brother's betrayal to pay much attention. Even so, she'd been aware of his brutish size, his coarse words and the way he'd looked at her: disgusted and calculating.

But was Busby's reputation and crude behaviour worse than her brother tricking his beloved sister? Or a sister that thought she was beloved?

She looked around for a distraction from her wayward thoughts. Unfortunately, the tall wet grass and the hopping insects weren't much of a distraction. But Robert was.

His fine dark figure cut against the wet green grass and sunshine. His broad shoulders, thick legs and even his relaxed arms, slightly swinging, were a braw sight. No movement was wasted; he walked, but saved his energy, as if he could make the complete journey just by his legs alone. Given his strength, she had no doubt he could.

She suspected he purposefully kept the pacing of the horses slow. He seemed to know what was needed for the children. Creighton was handling his horse well, but Flora was terrified and Alec and Maisie barely kept their balance.

Robert was a distraction to her, but that was not all and she had a terrible suspicion she knew what the rest of her feelings were. And she had only known him for two days.

Want. Pure and simple. She didn't know how it had come to be, but there it was. She tried to think maybe her feelings for him had to do with her longing for somebody, anybody, to get her out of the mess she was in.

After all, she had never begged God more passionately than for some help out of her situation. Then Robert had arrived.

Despite his scruffy appearance and rough manner, there was something solid about him. Unchangeable. Strong, not just in body but spirit, too. He wouldn't sell his sister. He wouldn't abuse his servants, or keep a mean, dirty, household. No, she suspected in Robert's realm everything would be neat, tidy and in its place. And she also suspected he wouldn't take to anyone upsetting that order.

And lying? She could easily imagine him slitting the throat of any man who would do so.

She could only hope that he would have some leniency with her lying. After all, she did it to protect some orphaned children...and herself.

'We'll need to find shelter soon,' Robert said.

The sun was beginning to parallel the earth. 'There's a thick copse of trees over the next hill. They aren't just birches, but some oaks, they'll provide more shelter than what we've got here.'

His eyes pierced hers before he nodded and returned to walking.

She tried to slow her heart when he turned away. Strong. Aye, that was the word for him, and just a little too knowing. There was no doubt he knew she had lied to him about the previous road they took.

Ah, well, there was no hope for it. She was lying to him and had been from the beginning. But her concern was for the children and getting them to the relative safety of Colquhoun land. She'd risk anything for their sakes.

Her only hope was that Robert wouldn't abandon them when he realised she had risked his life as well as her own.

It didn't take long to make camp, to find food or put the children to rest. Even Creighton fell asleep in only a few moments.

A pox on them all.

Without at least Maisie's crying, she had no barrier against the man who sat near the fire. His arms resting against bent knees, his manner relaxed, patient. Waiting to talk to her.

Gaira walked around the children one more time. She stared at Maisie, hoping that the slight fluttering of her eyelids would mean she'd waken and Gaira could take care of her. But it was only the gentle fluttering of sleep. Nothing more.

Chiding herself for the coward she was, she walked quietly around the fire and sat near him. She thought she had sat far enough away so his nearness would not affect her, but she was wrong. He'd probably have to be across the sea for her not to be aware of him now.

'I need some truth.'

She didn't take her eyes from the fire, but nodded once in acknowledgement.

'Are you truly from the Colquhoun clan?'

If he saw her brothers, he would not waste his questions. Every too-tall red-haired inch of her was from that clan. 'Aye.'

'Is their land north and along this trail we travel?'

'I said it was and 'tis just where I told you, too, by the Firth of Clyde.'

He nodded slowly. 'Is there a village or some place we can purchase a horse and some supplies along this route?'

She looked over at him; he was looking at her intently. Too intently. She turned her eyes to the fire again. For now his questions were safe and she saw no harm in answering them.

'Aye, we should reach there by tomorrow.'

'Why did we travel through the trees before?'

She bit the inside of her mouth, thinking. This was a question she did not want to answer. 'I must have been a little off in my direction.'

She kept her gaze away. She was not good at lying and dreaded any more questions of why they travelled through the trees.

He adjusted himself and turned his body to face her. 'Tell me of your family.'

Surprised, she glanced at him. She'd rather talk of trees than of her family. 'My family? You do have a sense of humour, Robert of Dent.'

He ignored her jibe. 'Just curiosity.'

'What is there to say?' She shrugged. 'My mother and father had three boys and two girls. It was not a large family by Scottish standards, but Mother died in childbirth with my sister, Irvette, and Papa broke his neck training a horse. So we were it.'

She stopped, clenched her mind from remembering too much. 'And now with what happened at Doonhill, we are one less.'

In the rush to protect the children, she had purposefully not thought of her sister. It felt like knives to her heart to have the merest thought of her now.

'Were your brothers kind to you and your sister?' he asked.

His questioning surprised her, but she could not

help the feeling of relief in avoiding the truth of her travel. Coward that she was. 'Nae, it was a battle from the beginning,' she said. 'They were gentler with my sister, but with my height and strength, I think they forgot I was a girl.'

She took a quick glance over at him. He was staring at her legs. She became all too aware of the length of her legs, but instead of her usual embarrassment, she felt like stretching them. It was the way he was looking at them. She became all warm, just as she did when he'd held her in the valley. Then she remembered how he had dropped her like a rat. Embarrassed, she tucked her legs under her.

'I gave as good as I got,' she continued. 'Or at least got cleverer about it.' She laughed softly. 'By the time I was twelve, I was running the keep. My brothers couldn't tease me any more about my hair, because they'd find stones in their bread.'

He made a sound that might have been close to a chuckle. 'I have no doubt of your authority. You did swing a cauldron at me.'

'You deserved it,' she reminded him. 'It was Irvette who grew up to be beautiful and even though I was the elder, the men started to court her. She never wanted power or wealth, so when Aengus Cathcart came with nae more than dreams of a little house in a pretty spot, she was in love. My brothers, too soft when it came to her, couldn't deny her wishes. They let her wed, though it did not prosper the clan.'

She shrugged. 'I was glad for her and by then I was firmly entrenched in Clan Colquhoun. I took good care of the boys and thought I knew what was needed and expected of me.'

She stopped suddenly and tried to keep her thoughts from crossing her face. He was paying too close attention not to notice her anger or her pain. She did not want to explain what her brothers had done to her.

'Something happened,' he said.

She turned her gaze away from him again. 'Aye, Irvette getting killed, that's what happened.' She stood and hugged her arms around her. 'Is that the type of information you were looking for, Englishman?'

She meant the question as a challenge, a way to push him away from the conversation.

But she knew the moment he took her words in a different direction. He still sat, but there was a slight movement in his cheek, a light to his eyes. Without moving, he answered her challenge with one of his own. It was a challenge that made her heart flip and her stomach contract. She lowered her eyes and tried to shutter her emotions.

'It depends,' he answered.

'On what?'

'On what you're not telling me.'

He stood and stepped closer to her. Gently, he caressed down her jaw until he reached her chin and lifted it.

Given her height, her eyes did not have far to travel to reach his. 'You reveal too little of yourself to me.' He lowered his hand, but did not step back. 'And I'm a damned man for being curious.'

She noticed the brown flecks of his eyes become cold, but it did not make him less warm to her. She knew the coldness was directed towards himself. He desired her and did not want to. She could think of only one reason, but she did not want to guess. She wanted to be told.

'Why?' she asked, clasping her hands in front of her.

The change in his breathing indicated that her question surprised him. Suddenly, she was not sure she wanted the answer to her question. If he thought he was damned for being curious, she was damned right along with him.

His fingers traced down from her elbow to her clasped hands. He found her exposed wrist and made tiny circles there, circles she felt to the very centre of her.

'Because of who I am.'

His eyes held hers and she felt the pull in them,

the wanting to be closer, and she knew that wanting came from her.

It couldn't come from him. Because he'd all but admitted what she feared. 'You are married,' she said.

Surprise flashed in his eyes. 'No, God, no, Gaira. I stand so close to you I can feel your breath fan my skin.'

'That does not preclude you from being married.'

'It does me. If I were married, it would be for life, Gaira. My life, my body—all my life and all my body.'

His words ran up and down her heart, making it tender in her chest. He was that deep river, constant, life-giving. But if he wasn't married now, did that mean he had never loved? She cursed her heart for needing to know.

'You were never married before?' she asked.

His hand returned to his side. 'No, I was never given the chance.'

Never given the chance to marry did not mean he had never loved. It just meant the love was denied. Her heart, already tender, stabbed her soul.

'We should get some sleep.' She stepped back. 'Maisie will be waking soon and I'll have nae energy for her.'

Robert did not try to stop her, but watched as Gaira returned to the children, who were asleep in a bundle of legs and arms. It was a warm night and Gaira's shawl was strewn between them.

He stood for just a few minutes longer, then he returned to his side of the fire and bundled a blanket under his head. The ground had dried sufficiently and he felt too warm for any cover.

Hell, he burned.

She had kept her hair bound since he'd asked her, but she kept it only in a simple thick plait and the effect was almost worse than it loose. He could imagine how easy it would be to untie the single leather string and slowly unravel the soft curls. He could almost feel how the bright tendrils of her hair would wrap around his fingers.

When he had stood so close to her, he'd felt how well her legs matched his own, how little he'd have to lift her to press her against him.

She had said her brothers had not thought her a girl. He could not seem to stop thinking of her as a woman grown, with a woman's curves and valleys.

Robert rolled roughly to his side. He wouldn't get any sleep if he let his thoughts wander too far down that path.

But he could not avoid thinking of her. So he'd force himself to think about her words and not the way she smelled or the lusciousness of her peach-coloured lips. Or her legs she tucked beneath her.

Robert rolled again to lie on his back and he hit

the blanket under his head to fluff it. There was much to think about what she had said. He had asked for truth, but he'd heard more than what she had said.

Something in her tale of her family had upset her, but he knew it was more than her sister dying. Her anger and grief over her sister was understandable, but that death had happened much later than her reminiscences.

Some of her hurt came before Doonhill. She had not told him why she had left her brothers. If she was as needed as she said, why had they let her go?

He had told her he was curious. What he did not tell her or what he didn't want to tell himself was why he was curious. He had no right thinking of Gaira's life or her legs.

She was a woman with a strength of will and spirit he never knew existed. When she felt or fought, it was with her whole being, her whole heart. She deserved a man who was as whole in heart, as well.

And he knew, all too well, his heart had stopped beating years ago.

Chapter Thirteen

Robert woke to breathing in his ear and a hot weight across his chest. Alec was sprawled across him. His face, soft and rosy, was scrunched against Robert's tunic and his rounded arms were splayed above his head and around Robert's neck.

'He looks different that way, doesn't he?' Gaira whispered.

Gaira was standing above him, her arms full of Maisie.

'How did he get here?' Robert mouthed.

'Must have been late. He was getting nightmares before you came.'

'What do I do?' he whispered.

She gave an enigmatic smile and turned away. 'I think that's up to you.'

Robert watched Gaira's departure and just barely stopped himself from calling to her. He didn't know what to do with the children on this journey and they mostly had left him alone.

Yet, sometime in the middle of the night, Alec had come to him and fallen asleep again. As if, somehow, Robert was somewhere safe.

Robert twisted his eyes to look at the boy. He saw the slight fluttering of eyelids, the soft down of his eyelashes, the pink lips allowing his gentle breath.

Robert stayed still, not only because he didn't want to wake the boy, but because he thought his legs wouldn't work properly. He was bewildered by the trust. He had done nothing to earn it. He had simply been lying there.

And that was the strangest of all, for how did the boy not wake him? Had he known in his sleep, somehow, that it was only Alec?

He closed his eyes again, imagining, thinking, and felt a little hand lightly tap his cheeks.

Alec, his brown eyes huge, stared at him.

Staring back, Robert felt something brush near his heart. 'Morning,' he said gruffly.

Abruptly, Alec's hand slapped against his cheek.

Robert immediately sat, blinking back the unexpected sting. Giggling, Alec slid in a heap in his lap.

'Oh, you think that's a fine jest, do you?' Robert growled. 'Let's see how you feel about this!'

Standing, Robert grabbed the boy by his waist

and hung him upside down as if he were a fish. The boy squirmed just as if he were caught on a hook.

'You had better set him down unless you want an accident on your clothes,' Gaira said as she finished straightening Maisie's clothes. 'He hasn't relieved himself yet.'

With a quick flip, Alec was righted and set free.

Gaira smiled and he found himself wanting to smile back. He turned his back before he did.

He hadn't truly smiled in years. Part of his reputation lay in that fact. His reputation… All thoughts of laughter left him.

Gaira had said they'd reach the next village before the day ended. Although he was further north than he'd ever been, he could not take the chance of being recognised. It would not only put him, but also Gaira and the children, in jeopardy.

His hand went to his beard and through his hair. He didn't have different clothes to wear, but there was something he could do to alter his appearance. It had been years since he'd properly shaven and had shorter hair.

Grabbing his knife from his satchel and a sliver of his soap, he headed to the stream running through the trees.

When he returned to the clearing, the children and Gaira were waiting for him. Gaira was sitting and talking with Flora. Their heads were bowed together as they picked long blades of grass and wove them into chains. Maisie stood next to them, swinging grass blades in the air, and Creighton, with rocks in his hands, sat watching them.

He knew they had been brought together in less than a sennight, but they already interacted as a family. A family brought together by fate and grief. But something about them still looked content with each other.

In all the years he had fought for King Edward, he hadn't found the peace they had in just days.

Gaira looked up. Her eyes flicked over him briefly before returning to the chain in her lap. In almost jester quality, her head swivelled back up, her eyes widened and her mouth dropped open. She said something to Flora, who also looked up.

He walked over to them. 'Are you ready to travel?' he asked.

Gaira didn't say anything to him. There was something in her gaze. Surprise, but something else that quickened his blood.

'Miss Flora, are you ready to leave?' he asked.

'What happened to your face?' She clapped her hand over her mouth and turned bright red.

He opened his mouth. Closed it. He could hardly tell her the truth. He'd have to bluster through. He made a big gesture of clasping his hands behind his back.

'I realised I was unfit for your august company. Thus, to look more respectable, I shaved my beard and cut my hair.'

He paused before meeting Gaira's gaze. It was more than astonishment he saw in her eyes. It was desire.

He had thought himself alone in his wanting of her. The fact she reacted even in the slightest way to him was too...tempting.

He did not need temptations or complications. And Gaira was both. He thought himself a damned man just for being curious about her, but his curiosity did not compare to his desire. If he gave in to it, his bloodstained soul would most certainly be damned.

But still he wanted her. Despite his obligations to the English crown. Obligations he had been neglecting since Doonhill. It had been too long since he was away. Hugh would have alerted King Edward by now.

They probably thought he had deserted them. And how was he to explain his absence? He had been acting like a besotted fool, not a trained warrior. He had to get this journey over with and quickly.

'As soon as I pack my items, we'll go,' he said.

Angry at himself, he turned roughly away and went to pick up his bag, blanket and longsword.

Something was missing. His blanket and bag lay on the ground where he had left them. But not his longsword. He looked over at his horse. The saddle was on the ground, the claymore and pouches were still attached. He glanced around the camp. More than his longsword was missing.

'Gaira!' he called. 'Where's Alec?'

She looked over at him and a smile broke out. 'Oh, Robert, if you could see your face! You look as if you've slipped in a bog. Did he steal something of yours?'

She began to laugh, and pointed towards the trees. 'I think he went that way.'

He didn't know what kept his feet planted for even that second longer—Gaira's beautiful laugh, or that a five-year-old boy had stolen a sword that could slice off his arm with the slightest scrape.

She stopped laughing, an expression of concern replacing her mirth. 'What's wrong?'

'My sword.' He lost his voice. 'Gaira, he's got my sword.'

All trace of laughter and colour drained from her face. She scrambled up, the many grass blades falling forgotten to the ground. Grabbing his arm, she momentarily dragged him until he felt the tug, which propelled him to action.

Good God, he never hesitated once in battle. If he had, he'd be dead. But just the thought of Alec hurt stunned him.

He knew now what his soldiers meant when they said they felt cold sweat and ice feet. He knew now what it felt like to feel panic, sure and swift. It hadn't happened because there was ten-to-one odds in battle, or because a Scotsman was swinging a double-headed axe at his head—it happened because of a little boy.

At what point had he started to care?

In the woods, Gaira broke off and ran to his right. The trees provided little cover, but the terrain was full of hills and Alec was short. A child. Searching the ground, he found it: the trail. Not of feet, but of something being dragged. The sword would be too heavy for Alec.

'Over here,' he called to Gaira. Following the trail, he ran down the hill.

Alec was raising a thick log over his head. But the size and weight of the log was not what made his knees buckle, it was the position of the sword that lay perpendicular to Alec.

It was raised and buttressed between two trees. If the boy slipped when he was bringing down the log, he could decapitate himself without the smallest of breaths.

Robert wanted to shout a warning, but he didn't

want to startle the boy. Yet if he didn't warn him...
He ran faster.

Gaira was still to Robert's right and just a little
ahead of him. She was hurtling herself down the
slope towards Alec. She must have seen what he
did, for her eyes were wide with fear, her running
frantic.

'Stop!' she screamed. 'Alec, stop!'

With her ankle unhealed and the ground muddy,
Gaira slipped and stumbled. Trying to run and gain
her balance at the same time, Gaira continued towards Alec.

And the sword.

There was not enough space to recover her balance. She was stumbling, flailing and, at the angle
it was at, she'd impale herself on the sword's tip.

It was a nightmare.

'Gaira!' Robert shouted. 'Run another way!'

Alec looked up, the log still in his hands. He
grinned when he saw Gaira, but then he began to
scream.

At Alec's scream, Gaira stopped trying to fix her
balance and increased her pace. She didn't even
know she was the one in danger. She slipped again,
her arms splaying out in all directions, her feet coming up from under her on the muddy slope.

Robert lunged forward and knocked her out of
the sword's path. But his body was too large and

too close. The sword effortlessly sliced his tunic and his ribcage.

At the sharp pain, Robert's fear quickly turned to anger.

Chapter Fourteen

Gaira didn't spare him a glance, but went straight
to Alec and wrapped the sobbing boy in her arms.

'Ach, now, it's all right, baby, it's all right.' She
wrapped him even tighter and the sobs turned from
hysterical to great gasping gulps of air and tears.
''Tis fine now. You're not hurt, are you, now?' Her
hands and eyes hurriedly inspected Alec's clothes
and body.

'The *boy* is fine.' Robert grabbed the sword's hilt
and moved away from the mud.

She was cradling Alec's face, her trembling hands
wiping briskly over Alec's wet cheeks. 'But he's
scared to death, though, isn't he?' Her head nodded
emphatically.

Alec nodded along with her.

Robert raised the blade. Satisfied it was only
muddy and not nicked by a random stone or, worse,

the boy himself, he said, 'The boy should be scared. He almost hurt himself and you.'

'Me? Not hardly. I slipped a bit, but my ankle feels fine.'

He searched for the scabbard. 'I'm not talking about your damn ankle. He could have decapitated himself on this sword, and you!' Robert's anger tightened. 'You tried to impale yourself on it in your rush to get to the boy.'

She clamped her hands against Alec's ears. 'What are you trying to do, scare him even more? He's a child. He doesn't need such graphic nonsense.'

'Nonsense?'

Her brows were drawn inward and she looked... stubborn. She actually believed what she was saying.

'He was just trying to help us. Couldn't you see he was trying to make kindling for our fire?'

He found the scabbard. It was damp from the grass and he laid the sword next to it. Both would have to be cleaned before he put them together again. 'I don't care what the boy was trying to do, what he did was wrong.'

Robert walked over to them and crouched down so he was almost eye level. 'Do you understand it was wrong to take someone else's property without asking permission first?'

The boy looked with his huge brown eyes and said

nothing. Robert felt his frown deepen. The boy did not understand.

'Never. *Never* do that again. You could have killed yourself. Dead.'

Alec kept his wide-eyed stare, but didn't say anything. Gaira glared at him. He didn't care.

His anger was coiled so tight now, the barest addition of an irritation would make it flare. He'd never lost his temper and the fact he was so close now, and the fact that a five-year-old boy was bringing him to the edge, only further angered him.

He stood to give himself some distance. He'd already explained to the boy about death and property, but Alec gave him no acknowledgement. Now he was forced to ask for an apology. From a five-year-old boy. If only King Edward could see him now.

He pointed his finger at the boy. 'I demand you explain why you would take my sword and scare Gaira terribly—'

'I'm sorry,' squeaked Alec.

Robert stopped.

Alec was worriedly looking at Gaira and back to him. 'I won't do it again.' Alec gave quick shakes of his head. 'I doona want to scare Auntie Gaira again.'

The boy had apologised. But to Gaira. That did it. Everyone in this motley family was mad. That he had agreed to travel with them was a serious lack of judgement on his part.

Gaira stood and patted Alec on the back. 'Why doona you return to the camp? There'll be some food for you there.'

Alec dragged his feet through the grass as he climbed the slope and disappeared over the ledge.

'Now look at what you've done.' Gaira turned to him. 'You doona need to shout at him. He's only a child.'

'I didn't shout.'

'Aye, you did, and you scared him to death, too. All that talk about hurting me. He's already lost his parents. He dinna need the scare of losing me, too!'

So that was the reason the boy had suddenly apologised, but that didn't change the truth. 'He did almost hurt you! He almost killed you.'

'That's ridiculous.' She gave a soft snort. 'How could he have hurt me? You were the one pushing me into the mud.'

He took a step closer and pointed to the sword. He was not in the wrong here. He couldn't believe he even *felt* defensive. 'You were hurtling towards a sword pointed right at your heart. I pushed you out of harm's way. I saved your life!'

By her expression, he knew she hadn't been aware of her own danger. She had been so focused on the boy's safety, she'd disregarded her own. He should not have been surprised. Since he'd known her she had done nothing but sacrifice herself for others.

She straightened to her full height and leaned towards him. 'Even if that is so, it is hardly the boy's fault. He doesn't deserve you glowering at him.'

He couldn't believe what she was saying. Just the mere thought of what had almost happened made his anger swirl with fear. 'Not his fault!' If he shouted now, it was only because this stubborn woman made no sense at all. 'It's entirely his fault. He took my sword. He hid in the woods. He used sharp steel as some sort of axe. He could have cut his head off! And you!'

He took a quick breath. 'You were just as careless as he! Crying out, running through mud, slipping right towards the sword tip. You could have been cut in half!'

Her face flushed, her eyes flared and she poked him in the chest. 'Ach, I had nae caution, you brastling gaupie! What about you? You recklessly left the sword out when there are children around!'

Anger crackled in every fibre of her body. He felt it. He saw it in the flash of her hair, the light of her eyes. But she was standing right in front of him and she was so very *whole*.

'Reckless!' He grabbed her arms and yanked her to him. 'I'll show you reckless!'

He felt satisfaction in the widening of her eyes and the slight parting of her lips. But satisfaction was quickly swamped by the stronger feeling of how she felt against him. She was all slender, tall limbs, moulding to his body.

If she had pushed him away, if she had protested, even if she had just kept her anger, he might have been able to pull away. But her eyes turned to clouded whisky and he didn't stand a chance.

Gaira had felt his hard male body when she had accidentally slid into him. She had even felt his arms support her before, but she hadn't felt his intent before. His desire swept over her in great rolling waves and she knew she would have drowned if he hadn't locked his arms around her.

Then his lips captured her mouth and she knew she was drowning, swimming in liquid heat. Hot, feral and so very greedy.

Reaching around his waist, she leaned further into him. She felt his breath, felt the firm pressure of his mouth, the insistence to open. She did.

The feeling of his tongue upon hers, tracing the inside of her lips with a light, wet caress, pooled across her heart and lower. She pressed against him, wanting to be closer.

He complied. Lifting her, curving his hand around her, pressing her against him. She gasped at the sweep of heat to her breasts and she dug her fingers into his sides.

He growled and pushed her away. She felt the panting of breath fill her chest, the cool air brush across her breasts and a warm sticky wetness covering her right hand.

Looking down at her hand, she blinked through her haze at the bright red covering her fingers.

'It looks worse than it feels,' Robert said.

'You're hurt!'

'In more ways than one.'

She grabbed his tunic and pushed his arm roughly out of the way.

'I'll not like further injury,' he added.

'Oh!' She dropped his arm. 'Does it pain you?'

'It does now.' He laid a hand on her shoulder. 'But I think it has more to do with my mind being occupied with the wound rather than with other... thoughts.'

Her face flamed.

He took a step back. 'I should not have done that.'

She swallowed to cover the sudden lump in her throat. 'Aye, your...lecture to Alec was unconventional, but he is a child and I'm sure he has recovered.'

He glanced at her. Already, the heat in his eyes was cool, distant, but she saw something swirling there before he turned his head away. Anger?

'That is not what I meant.'

She nodded. She knew that. She just didn't want to discuss why he shouldn't have kissed her. She wanted to be kissed. She didn't want to hear he hadn't wanted it, too. 'We should take care of your wound.'

'I brought thread for stitching and cloth for bandaging. It will be fine.'

'I'll help you.'

'No, I have done it before and it won't take me long.' His voice was level and so removed. 'If I need further ministrations, I'll find some when we reach the next village.'

'But you could go into fever. At least let me stay with you until we are sure.'

'There won't be the time.' He turned and picked up his sword and scabbard. 'This scratch changes nothing. Once I get your supplies and a horse, I will be gone.'

So he still planned to leave them, even after they'd kissed. Had she imagined she felt something for him when he'd held her?

And what about Alec? She thought he had been genuinely concerned for the boy's safety.

He was not even looking back to see if she followed him up the hill. It was as if he was already getting ready to leave them.

How could he change so fast? She still reeled from the feeling of his kiss. He'd left as if he felt nothing.

She pressed her lips and felt the tender, swollen feel of them. He had roughly kissed her, his arms and hands had shoved and pressed her to him, as if she was his air, food and shelter.

She had not imagined that. Nor had she imagined the worry in his features when he'd raced down the hill and lectured the boy. He had been worried for Alec and worried for her.

He did have feelings. She knew with her heart he wasn't being cold and distant because he didn't feel. It was because he didn't *want* to feel emotion for a five-year-old boy and didn't want to feel anything for a woman with gangly legs.

But he had displayed both just moments before. And that thought made her feel just a bit lighter.

She swung her single plait over her shoulder and followed Robert back to camp.

Chapter Fifteen

It was late in the day when they reached the village. It took some time for Robert to clean and stitch his wound and even longer to clean his sword and scabbard. She argued with him to help, but he wouldn't let her touch him.

The road into the village was not much wider than the two horses and at first there was nothing more than a few crofters' huts surrounded by gardens. When the road narrowed even more, the huts became tightly built buildings sharing common walls. Taking the reins of Creighton and Flora's horse, Robert slowly manoeuvred them through people and farm animals until they reached the square. The busiest building was a little taller than the others, with dark slits for windows. The doors were open and a din of voices echoed.

'This isn't a mere village,' Robert remarked. 'Did you stay here?'

'Nae.' Gaira relaxed her tight hold on the reins. It was more of a town. When she'd fled, she had avoided the many huts and buildings. But now she was relieved it had accommodation. Storm clouds were moving in from the north and they needed the protection.

He soothed the side of the horse's neck. 'I thought you travelled this way before.'

'I dinna spare the time for rest.'

He looked at her a moment longer and shrugged. ''Tis late now. We'd be lucky if they have rooms available for the night.'

Relieved at a change of subject, she rushed her words. 'I'll see to it. Despite your using our tongue, you are still English. At best they'll quote you a higher price, at worst they'll lop off your head.'

He spoke to her in Gaelic. 'But you are a woman and it's not safe for you to go in alone.'

She smiled. 'You doona stand a chance with that pronunciation.'

'Even so, I think it's—'

Loud laughter poured out of the inn. Three large Scotsmen, wide grins plastered on, came stumbling out.

Blinking rapidly, one of them waved. 'Ho, ho, greetings, welcome, welcome on such a happy day!'

Gaira laughed and inclined her head. 'It is a happy day with such a welcome.'

One of the men stumbled and another clutched his waist. The more sober, but no steadier, man answered back. 'Ach, lass, it is a happy day with your fair face, but we have great news!'

'Great news!' one of his comrades chimed in.

Gaira's horse shied. 'What news is this?'

'Haven't you heard?'

'Nae, we just arrived,' she answered.

'"Black Robert" is dead!'

'Dead! Deaded, deader.' Stumbling, the Scot landed in a heap on the ground and he took his comrade with him.

'Dead!' Maisie clapped her hands in front of her face. Alec giggled into Gaira's back.

The two fallen comrades were failing to right themselves again. They were both as big as oxen and looked just as graceful. Gaira swivelled her attention to the still-standing man.

'Black Robert?' she asked.

'Doona you know the dirty Englishman? Fights as though he's possessed, he does. Must've sold his soul. He's black as night, bigger than any Scotsman and has eyes that…glow. Yellow. And worse, he's taken the Scotsmen's right arm, the claymore, and can wield it with just the…tips of his fingers.' The man rubbed his fat belly. 'Too many good Scots have been gutted by that English scourge.'

'I see,' Gaira answered. She was unsure what to say. To be polite she added, 'What happened?'

'None sure, fair lass. Wasn't there. Too far east. The English dog King and his army were there, to which...' The Scotsman belched. 'Sorry to say... Lost many... None were victors. But we received vital news, vital news. Black Robert's men were there, but nae Black Robert. A couple of days this battle took place, but he never. Showed. His beard.'

'Was he found afterward?' Gaira asked. 'You know...' She gestured towards the children, hoping he'd tell her without details.

The man rocked precariously. 'Nae, nae body, miss, but he's never missed a battle, has he now? He would've been by the King of side Edward.' He gave a wide grin again. 'He's a bloody mess dead, he is.'

The two fallen comrades came unsteadily to their feet and stumbled down the road.

The one talking to Gaira swivelled his head, swayed and seemed to lose focus before he shouted, 'Ho, ho, to home they go!'

He gave Gaira a cheeky grin and a wink. 'Can't hold their drink, they can't.'

Gaira watched as the man took a stumbling step, righted himself and walked after his comrades. She turned her attention to Robert, Creighton and Flora. Creighton and Flora watched the men with rapt interest, but Robert averted his head and his hands were tight on the reins.

With the three men gone, the sounds from the inn roared out to them again. She moved her horse closer to them. Leaning over, she whispered, 'We at least know their feelings on the English if they celebrate one of their deaths. Can you agree now, it'll be better if I go and see if rooms are available?'

'You'll go,' he whispered in Gaelic. 'You'll go and see if there's a room. But I'll be leaving this night.'

She gave a snort. 'Ach, now, nae reason to be afraid, I'll protect you, I will. You should stay.'

He glanced up at her, his eyes blazing with an emotion she could not name. 'No,' he answered.

She ripped her eyes from his. He was acting too strangely to argue with. Without a word, she handed him Maisie and helped Alec dismount.

When she walked out of the inn, Robert was holding the horses and Alec and Maisie were jumping up in front of him to gain his attention. Alec was laughing, but Robert's face was turned away from her and she couldn't tell what he thought of their play.

She looked around the square. Creighton and Flora were at the opposite side, watching the blacksmith work.

Robert, his shoulders rounded, his face lowered,

wasn't even watching them. Perhaps he was only spooked by the celebrations. But Robert spooked over anything was worrisome.

Whatever was happening with him, they still needed his protection. He had told her he'd help her only to the nearest village, but she'd hoped he'd help her some more. She dared not travel further west or they'd be too near Busby's keep. In order to avoid that, they had to go east and over Buchanan land. Since the Buchanans and Colquhouns had been fighting for years, she would not be a welcome sight on their land. The children needed his protection.

'Good news.' She ruffled Alec's hair. 'The innkeeper says he has one room large enough for our party. We'll only need one room anyway, since we have children.'

Robert did not raise his face.

''Tis too dark to travel now, and it's going to rain,' she added.

He turned to her, his face implacable, his features cold. She almost wished for his earlier anger or at least his gruffness. This was a Robert she knew nothing about.

'I'll leave by first light,' he said. 'You'll have to be on your own to get your supplies. I will not stay any longer.'

She had a feeling it was the worst possible time

to ask for any favours, but then again, the past few weeks had been the worst possible time for her. 'I'll still be needing your money, as I have none.'

'You'll have it.' His lips almost curved, but it wasn't in humour. 'Isn't that the reason you goaded me on this trip?'

He mocked her. How could she explain needing money hadn't occurred to her until they'd started travelling? When she had asked him to help her, she had only been thinking of using Robert's horse and Robert's protection. Embarrassed, she stated, 'I had nae...'

Simultaneously, Robert whispered, 'Beg pardon.' He grabbed Maisie's hand and pulled her up from the ground. 'I did not mean to embarrass you.'

He'd apologised. He never apologised. She didn't understand him. If he had displayed this icy cold-ness before, she wouldn't have asked him to travel with them. He looked every bit as unsafe as she could imagine. She couldn't imagine staring in want of him now, let alone...kissing him. Her cheeks flushed. He had been acting oddly since they'd ar-rived here, but she realised that since she had met him, she'd been acting just as oddly. Kissing and wanting a stranger, demanding his protection and money. Demanding...him.

'Nae, it's I who should beg forgiveness,' she said. 'I really had nae intention of—'

'Enough,' he said. 'This journey is full of unintended actions. Let us see what they offer.'

The moment they opened the door, the innkeeper came barrelling towards them. She grabbed Alec's hand and addressed the rounded man. 'We are all ready if you are.'

'Aye, lass, my wife has got the bed ready for you and I'll find some shelter for the horses in the back.'

Gaira called for Creighton and Flora, then followed the innkeeper into the building.

Her eyes had hardly adjusted to the dim light as the innkeeper manoeuvred them through the tables and boisterous patrons leaning against whitewashed walls.

The room was in the back of the dining room. It was a simple, crude room and consisted of a low fireplace, one bed and one very tiny stool. What it did not consist of was space. She had agreed to the room because the innkeeper had said it was big enough for them.

The bed was hardly big enough for two people, let alone six, and she could hear talk through the thin walls.

Even if she put the children in the bed, there was no place for her and Robert to sleep. There was only enough floor space for one to sleep in front of the fire. It might be suitable for a married couple, but entirely unsuitable for a man and a woman not married. They couldn't possibly stay here.

Chapter Sixteen

Turning, she fixed a bright smile on her face. The innkeeper and Robert were not going to understand her sudden change of mind. But her feelings for Robert were too confusing to be put in such tight quarters. What if she did something foolish, such as…demanding him again?

The loud crack of thunder made her jump and the deluge of rain made her smile fall. The storm had reached them. She couldn't ask the children to travel now.

Robert, at least, would be happy they had shelter for the night. The man did not like getting wet. She almost giggled at Robert's secret weakness.

Giving the innkeeper a true smile, Gaira said, 'I suppose we should have some food. Do you have any?'

'Aye, mutton soaked in ale and a bit of bread.'

Gaira gave him a grateful grin. 'We'll take bowls and bread for everyone, please.'

'And honey!' Alec piped up.

'And ale,' Robert added.

Gaira glared at Robert, but he ignored her. She turned to the innkeeper. 'You doona happen to have any honey here?'

'Ale, aye, but honey, nae.'

'I'm sure your stew will be delicious and we'll take the ale. Thank you.'

The innkeeper nodded and opened the door. Great sounds of laughter and loud talk filled the room before he closed it again.

Gaira waited before she turned to Robert. 'You spoke!'

'I've been known to do that before.'

She put her hands on her hips. 'I thought we agreed you wouldn't.'

'I couldn't take the risk of you not ordering me ale.'

'Ale is worth risking your life for?'

'In certain situations.'

'Now?' she asked incredulously. 'Now is that time?'

'Being shut up in one room with four sleeping children and you, Gaira, warrants the numbing effects of ale,' he replied. 'I only hope he brings me enough.'

* * *

Busby couldn't believe his luck. Just when he thought he was wasting his time drinking and resting his nag, in walked the reason for his drink and rest.

It was her red hair. A man could use that for a beacon in the foulest of Scottish weather. But the rest of her was so changed, it took her coming in a second time for him to recognise her.

She was still too tall and skinny and she walked with a slight limp. He couldn't remember a limp. But the limp was not what marked her different. 'Twas her face that was no longer red and puffy; instead it was slender, well-shaped and her eyes were...not ugly. He realised it wouldn't be so bad to bed the wench now.

Luck and fate were on his side. Fate that his betrothed walked into this particular inn, and luck that he was far enough in a dark corner she didn't see him as she talked incessantly with the innkeeper.

But fate dipped a second hand because she wasn't alone. Four children and a man followed behind her like ducklings and a protective papa duck.

Busby kept his eyes on the man, who moved with assurance. The man's head was bowed, but Busby could see his eyes scan the room. Busby had no fear of recognition because he had never seen this man before.

Keeping his tankard to cover his face, he watched them go to the back rooms. When the back door opened again, he carefully averted his head, but it was only the innkeeper. He ordered more ale and watched as the innkeeper gathered food and took it to the back.

So they weren't joining the diners for food and they intended to stay the night. All the better for him. Luck seemed to be evening the odds.

Busby's only concern was the man with the sword. The man wasn't as large as him, but he could still be dangerous. Busby wouldn't take chances. He would use the element of surprise. He would be victorious for his children and for himself.

At the thought of his children, he felt the familiar stab of pride. He couldn't let them down. He would get the wench and teach her a lesson for not wanting to be their mother. Those brats she had in tow were not her responsibility and he didn't care what happened to them. His bargain was for her.

Fully satisfied with the turn of events, he drank long from his tankard. Now that she was here, he no longer needed to chase. He just needed to capture and kill any man that got in the way.

'I thought the stew was delicious,' Gaira said loudly to be heard over the rain pounding on the roof above them. 'I think the innkeeper must have used a touch of mead to finish it off.'

She walked to the stool and looked down at it, then turned on her heel and began to walk towards the opposite wall. 'I thought it would have made the stew too sweet, but it was quite good.'

Robert leaned against the door and took a drink of his ale.

'It must have been Alec's request for honey that made the innkeeper put it in. Or do you think he always makes it that way?'

Robert swirled his cup, but he did not reply.

She walked back to the stool and circled it. 'This evening will hardly go faster if you are silent.'

He shrugged. 'It's easier.'

She clenched her hands at her side. 'What's easier?'

He pointedly looked at her and over at the four sleeping children in the bed. When he gazed back at her, his eyes lingered on her lips, her breasts, her hips and then slowly, slowly, down her legs.

She felt every bit of his gaze. It was most effective in getting his point across. 'Oh!'

He took another drink.

'Why do you not go outside to drink?'

'I've been asking myself the same question.'

She raised her brows. It wasn't clear to her why not.

'You are on the same floor as those men outside.

There is no lock on this door. If I stand outside this door it would only look like a challenge to men too drunk to see they shouldn't fight with me. Therefore, I stay right here and when I rest, it will be against this door.'

She looked at his face, unreadable, but his body was held rigid despite the ale he'd been drinking in copious amounts. Neither had sat on the stool. She had paced, while he had remained by the door.

Yet he had not remained still. In fact, every time she paced near him, he had moved. A step here, a step there, but always away from her.

That shifting, that trying to stay away from her, confirmed he had feelings. His arrogant gaze at her body had been meant as a defence. It was a way to embarrass her, to make her wary.

And she had been. For a moment.

But maybe it was the pounding rain, or the laughter of the men outside, or maybe it was because she seemed to have too much energy for this tiny room, but she didn't feel wary any more. She took a couple of steps towards him. She knew she was demanding again. But he had been acting oddly since they arrived in town and she had to know. He could forget the kiss, but she couldn't.

He did not move, but he lowered his tankard and kept his eyes on her.

In the fire's bright light, all his braw features were

highlighted for her. He had shaved his beard and cut his hair. Such simple things and yet it greatly altered his appearance. His eyes, eyes that already compelled her, were not hidden behind unruly locks.

His cheeks and jaw were square, strong. He had a smattering of white scars along one cheek. They weren't cuts, but flat and just a bit lighter than his skin. There were so many and they continued down into his tunic, but they did not hide what his beard had.

Robert of Dent was a handsome man.

Since he had emerged from the forest, she had stolen glances at him. She couldn't help it. Where for some inexplicable reason she had been drawn to him before, now, with his features revealed, she was...fascinated.

She took a step closer and he began to make his own adjustments to avoid being near her.

He was wary of her. She almost smiled. 'What are you so afraid of?'

Surprise flashed in his eyes before he could hide it. 'I thought I made that clear,' he said.

She took another step closer. 'Nae, you are not wary of the men outside this door, there is something else.'

'There is nothing else,' he said.

She couldn't seem to help whatever curious or

foolish part of her heart that made her take the chance. 'There's me,' she said.

She saw his hand jerk before he lifted the tankard to his lips again to hide the telltale movement. He swallowed deep, draining the cup, and lowered it. 'Aye, there's you and the children and this damned journey you have me on.'

'It would be damned if you did not come.'

'You keep forgetting I am only on this journey part way. In the morning I will be gone.'

'I think of little else. I had hoped...' She stopped, unsure of whether to ask, but knowing she needed to. 'I had hoped you would take me and the children the rest of the journey.'

He looked stunned. No, he looked terrified. And his reaction hurt. Perhaps now wasn't the time to ask him, but necessity required her to ask him again.

She lifted her chin. 'Will you at least wait until I have my supplies?'

He bent down and set the tankard on the floor by the door. 'An hour at this point will not make much difference. The damage is done.'

She turned and looked at the children. Except for Alec, they were curved into each other. Alec, in the middle, was sprawled, his arms flung out across the face of Maisie and the chest of Creighton. They slept knowing they were safe. Robert, reluctant as he was, was making sure they were safe.

'I see nae damage done,' she said.

'No, you wouldn't.' It was his turn to take a step forward. 'But you never asked if it would hurt me to help you along this journey, did you?'

Guilt hit her like a ram to her gut. She knew he risked his life by going further into Scottish territory, but she hadn't thought about the journey hurting him in any other way. How could it? He was just one of thousands of soldiers in King Edward's army.

She was the one who had to get the children to safety through hostile land. She was justified in asking him. Her guilt was quickly replaced by frustration. 'I asked you to come only because of our safety.'

'Aye! You were only concerned for your *own* safety, for your *own* convenience,' he continued. 'And I am a damned man for caving to any guilt.'

Anger swamped her frustration in one swift wave. How dare he say he was damned! 'That's not true! By returning to my brothers, it is I who will suffer!'

His eyes narrowed. 'What do you mean?'

A pox on her temper and her tongue. ''Tis naught.'

'What danger have you put us in by taking us here, Gaira?'

She tried to act affronted. 'I haven't put you or the children in any danger.'

'What about you?'

She turned away, but there was nowhere she could

go and there was no way she was going to be able to avoid the question. 'My brothers may not be happy to see me when I arrive home.'

'Why?'

Oh, she didn't want to tell him the whole humiliating truth, but she was terrible at lying. 'I ran away to my sister's.'

'Why?' he asked again.

She hated his persistence. 'Does it matter why?' She turned to face him. ''Tis my worry, not yours. You, as you so often state, are leaving in the morning to your precious England.'

'I have reason to return.'

'Secrets, you mean. Why do you hound me to tell you everything, when in fact you are hiding things, too?'

'Are we to have this conversation again?' he asked. 'I thought it did not matter who I was and what my obligations were as long as I was at your beck and call.'

His level tone did not hide his anger. But his anger did not match hers, which crested like the waves of the Clyde.

'I!' She pointed to her breast, her whispered voice harsh with wanting to scream. 'I would do anything to help these children. Even if I have to beg some churlish, English, scrubby murderer of Scots to help me, I am going to help those children!'

She stepped closer and glared directly into his deep brown eyes. 'I did not ask because I wanted your company, Englishman. I asked because fate, God or the devil gave me nae choice.' She took a deep breath. 'I asked because you were the only one who showed up!'

She watched how his breathing changed, saw his eyes darken to a terrible black and in their depths she saw heat war with his anger.

'Aye, I showed up,' he said, stepping closer and lowering his voice. 'Aye, I agreed. God knows I will not allow such a whim in the future. The cost has been too high.'

'Do not speak to me of cost.' She wanted to take that one step separating them so she could hit him. 'I have paid doubly to whatever your whim may cost you. First with Irvette's death, then with my—'

She stopped and caught herself before she said anything further. Just thinking of Irvette fed her need to hurt, stab, to free the sudden frustration she had.

She saw his eyes flick over her features, take in her pent-up emotions.

'Don't take a step closer,' he said, his breath heavy.

Anger no longer held Robert still. Desire had won and it was consuming him.

And he asked her not to step closer? She knew

that heat would release her feelings. She *wanted* to feel that heat.

'Don't,' he said his voice harsh. 'Whatever feeling you have right now, don't follow it. What little power I have is keeping me rooted to this spot, but it will vanish if you so much as lean towards me. Not even the children will make a difference.'

The children.

She stumbled back from him. 'I dinna mean...'

'Don't speak!' He let his breath out roughly and rubbed the back of his neck. 'You were right to ask me to help with the children.' He lowered his arm. 'It is I who should apologise. I have no right being angry or making you feel wrong for the decisions I made.'

He reached to touch her face, then clenched his fingers and dropped his hand to his side. 'I didn't mean to hurt you. You have lost much in a fight you did not ask for.' He gave a wry smile. 'I, at least, should pay some cost for my deeds. If that means making sure you and the children have what you need for the rest of your journey, so be it. I will not travel with you, but I will wait for you to receive your supplies.'

She could not return his smile, but she tried to make her voice light. 'Doona worry, Englishman, I'll make sure you pay. I have high plans for buying a right nice horse for Alec.'

Chapter Seventeen

It was still dark when Gaira woke to soft choking sounds coming from the bed.

She shifted, felt her legs rub against much larger and rougher ones and stopped with a jerk. She had fallen asleep by the fire long before Robert. But he was near enough to touch and it appeared she had— her feet were warm and plastered against his.

Another soft sob from the bed turned her attention away from the feel of Robert's skin against her own.

She moved slowly and hoped she wouldn't wake him. When he remained still, she rose from the floor and stepped quietly to Flora, whose sobs had become shakier.

Gaira knelt beside the bed and laid her hand on Flora's arm.

'Nae, doona hold the tears back,' Gaira whispered. She wished she could take Flora and hold her, but she knew that would wake Maisie or Alec. 'It helps to let them out.'

Flora turned over. There was only thin streams of dawn entering the room, but Flora's eyes were wet, red-rimmed and the dark circles shadowed pale cheeks.

Flora sniffed. 'I never hear you crying.'

Gaira didn't know how to answer. She hadn't cried for the death of her sister. Not once. The pain in her chest wouldn't let her. But Flora needed to see her grief, to see that she loved and lost just as they had.

'I grieve, Flora. I haven't shown it because it's stuck, here.' She rubbed over her heart. 'I haven't wanted to hurt you with my grieving so I haven't talked. But I guess that was nae a good idea.'

Flora's eyes began to dry as Alec and Maisie wiggled. They were listening, too.

Gaira pulled away the thin strands of hair sticking to Flora's cheeks and forehead. 'I miss my sister very much, Flora, and you're supposed to miss your parents, too.'

'I...do.'

The too-loud stretch and noisy yawn behind her let her know Robert was waking. She wondered how long he'd been listening.

Gaira rolled her eyes for Flora, who giggled.

She stood and looked over her shoulder. 'Good morning, Robert.'

'Did I wake everyone?'

'Nae, I was just waking the children.' Gaira lifted Maisie. Alec sprang up with his usual verve, hitting Creighton in the chest with his elbow when he bounded out of bed.

'Creighton, it's time to rise.'

Creighton did not answer. The cover was still over his head.

Gaira, her arms full of a sleepy Maisie, marched over to Creighton's side. 'Creighton, time for you to get up, too.' She kissed the top of Maisie's head and carefully set her down before she yanked the cover from Creighton's shoulder.

The sudden and violent swing of an arm surprised her. She didn't even move as the full force of it hit directly below her belly.

But Creighton didn't stop and he was already rising, his fists swinging. Gaira could do nothing until she gained her breath, but the boy's fists were waving towards her and she shuffled backwards.

It was Robert who reacted. In two swift strides, he lifted the young boy from the bed and, with arms locked hard, held him against his chest. The boy was nine and already growing into a young man's body, but against Robert he looked as childlike as Maisie.

Creighton, still silent, his eyes unfocused, kept swinging his fists, his strong arms and legs making contact with Robert.

The pain dissipated enough for Gaira to straighten. Flora was clutched to her side. Alec was slumped on the floor, Maisie was crying, but Gaira could only stand and stare.

Robert hummed a song as he took Creighton's pounding to his back and the sharp kicks to shins. Gaira didn't recognise the song, but his voice was calming and the tune was a haunting lilt.

When Creighton woke, his fists and kicks stopped immediately, but anger blazed in his eyes when he realised where he was and he pushed with all his might to get out of Robert's arms.

Robert let him down immediately and the boy tugged at his clothes. Robert did not say anything to Creighton, nor did he look at Gaira. He just walked to the door and put his hand on the handle to open it.

'I'll see what they have to break our fast.'

After the door closed, Maisie still cried and Gaira rushed over to soothe her. Flora had moved to Creighton and was giving tentative pats to his back.

Creighton was not acknowledging anyone in the room and Gaira didn't know what to say to him. But she had to say something.

'It was I, Creighton. I dinna mean to wake you abruptly. You were nae awake. Everyone knows you knew not what you were doing.'

Creighton looked up. His wide blue eyes were filled with remorse, but he stayed silent.

She wiped Maisie's face and gave her a quick squeeze before she knelt in front of Creighton and Flora.

'It's been a rough morning for all of us and, given what we've all been through, that's nae surprising. 'Tis going to take us all some time.'

Flora rested her head on Creighton's shoulder and Creighton nodded. Not exactly a positive response, but it was a response. She just hoped with time that they'd all be able to heal.

'However, I'll tell you what is surprising.' She gave a wide conspiratorial grin. 'Who knew that that grumpy Englishman could sing?'

Gaira adjusted the cloth bundles in her arms and walked to the shade of trees by the inn. The late morning sun was quickly drying the wet ground and causing the air to feel thick and hot. She couldn't wait to get moving to feel a cooler breeze.

Robert was adjusting straps on the new horse. She set her bundles down beside him and swiped her plait back over her shoulder.

'The money you gave me bought us enough oat-cakes for three journeys.'

'You'll still need fresh meat. But the dried supplies will help.' He looked at the children patting and talking to the new horse. 'It seems the horse has met with approval.'

Even though the horse had been ill used by its previous owner, she was the gentlest horse Gaira had ever seen. Even Flora banished her fear and was brushing the soft muzzle.

Gaira smiled. 'More than sufficient, I think she realises she's about to become a pet.'

Robert continued to secure the satchels. She loved the smooth, confident way his hands worked.

The horse shied nervously as he tugged. 'I doona think she likes you, however.'

He turned around. 'She doesn't need to. All she has to do is her duty.'

So like the man to say such a thing. 'She's a horse,' she pointed out.

'We're all just something.' He moved to attend his own horse. 'It doesn't preclude our duty.'

And that simply, the river revealed some of its depths. Gaira finally understood part of what drove Robert, part of what made him the man he was. He said it was duty, but she knew otherwise.

She was running out of time. He had not agreed to take them further on this journey, but he had to. Maybe, just maybe, her further understanding of what drove him would help her persuade him. Because what drove him drove her, as well.

'Is that why you are here?' she asked. 'Is that why you're going to leave us? Because of duty?'

He shifted, took a couple of steps away from the horse and the children. 'It is what drives most men.'

'But not you,' she said. 'Oh, it's there, in every care you make to your swords and to your horse, but it doesn't explain why you came to Doonhill, why you helped us, or why you are leaving now.'

His eyes had become wary. She was close to the truth now. She knew it.

A loud guttural cry broke through the quiet of the town.

Gaira, startled, looked past Robert's broad shoulders. She screamed.

Robert whirled and ducked. He just missed the sword sweeping above his head.

Her legs weaved beneath her. She was still standing close to Robert, but didn't duck, and the tip of the sword had been close.

'Get the children!' he shouted.

She ran. The children, standing behind the horses, didn't see what was happening. She scared them when she swept them further away from Robert.

And from Busby of Ayrshire.

She could not mistake that huge thick-gutted man.

Her betrothed had found them. And he meant to kill Robert. His blue eyes were filled with rage and his black hair bristled around him. His sword was even now making another swing.

Robert was without any shield or any sword. In

his quick movement to protect her and the children, he had run away from the horses and away from his weapons.

He didn't stand a chance.

She gripped Creighton until he looked at her. 'Stay here!'

Running to Robert's horse, she looked at the two swords in their scabbards and yanked at the largest one. It stuck.

Another scream of rage from Busby—followed by a quick shout from Robert. Oh, God, was he already dead? She couldn't get his sword free. She didn't dare look over her shoulder. Her entire concentration was on his weapon.

She yanked again. The sheath swung, but the sword was firmly in the leather's hold.

Creighton was suddenly by her side, his fingers quickly releasing the scabbard. The sword fell with a clang on the ground. The horse stomped his feet with the sudden movement, but she didn't hesitate to fall to her knees beside it.

With shaking fingers she unlatched the scabbard and pulled the heavy instrument free. Half dragging, half lifting it, she turned towards the two men fighting.

And quickly wished she didn't have to look.

Robert was fighting for his life. She had not even seen it coming. One moment they were saddling the horses, the next she'd seen Busby come out of the copse of trees beside them.

Robert had managed to grab a large branch, but it was too short as a weapon and was making a paltry shield. Already it had been chopped smaller by Busby.

Busby's back was to her, but Robert saw her and the sword. A gleam of victory flashed in his eyes.

She was not that certain.

She couldn't move any closer to Robert because Busby was swinging his sword for all he was worth.

To get to the sword, Robert would have to get past Busby.

Robert feinted low right. Busby raised his sword to swing. It was just enough opening for Robert to dive towards Gaira.

There was too much gap between her and Robert and Busby was already recovering from the missed swing.

She pushed the sword in front of her with all her might. It went wide, but the handle stayed straight. Robert hit the ground and grabbed the long handle with both hands.

Her yelp of elation was covered by her gasp of fear.

Busby was directly over Robert. His sword, clasped in both his hands, was raised to strike Robert.

Robert still had his stomach on the ground. Swiftly turning, he blocked the brunt of Busby's sword and strength. The two swords reverberated through the small square.

Busby had the advantage. He leaned his great weight into his sword. Robert was rocking to throw Busby off balance, but it wasn't working and he started to shake.

He wasn't going to have the strength to hold out. And even if he did, how could he roll away fast enough from Busby's pressing sword?

Without thinking, she screamed and started jumping up and down. Busby's eyes flew to hers. It was the distraction she was hoping for. Robert rolled and Busby's weight, off balance, fell forward.

Gaira's elation swelled and was dashed again as Busby recovered. He swung himself to face Robert.

But now, Robert was ready for him.

She had forgotten how huge Busby was. Robert, broad and thick, was still a head shorter.

But their swords matched in length and breadth. They both held them with two hands. She looked at them closer. They were claymores, the Scottish sword.

In rage, Busby swung to kill, his aim inaccurate like a hammer and just as relentless.

Robert parried and thrust and blocked Busby's

moves. He stayed crouched and moved his legs to keep distance between them.

It worked. The majority of Busby's swings were hacking through air. If they struck Robert's sword, Robert still maintained his distance. His sword took the blows, not his body.

Robert was skilled with the claymore. Whereas she had trouble lifting it, she watched as it danced in his hands. He used speed and balance as a weapon to counteract Busby's size and strength. His feet kept close to the ground and he used the muddy terrain as another weapon.

She had three brothers, who trained every day. They were skilled, strong swordsmen, but she had never seen a man fight like Robert did.

He was a master and used the sword as an extension of his body. He was fluid. Busby hacked. Robert used skill, Busby his strength.

What did her brothers tell her? Strength always ran out, but never skill.

Robert, still dressed in his customary black, was like a shadow of Busby.

There was no doubt he was a formidable English warrior.

She jolted as if she was suddenly grabbed and dunked in cold water.

Black. Claymore. Robert. Warrior.

She looked around her. Her legs gave way and she struggled to stand. She had been so concerned for Robert's safety she did not see the crowd gathering. She recognised the faces of the innkeeper and the blacksmith. She even spied the three Scots who had talked to them yesterday—the exact three Scots who had celebrated Black Robert's death.

Taking in a steadying breath, she looked at the children, who were crouched and not watching. Even if they did, she doubted they would draw the same conclusion she had.

She knew she no longer needed to worry over Robert's safety.

At least not from Busby.

But they were in the centre of town, surrounded by hordes of Scottish people who hated the English and most especially one man they thought dead.

She wondered how they were to going to get out of town without the people realising whom they were watching.

Black Robert was not dead.

Chapter Eighteen

The man fighting him was tiring. His sword shoulder dropped and his shifting weight was more pronounced. Robert made more wide-swinging cuts at the man's legs. While the cuts weren't enough to fell him, more cuts meant more blood loss and a slower target.

He allowed himself only to feel the rush of his blood and the tremors of his strength. He could make no mistakes. He knew he had the better skill, but there could be some misstep, some miscalculation, and he would be killed.

Then Gaira and the children would have no protection.

After the first attack, he stopped trying to reason with the man who was trying to cut him to shreds. He had no idea who this man was or where he came from. The man could be holding a grudge from a past battle or have discovered Robert was English.

He didn't know and didn't care. After his first battle, Robert stopped looking his enemy in the face. It made killing easier.

Robert made another leg cut. The man stumbled. It was time. Without warning, Robert dropped to the ground and swiped his sword deep into the shins of the man. The man lost his balance.

Robert twisted his body, rose up and sliced the man's neck with one fluid movement. He rolled out of the way before the corpse hit the ground.

He stood. The last effort had cost him his breath and he wiped the sweat pouring from his brow so he could see.

The crowd of people was thick. He could not see Gaira or the children. 'Does anyone know this man?' he called.

The crowd of people stared at him. There was no yelling, screaming or crying foul. Some shook their heads, but no person spoke; no one stepped forward.

Either they were scared or the dead man was a stranger to them, too. Robert looked at the man with blood rushing out from his neck. The man had been intent on killing him. From his anger and rage, Robert knew it had been personal. But he still did not recognise him.

He leaned down, flipped the man's tunic and looked for a pouch. The man carried nothing.

The man had attacked him, had come from behind. No witness could claim he had killed wrongly. What they did with his body, he didn't care. Robert wiped his sword against the man's tunic. Reaching into a small pouch still attached to his waist, he threw some coins on to the body. The man was a stranger, but he would have to be buried.

Straightening, he searched the crowd again until he saw Gaira and the children far behind the horses.

Her face was so white, she looked no darker than the birch trees shading her. Her eyes were wide with fear, but she was not looking at him. She was looking at the people surrounding them, gazing at each face as if she was a child lost, searching for some recognition in the crowd.

The crowd parted and murmured, but he paid no attention. He waited for Gaira to acknowledge he was heading her way, but she didn't notice him until he stood directly in front of her. Frantic, she grabbed his arm and tugged at him.

'Ro—!' She stopped, looked around and lowered her voice. 'We have to get out of here. Right now. You have to come with us. The horses are still packed and the children are ready.'

She was in shock. Panic was etched in her brow and around her eyes; her hands on his arm were shaking. She had watched the fight.

He had not thought. He had killed. In front of her. He should not have allowed her to see that happen.

'Gaira, I am sorry. He came out of nowhere. I did not think about you or the children witnessing—'

She tugged harder and he took a couple steps forward. 'We have to leave!'

She was terrified. Maybe she hadn't seen what had happened. 'All is well, Gaira. He is dead. The children are safe.'

She raised her voice. 'I know, I know, it's just you!'

It wasn't panic in her voice now, but frustration. He was missing something. 'What is wrong?'

He looked at the children. Creighton looked at him as if he were seeing him for the first time. Flora's eyes were not fearful, but thoughtful. Alec and Maisie were unaware and playing with rocks in the sand. The children gave him no hint of what was troubling her.

'Gaira?' he asked.

'Please, Robert, leave with us now.' She tugged at his sleeve again. 'When we are far enough away, I promise I'll explain everything.'

Terrible realisation dawned. 'Did you know that man?'

'Robert, please!'

He yanked his arm away. 'Answer me.'

She took a deep breath and paused. He almost interrupted her before she said very fast, 'He was my betrothed.'

'Your betrothed!' he roared. 'Explain yourself!'

Glancing quickly to her left and right, she hissed, 'I won't, Robert. Nae here. It isn't safe, you daupit eel-drowner! You fought him with a claymore!'

''Tis the sword you threw to me!'

'But, Robert, you're English and you fought with a claymore. If I know who you really are, how long do you think it'll be before these people realise it, too?'

There was absolute silence. Then Robert of Dent let off a stream of invectives that shocked Gaira of Colquhoun.

Gaira couldn't still her racing heart. They were out of town, but on the main road. Every few moments she looked behind her, sure she heard pounding hoof beats.

She dared not glance at Robert, who rode with Alec in his lap. He hadn't said anything since they mounted the horses. His demeanour didn't encourage any speeches, either. Even Alec was quiet.

She was sure Robert would leave her at any time. There was no reason he travelled with her this far other than for her asking.

She glanced behind her again.

The extra horse allowed them to travel faster, but Creighton and Flora rode on their own. They couldn't travel fast enough should the townspeople try to pursue them. She couldn't believe there wasn't a crowd of villagers following them. They had just been celebrating Black Robert's death.

Maybe that was a blessing. If they thought he was alive, anyone watching him fight today would realise who he was. He was a warrior, all in black, and he had swung that claymore as if he were born to it.

She felt a hysterical giggle. She had been in the company of Black Robert and she didn't know. She hadn't even suspected when the drunken Scot had given a detailed description of him.

How could she recognise him? All this time she had not seen Robert use his sword. He had not seemed like so much a warrior, a legend, a killer of her kinsmen, but...a man.

A man stating his only motivation was duty, but she knew there was more to him than that. He had buried her dead. He had taken them to the town to obtain supplies. He had saved Alec from getting hurt and held Creighton as the boy battled his demons.

No wonder she didn't recognise the description given by the stumbling Scotsman yesterday. Everything she knew of her Robert conflicted with the Robert described by the Scot.

Her Robert.

She risked looking at him. His face was hard, his eyes staring straight ahead. He had not disappointed her, like Busby, or betrayed her, like her brothers.

He had done everything possible to help them. Reluctantly. Aye. But now she could understand some of that reluctance.

She glanced behind her again.

She had just seen Robert kill her betrothed. It didn't seem to matter that she didn't like Busby. The fact was he was dead and she rode with the man who had sliced his neck and wiped the blood on his clothes. But the hardest fact of all was she felt not a drop of horror or repugnance for what Robert did to her own countryman. No, not to her countryman. To Busby, who had swung his sword towards Robert's back. Busby had launched a coward's attack. Robert had simply had no choice.

But what of his reputation? The Scotsman had said Robert had killed many of her countrymen. Did he kill like the men who had killed her sister? Was that the kind of man she travelled with?

She tried to understand her feelings, but there was too much confusion. She looked around, momentarily forgetting where they were heading. Safety. She had to get them all to safety.

'We'll need to stop.'

Gaira's voice was louder than she intended. Everyone looked at her sudden declaration and it was no wonder. They had been travelling for hours and no one had spoken a word. She didn't want to stop. She was still terrified of being caught. But she had to stop. Maisie was wiggling in her lap.

'Maisie needs a break,' she added.

Robert pulled his horse over to the side and dismounted.

He got Alec to the ground before he took Maisie from her lap and set her on the ground.

'Do you need help dismounting?' he asked.

She was loath to admit it, but she knew from the numbness in her legs she did. 'Aye.'

He lifted his hand up for her to take. She did and felt the warmth and calluses before she adjusted and placed her hands on his shoulders and swung her weight over the horse.

She gasped at the sharp shooting pain in her legs.

'You were too tense on the ride.' He released her waist.

The cool air hit her sides and she missed his hands, but he waited. She smelled his sweat, the very personal scent that was his alone. Desperately, she wanted to rest her head against his chest and curl her arms around him. She wanted to feel his arms around her as well, clasping her close against him until all her worries and confusion went away. Instead, she straightened and flexed her legs. Without a word, he walked towards the woods and she turned her attention to the children.

Creighton and Flora had gone the opposite way of Robert. She grabbed Maisie by the hand and slowly walked her over to a plush length of grass.

'There now, let's see what we have here.'

She removed the linen and gave an exaggerated gasp, waving her hand before her nose. 'Ach there, I dinna know you had weapons more powerful than a wild boar!'

Maisie grabbed Gaira's plait and let out a peal of laughter. Gaira's heart stopped. Maisie laughed Irvette's laugh. It was a high tinkle that ended in giggling. Irvette's laugh. She never thought she'd hear it again.

Maisie put the tip of the plait in her mouth and Gaira leaned forward, staring at Maisie, staring at Irvette's baby. The resemblance was there, in the shape of the mouth and chin, in that unmistakable laugh. Her resemblance was just a wisp of Irvette, but her sister was still *here*.

Trying to breathe through her revelation, Gaira removed her plait and wetted clean linens to wipe her bottom. She let Maisie lie there, bare-bottomed, as she went to a tree and roughly cleaned the dirty linen. Maisie scrambled up and began to run towards the trees where Robert had gone.

'Oh, no—I'm nae done with you.'

Maisie ran even faster. Her legs, chubby and still

curved, were making a hasty but sloppy retreat. Her arms were pumping as fast as they could, which caused her tunic to rise up and Gaira caught sight of her small dimpled bottom beneath her short tunic.

It was about the dearest sight she'd ever seen.

Without warning, great bursts of grief rose out of her chest. Crushed at the stab and weight of it, she fell to her knees and wept.

Her sister would never see Maisie's bare bottom or how she would grow. She would never hear Irvette's voice again or see the gentle way her eyes softened. She'd never have her counsel, though she desperately needed it now. Never, never, never again.

She cried even after her eyes could no longer produce tears, for the pain still racked through her body in great gasps. She cried until even her choking sounds could no longer escape her dried lips. When she could make no sound at all, the pain still made her eyes clench tight and her fists curl in her lap.

She felt rather than heard the hesitant steps and motions around her. They were quiet, but she was no longer alone. She wiped her cheeks and pushed her hair away from her face.

Flora and Creighton were hand in hand, sitting on the ground to her right. Alec was fast asleep and laying in both their laps.

Robert was standing in front of her. In his arms

was Maisie. Her bottom was still bare and her mouth was full of his tunic.

'We need to keep moving,' Robert said quietly.

She didn't know what to say. So, she stood and wiped the dried grass and dirt from her clothing. She reached to take Maisie, but Robert shook his head.

'I'll do it,' he said. 'There's a stream just behind me. Take your time.'

She was relieved nobody wanted to talk to her. She wasn't ready to talk. She was too shaky, too raw. When she returned to the horses and children, she felt exhausted and little like herself.

Creighton and Flora were petting the new horse while Maisie pulled grass nearby. Alec was jumping in front of Robert, but this time, Alec's hands were in Robert's and he was pulling the boy up.

Gaira's heart eased a bit. Robert was playing with Alec. Robert looked perplexed, but Alec didn't seem to mind. He laughed great squeals as Robert pulled him higher and higher. The sight was almost as good as sound counsel and her heart calmed even more.

They found shelter with some shallow caves late in the day. The sun had set and a cool wind had picked up. The caves did not provide much protection if it rained, but the rocks were warmed by the sun and the curvature buffeted the chill of the air.

'I'll go and see if I can get some food,' Robert said.

''Tis late and dark.' Gaira hugged Alec in her lap.

'Aye, and I'm hungry.'

She could do nothing to keep him there. She tried to release the emotion that something could happen to him. They were far from the town and no one had pursued them. It was ridiculous for her to feel he needed to stay within sight.

She stayed busy with the children, gathering wood and leaves for beds and a fire. She tried not to think of danger or losing him. Soon, Robert returned with a couple of mountain hares.

'You must have the eyes of a cat to see in such light.' Gaira took the hares and helped him prepare them.

They hadn't stopped to eat since leaving the town and they ate like starving foxes. Once fed, Alec and Maisie fell asleep sitting up and Gaira adjusted them to a more comfortable position. It didn't take long to settle Creighton and Flora next to them. They had blankets now. The children would not get cold.

Robert had left the shelter of the cave as soon as she started preparing the children for sleep. He hadn't returned. When she was sure they were settled, she grabbed her shawl and went to find him.

Her emotions were still confused, but she knew she owed him her entire story. Whether he wanted to hear it, she didn't know. Something had possessed him to continue north with her and it was time they talked.

He was near the stream. The moon illuminated and shadowed the night. The water sparkled and the open ground lay so clear that she could see each pebble and blade of grass. But Robert and the trees were black silhouettes and their shadows long.

She stopped behind him and listened to the water lapping around larger rocks.

He did not turn around to face her, but he knew she was there. She had not walked silently.

She looked down at her feet, not surprised to see Robert's shadow had reached her. She stared at it, feeling strangely comforted and yet apprehensive about the breadth and length of it. It was how she felt about the man. How, despite his gruffness, despite his killing a man, he had reached into her heart, into her very soul.

And because of that, she didn't want to tell him her painful past because she owed him; she wanted to tell him because she wanted to share it with him.

But still he did not turn to face her and his back was wider and darker than the shadow. But unlike the shadow, she knew his strength and character were solid.

Oh, aye, he was solid and so very angry. At her. She couldn't blame him. By forcing him on this journey, she had jeopardised his life.

'I met Busby of Ayrshire less than a sennight before you came to Doonhill.' Her voice sounded unnatural in the quiet of the woods. 'That was about the same time I realised my brother, Bram, the eldest and laird of our clan, had agreed to make Busby my betrothed.'

Robert did not turn around. But not facing him somehow made it easier to talk to him. 'Busby and my sudden betrothal were a…surprise. I was very happy where I was. But my brother had given his word. I could defy my brother, but not when he acted as laird. That would have resulted in my immediate banishment without somewhere to go.'

He turned around. 'Why did he do this?'

She had not expected his acknowledgement so soon, nor his gaze to be so intent. She was suddenly unsure how to proceed. She tried to discern what he was thinking, but the moonlight obscured his features.

'I dinna understand it at first.' Embarrassed, she took a step away from him. She doubted very much Robert had ever been thrown away.

'I ran the keep and made sure we had profits,' Gaira said. 'Irvette had married happily and I had found some purpose to my life at the keep without her.' She gathered her breath. 'I guess I ran the keep a little too efficiently. My older brother kept bringing women home to marry, but they never stayed.'

He made some sort of noise in his throat.

'Some of them were quite nice, but they'd…' She didn't know how to explain the women who came. How they'd behave with her brother; how annoying all the simpering and flirting was.

The corner of his mouth lifted and he took a step closer. 'Get in the way?'

'Aye, I guess that was it.' She flushed. 'It was apparently me in the way. Bram put a dowry of twenty sheep on my head and made an alliance with Busby of Ayrshire.'

'Why with him?'

'Busby's keep is poor and he has a horrible reputation. But at the time I hardly wondered about that. I was just so stunned by my brother's betrayal. He hadn't told me what was happening. He did not allow me to fix it. If he had, I would have stepped back.'

He raised his eyebrows.

'I would have tried at least,' she corrected.

Robert took a step closer. He cupped her neck, his fingertips tracing her jaw from ear to chin. His hair was slightly damp. She wondered if he had washed in the stream.

'Did you know your chin juts out just a notch

when you are determined to get your way?' he said, his voice low.

Arrested by the feel of his skin against hers, she did not answer him.

He dropped his hand roughly away. 'I imagine your brother has seen that particular angle of your chin for years.'

She did not protest. She could still feel the slight friction his fingers had left. 'Aye, I suppose Bram did.'

He took a step away. 'You probably berated him heavily for his lack of consideration in not telling you of his plans.'

Her embarrassment escalated with his comment. Under normal circumstances she would have cursed her brother, but the fact that he had just given her away had been too much to take in.

She shook her head. 'Nae, I dinna.'

His gaze took in every facet of her face. 'He hurt you.'

'When Busby arrived and they told me, I was too stunned. I just stood there while Bram placed my hand in Busby's and said the words to the clan. With his words we were handfasted, which in Scottish terms means—'

'That you were married,' he interrupted, his voice grim.

'Only if—' she started.

'You said you met Busby almost a sennight ago and your brother handfasted you that very day,' he interrupted. 'You were married to that man for almost fourteen days.'

His voice was tight and angry again. She did not understand it.

'I've made you a widow.' He paused. 'Do you grieve for your Busby from Ayrshire?'

She wanted to take a step away, but didn't know how close she was to the stream. His demeanour had changed from soft to hard so fast she didn't know how to react. She didn't know what had changed.

'There were nae celebrations,' she said. 'Busby did not want to stay with the clan. By the time Busby arrived, my things were already packed.'

'That does not answer my question. You travelled with this man. Yet you tell me you have nae feelings for him?'

'Aye, I travelled, but I hardly had enough time to know him. The further south we went, the more my shock left me. I realised we were getting close to my sister.'

'You asked him if you could visit her,' he concluded.

She shook her head. 'Nae. I knew it would be useless. Busby had got what he wanted, which was my dowry of twenty sheep. When I could, I took some clothes and his horse and went south to my sister's.'

'How long did you travel with him?'

'A day, two days?' She waved her hand. 'What does it matter?'

'You were handfasted.'

'I explained that to you already.'

'He pursued you.'

'That was apparent.' She did not keep the exasperation from her voice.

'Why did he pursue you?'

'Who knows?' she answered. 'For his sheep is what I suspect.'

'Sheep!'

'Aye, Bram made it apparent if anything should happen to me, he would expect the twenty sheep returned.'

Robert took a step closer to her. She had to tilt her head to continue looking at him. The moonlight made his face hard angles and planes. The evening breeze did not hide the smell of cedar and the heat of his body.

'You think a man had you for two days and pursued you because of some wool?' he asked.

The night hid the colour of his eyes, but incredulity was visible in their depths and heard in his voice. She suddenly felt as if she didn't have the right answer to his question, but it was his manner that gave her the first clue.

He acted angry with her, but she was beginning to

think maybe it wasn't because he had almost been killed or his identity revealed.

'What other reason could there be?' she asked.

His lips parted and she felt his warm breath. His gaze travelled to where his fingers had traced her jawline. She felt the pull to bend her neck, to expose more of her skin to the moonlight and to him.

He didn't touch her, he didn't move any closer, but she felt him reaching for her.

'Do you not know your worth?'

She was finding it hard to think with him so close. 'I doona understand.'

'Your strength, your will, your ability to laugh in the face of all your grief, Gaira, those qualities are rare, like suddenly finding gold beneath your feet.'

She snorted. 'Aye, I think that's what my brother thought of me, beneath his feet.'

He moved back almost imperceptibly, but she felt it. 'No, you do not understand.' He rubbed the back of his neck. 'Or maybe I am explaining it wrong.'

He turned slightly away from her. She did not think he would say any more, but she didn't know what to say to him. She again heard the lapping of the water, the scurry of the nocturnal animals hiding in the low brush. The breeze had settled, becoming no more than a soft zephyr across her skin. She tried to find some words to say, but Robert was so tense, his thoughts almost tangible, she could not.

When he turned his head to face her, she was stunned by the pain she saw there. His eyes were trying to conceal it, but it was there in the drawn cheekbones, the way the white scars along his face were more pronounced.

'I have to know,' he said. 'I cannot stand here, cannot return to England, without knowing.'

She waited.

'He had you for two days, Gaira—do you grieve for him?'

Grieve for Busby? No. In order to grieve for him, she'd have to care for... She stopped her thoughts. It all made sense. He had killed Busby. His identity had been almost revealed. But his anger and his pain were not in those facts. He thought she belonged to another.

'Nae, Robert of Dent, I do not grieve for him.'

He did not look relieved. She'd have to tell him more.

'He put me on a separate horse and I rode behind him. He did not talk to me—he barely looked at me and he did not touch me.'

He did not relax his rigid pose, but she sensed something had eased in him.

'But because he was a proud man,' she continued, 'a man desperate for the wealth of my clan, I knew he would come after me.'

He turned fully to her. 'That's why you were demanding me to be quick.'

'Aye. By the time you arrived, Busby would have had some days to come after me. But I thought he'd go to my brothers and wait there. I dinna know he even knew about my sister to travel south.'

'Maybe he did both.'

Thinking he was joking, she laughed. 'You doona know him as I did. He was hardly industrious.'

'He could have sent a messenger to your brothers and that's how he found out about your sister. Then he was free to go south to your sister's.'

'If he sent a messenger north, it would have given my brothers enough time to travel at the same time Busby travelled.' She began to chew on her bottom lip. 'If Busby found us, my brothers could find us, too.'

'Doonhill was burned to the ground,' he pointed out. 'They'd have no idea where you are.'

'They couldn't have reached there by now. We would have seen them on the road or in town.'

He didn't say anything to her, his eyes shifting away.

'I should never have let you see me kill him,' he said.

She was wondering when he would broach that subject. If she knew anything about him at all, it was his need to protect her.

'I was already there and it wasn't as if he gave you a choice,' she said.

'I could have chosen not to kill him,' he argued.

She touched the frayed slice in his tunic where Busby's sword had reached. 'Nae, Robert, the moment your back was turned, he would have killed you. He gave you nae choice.'

'Choice? There are always choices, Gaira.'

He turned away from her.

She looked at his back and the rigidness of his shoulders. He had felt so warm near her, now he looked removed from any heat. Not cold, just… alone.

He had looked that way before Busby attacked. When he was packing to leave her and the children; he was there and yet alone already. She had argued with him regarding his so-called duty. But it was not duty driving this man.

'Do you want to know what I think drives you?' Wanting to know what he was thinking, she walked around to face him.

'Do you want to know what I think made you go to a destroyed village? What made you help a woman and four children bury their dead and protect them until they obtained supplies for their survival?'

He barely glanced at her. 'No,' he answered.

''Tis not duty as you so put it, Robert of Dent,' she said simply. ''Tis grief.'

Chapter Nineteen

He looked as if she had taken his claymore and thrust it tip-to-hilt straight through his stomach. Just as pale; just as surprised.

'You are wrong.' His voice was hoarse.

'Ach, nae,' she said. 'Do you forget I grieve as well? Do you think me so naive I would not recognise it?'

'You do not know me.' His eyes returned to hers. 'I am an English soldier. I have fought for King Edward my entire life. Grief is hardly a motivating factor.'

His face was unreadable, his mask in place. It did not matter. She had seen his expression before he tried to pretend otherwise.

'You are right. I doona know all your past and maybe you do not grieve for the men you have killed. But there is something or someone you do grieve for. Maybe 'tis your family?'

'My childhood is hardly unusual enough to cause any sadness.'

He tried to make his tone mocking. She did not believe him. 'Tell me about it,' she pressed him.

'There is no reason for you to know. If it wasn't for the fact that I—' He stopped.

'You what?' she asked. She was getting irritated at his constant nae-saying. 'Why doona you want to tell me? My entire humiliating history has been laid bare to you. You know my brothers abandoned me to the worst possible man they could find. You know my sister died a horrible death. Why do you not want to tell me one thing about your life, you surly reebald!'

His lips pursed. 'You aren't afraid, are you?'

The humour and cynicism underlying his question made her suspicious. 'Of what?'

'Of me,' he said.

'Why should I be?' she asked.

'I thought you understood, back in town, back when I *murdered* your husband, that you knew my identity. I *am* Black Robert.'

The name meant little to her. 'I see you wear black, but I haven't noticed your eyes glowing yellow or having any such conversations with the devil.'

'No,' he said impatiently. 'That is myth, but my killing, my ability with the claymore, is true. I have murdered hundreds of your fellow Scotsmen at my sovereign's request.'

She knew he was being graphic to shock her. It didn't. She had had some time to sort her thoughts. 'Even if that is true, I have seen another side of you. Maybe I do not know all you have done in the past, but I have seen a man willing to risk his life to help a stranded woman and children survive.'

'That is—'

'I have seen a man, not a myth,' she interrupted.

She took a step closer to him. She was tired of him putting up defences. 'A man who was angry because he thought I belonged to another.' She placed her hand upon his sleeve. Beneath her fingers, his muscles contracted. 'I do not belong to another.'

He did not move, but his gaze remained riveted on her hand on his arm. He did not move, but he wanted to.

'You're afraid of me,' she said, realisation dawning.

'No,' he whispered.

She remembered that first morning when she woke. He had been making breakfast for the children, but when his eyes reached hers, all time had stopped. She had watched him ever since, fascinated by the way he moved, the way he cared for his horse, his sword, the way he was awkward but gentle with the children.

She remembered the way his lips felt against hers. The heat, the desire, the need. Both his...and hers. She wanted to be closer to him then. She wanted that again now.

'Then prove it,' she said.

He moved and brought his foot between her own; he leaned until his leg separated hers. He was so close his hips almost touched hers. The rise and fall of his chest brushed against her breasts, making them sensitive. The night's humid air was suddenly too thick to breathe and her lips parted to take in more air.

He hissed. With an imprecation under his breath, he pivoted and took several rapid steps away.

With the removal of his body, she was cold, stripped. Restless. Her breathing would not return to normal.

He straightened, but he did not turn to face her. 'Damn you, Gaira. You pick at my soul until I hardly know myself anymore.'

He was so far away from her, not in distance, but in spirit, that she didn't know if she could reach him. 'I doona know what you mean. I doona know anything anymore. You're nae making it easy.'

He looked over his shoulder. Her eyes probably betrayed every grudging feeling she had for him.

'There's no reason to make it easy,' he said. 'I have

fulfilled any bargain you and I had. Regardless of what happened today, I will leave tomorrow.'

Oh. He was a stubborn man. Why she cared for him at all was beyond her. 'Fine! Leave tomorrow. Keep running. You wear this image of Black Robert as if it's a cloak to hide behind.'

He gave a small mirthless laugh. 'I do not hide behind my image. I *am* that image. I have slaughtered men with my hands. Why can you not see that and leave me alone?'

'Because I have seen nothing of that man in you. I cannot deny you have killed. But I have seen you are good, kind—'

He turned, his movement wide, erratic in his anger. 'What do I have to say to make you go away? Why can't you believe I am leaving and want nothing more to do with you!'

His statement was so vicious she was taken aback. And it was that pause that made her see him clearly. He was throwing up defences again. Cruelly. Angrily.

Desperately.

She could see it now in every muscle highlighted by the moonlight. His body tense, shivering with barely contained emotion. He was a great river, waiting only for the boulder in its flow to crumble. She felt like that boulder with his words crashing against her. But he wasn't going to make her crumble. The river was going to have to bend.

Her anger quickly evaporated and when she gave him a slight smile, she revelled in the wariness entering his eyes. He wanted her. She knew it. She'd just have to break his control.

She grabbed the end of her plait, her fingers deftly releasing her hair, while her eyes never released him.

'What are you doing?' he asked.

'Unbinding my hair,' she said.

He leaned back as if she had suddenly caught on fire. She saw anger, frustration and something else flash across his face before he gave a low sound that was part growl, part moan.

'You don't know what you're doing,' he said hoarsely. 'What you're feeling.'

She felt as if she'd run up a steep hill, but hadn't reached the top; her body was held suspended by something she couldn't name. It waited, wanted and hurt all at the same time. Oh, she might not know how to name it, but whatever she was feeling, she'd been feeling it strongly from the moment he'd made breakfast that first morning.

And she had a feeling Robert knew what to do about it, too.

She released her hair and started to run her fingers through the thick waves. She felt his eyes devouring her. She saw him shudder.

She felt her own body respond to the heated current flowing between them. 'Ach now. I know I'm feeling my breasts rise and tighten and my belly filling with heat. My lips aching be—'

With hands that wielded steel swords, he seized her arms and shoved her against a broad oak. She felt the coarse, splintered surface of the bark before he slammed his body against hers. Matching hip to hip, he knocked the breath from her, but then she had no breath as his lips, hard, crushing, covered hers and his calloused fingers dug into her arms, pinning them to the tree behind her.

She felt the sharp pull of her muscles, the hard uneven surface of the tree, the force of his body pressed into hers.

But she also felt his desire.

She moved to free her arms, only knowing she wanted to be closer. Wanting—

He suddenly stiffened, released her arms and she fell against the tree. His breath was a hot sear against her mouth.

'I cannot do this,' he said harshly. 'You have to free me, Gaira—push me away. Run.'

She saw the change in his eyes: the heat and need dimming with something akin to devastation and anger. Her heart ripped a little. He was denying

himself, but she would not let him. Because in denying himself, he was denying her. Denying them.

'Aye, you can do this, Robert,' she said. 'You can
and you will.'

'You are untried, Gaira. It has been too long and
I want you too much. I will not be what you need
me to be.'

'You are what I need,' she said. She worked on
instinct and rose on her toes, quick, and flicked her
tongue over his lips.

He jerked and bowed his head. The curls of his
hair fell loosely forward and she shaped her fingers
around them.

'You don't understand everything. I have not
told—'

She didn't want to listen to excuses any longer.

'You.' She wrapped both hands around his neck,
bringing her body closer to his.

His breath came in discordant rhythm. His cheeks
were hollowed out and flushed. She felt sweat bead
against his neck.

'Then damn me—' he leaned into her '—for this.'

His lips softened, his body no longer felt tense,
but warm, firm and so very masculine.

Wrapping his arms around her, he pulled her up
and into him. She didn't know a body could melt,
but hers did, right against him, curve for plane, soft
for hard.

She felt his hands slowly trail from the base of her shoulders down the length of her spine to the crest of her bottom and below. There, he pulled her tighter towards him.

The coarse wool of her shawl confined her and she stretched to release its grip. He set her down. She leaned against him, shivering in anticipation while he untied the knot. She watched his fingers, saw the rapid rise and fall of his chest. She felt his eyes on her, but she did not look up as he pulled the fabric, unwrapping her slowly and letting her shawl fall around her ankles.

He quickly freed her of her tunic and leggings until she stood only in her released chemise, the thin white fabric covering her, but providing him no barrier to what was underneath. The night breeze curled around her. Her sight was blocked by the expanse of his chest, the cadence of his breath harsh, fast, matching her own.

At her hips, he fisted her chemise into his hands and stopped. She felt the strength of his hands gripping the fabric, felt him pausing, felt as if it were her he held in his tight grip. Suspended.

His entire body shook with restraint; imprisoned by something she did not understand.

'Robert?'

He shuddered. 'No!'

He loosened his grip. He had not moved otherwise, but she felt the coldness of his withdrawal all the same.

'Why?' she said, proud her voice did not sound as broken as she felt. Rejected. Again.

He raised his head. Regret might as well have been written on every line and plane of his face. It was certainly in his eyes. It was not the look she wanted to see.

'I have hurt you,' he said.

'Aye!' she said, exasperated. 'But only because you've barely given me a breath before that wasteful reluctance is between us again.' She waved her hand in front of her body. 'And I feel…empty.'

He groaned and his fingers flexed against her hip. But he did not remove her chemise. Instead, he set her on her shawl and lay beside her. She could feel the weight of him, the want of him. She closed her eyes. If possible, she felt even more. His breath, the very smell of him, permeated her senses. Lying next to him, she felt poised on some precarious cliff that they would soon fall off together. She didn't know what was waiting for them below and she didn't care.

'Here, let me… Maybe I can…' He pushed her chemise up, revealing her legs. He kept his hands buried in the material. The fabric had never felt so soft or rough before. He stilled and she opened her eyes.

She felt his gaze on every freckle, every earned scar. When he looked up, his expression was of a quartered man, his limbs being pulled in different directions.

'I can make you less empty,' he said, 'but I fear to touch you. Do you know how many times I have dreamed of your legs around me? Just the sight of them laid bare is enough to make me forget every hell-bound part of me.'

His words warmed her again. She wanted to stretch before his admiring gaze. She had never felt desired, wanted, as Robert wanted her. 'Then forget,' she said.

His expression became shuttered. 'I will not forget. It is all I am now. Damned. I ache for you, Gaira.'

He released the fabric; his hand hovered above her belly. She felt the warmth of his hand, tangible to her bared skin, and she stretched a leg.

A predatory gleam returned to his eye. 'Do you ache for me?'

His eyes were like a riptide pulling her down with him. Her stomach flipped at the sensuous curve of his lips, the flush of his cheeks. She pulled back her leg, lost her ability to breathe.

He watched every move. 'Aye, you do,' he said, satisfaction entering his voice. 'So do I. Ache. And

I...should not touch you.' He shifted. 'Move your legs for me.'

She swallowed and wetted her suddenly dry lips, but she moved her ankles apart.

'Wider, Gaira, or I'll need to touch you.' A ghost of a smile glided over his eyes. 'Where is your bravery?'

She moved her ankles a bit more, now feeling the breeze tease her thighs and flow under her knees. Vulnerable, she stopped moving. He was fully clothed; her chemise barely covered her. He had moved the chemise so far up she'd be bare to him if she moved any more. No one had ever seen her this way.

Robert's brow furrowed, his gaze questioning her. How could she tell him that she wanted to, but...?

The sudden heat and possession of his calloused hands on her inner thighs shocked her. She gasped. He hissed a word she couldn't hear.

Roughly, desperately, he shoved her legs apart and moved between her legs. As quickly as he touched her, he released her.

'You won't deny me this now, Gaira.' Breath uneven, he settled between her legs. 'I can't touch you and I need you to help me. Help me while I'm pulled between my want and your need.' His gaze changed, questioned. 'And you do still need, aye?'

He asked for her permission. Even as his body

shuddered and toiled with need, he asked for permission. He already had it. 'Aye, I need,' she answered. But she felt the loss of the roughness of his hands and their purpose. His hands no longer touched her, but his legs pressed against her legs, the fine wool of his trousers now a sensuous friction against the tender insides of her thighs. 'Doona stop.'

He exhaled. 'I'll open you for me now.' Watching her reactions, he shifted and pressed his legs more. 'But you mustn't touch me—mustn't move your body, any part, unless I tell you to.' Slowly parting her legs, he moved his knees again. 'Do you understand?'

Did she? She couldn't think; she only felt everything. Further and further he pressed until she was laid bare before him, her chemise now bunched tightly around her waist. Utterly vulnerable, but she didn't feel that way as Robert gazed at her. His head bowed, she could not see the emotion in his eyes or know if she pleased him, but he told her in other ways. His hands trembled at his sides; his fingers clenched and released. He shuddered once, twice, his hands moved closer to her. She wanted them closer still.

'Aye,' she finally answered. 'I understand.'

No longer vulnerable; there was only Robert. The night, the air, the way the shawl and cool grass felt beneath her no longer existed. Her need increased and she still waited.

'I fear I will not survive your heat,' he said.

Pressing his hands beside her arms, Robert leaned forward. Gaze intent with hers, he slowly lowered himself, but again he was touching and not touching; the heat from his body the only caress. He leaned again until his chest brushed hers. The faint caress tightened her breasts, made her nipples ache. He lowered his head just enough until his lips grazed against hers. The kiss was slow, lingering. His tongue, tracing, coaxing a response. When she gave it, when her lips softened beneath his, when her lips opened to deepen the kiss, to invite a response from him, he lifted his body away.

She protested as her breasts felt the immediate chill of the air.

He half groaned, half laughed. His eyes went to her face, to her breasts. Her nipples were visible through the thin material. She wanted more than his gaze on them.

'Please.' Begging, she reached to pull him down, to force him to kiss her, to touch her.

He quickly pulled away. Confused, wanting, desperate, she lowered her arms.

'You cannot touch me, Gaira,' he said again. 'I could not control... And you need my control, even if you do not realise.' He shook his head. 'But I think I can touch you.'

She listened and sunk her fingers into the dirt.

He waited until she stilled. 'I will touch, but not in the way...' He clenched his eyes and opened them, searing her with his need. 'I'm stretched till I'm about to break. I can't have what I want, but I will have some part of your need. I'm damned, but I have to know. Are you wet for me?'

His hands returned to her legs, but they were not rough now. His fingertips, whisper-soft, trailed from her knees to the very centre of her. They stilled until one finger glided through her slickness, parting her.

She couldn't stop the rise of her hips nor the shortness of her breath.

'Aye, you're wet, wanting me to fill you.' He immediately removed his finger and gave a harsh laugh. 'God, you've weakened me, but I will ease your emptiness.'

'How?' she whispered. Her body now only felt the cool breeze where his fingers had been. She needed his hands, his body, his touch. Her body clamoured for it.

'There is a way.' Staying between her legs, he shifted his body again. He moved so that he touched her not at all. She wanted to protest, but she didn't get the chance. Not when his lips kissed just where his finger had been. Hot pressure, and she gasped,

'Robert!' Moving, shifting, the shawl bunching beneath her, she tried to escape.

But he wouldn't let her.

His hands returned, lifted her legs to give him more access; his tongue pressing intently. She couldn't do anything, but dig her fingers deeper into the dirt as she was pulled into his rip tide. He kissed, licked, caressed with his tongue. His hands released her as she bent her knees, raised herself to him. Compelled to drown in heat, want, desire.

'Robert, please, I cannot—' She exhaled sharply, and jolted as her body buoyed up then crashed to the surface in a thousand pieces.

When she fell back to the cool earth, Robert lay next to her.

She felt as if she was floating in a gentle stream when she opened her eyes.

Robert did not touch her, did not look at her. Breathing harshly, his body was rigid, locked in a prison he had created.

She moved on to her side. He had given her pleasure, but he had rejected his own. She didn't understand.

'Is it this journey? The fact I'm Scottish? Is it me?'

He looked at her. Pain clashed with anger in his eyes. 'Aye, it's you. It's me. It's this whole damn mess we're in. I want you. Want you like I've wanted no other woman in my life, but I can't give you that want. Because that's all it would be. All it could ever be. I'm barely a man.'

A dull flush crept up her neck and she was glad it was dark. She hadn't thought his rejection was for a physical reason. He was so physically fit, but he did have those scars along his face, neck and arms. Maybe he had hidden injuries as well.

'Were you hurt?' She bit her lip. She didn't know how to finish. Guilt over what she might have put him through was quickly taking away her contentedness. She waved her hand towards the lower half of him. 'In a battle?'

He rubbed his eyes. 'Hurt, aye. But not in the way you think.'

She didn't know what to think. He wanted her. Even if he hadn't said it, she would know. She also knew she wanted him. But if he wasn't hurt, was actually capable of being with her, why wasn't he?

She knew so little about him. What she did know was contradictory. Was he an evil right-hand man to King Edward? Or a man filled with wonder and trepidation by the attention from a five-year-old boy?

He wasn't giving her any clues, but she wanted to know. She was determined to know something of him at least.

She briefly touched the side of his face. His skin was still damp with sweat, but it felt cooler to her now. He did not pull away from her, but he didn't acknowledge her, either.

The white scars scattered across his cheek and down his neck. There were some against his shoulders and many she could see beneath the hairs on his arms. She laid her hand back at her side.

'How did you get these scars?' she asked.

His face instantly froze. His brown eyes, already cooling, became like ice. An invisible barrier so suddenly erected between them she felt it would have sliced her arm in two if she was still touching him.

Chapter Twenty

He turned his head away and stared at the night sky. 'So you've returned to picking at my soul?'

His taunt hurt. But she wasn't giving up. She knew it wouldn't be easy to make the river bend. With her fingertips, she touched the side of his face covered by scars. He flinched, but she kept her hand on him.

'What happened to you here?' she persisted.

He looked at her. His hair had fallen back, the waves curling around his ears. Her fingers continued to trace the outline of his face, his cheekbones and the square of his jaw.

He gently grasped her fingers and pulled them towards his chest, laying the flat of her palm against his heart.

'What happened between us doesn't change anything.'

She tried to keep her voice level, but she could

not stop the tremor in her hand. 'I did not think it would,' she lied.

'I only wanted to help you. I will be leaving in the morning.'

She felt her heart crumbling into tiny fragments. The river had won. She'd given him her heart and her body. She thought she could understand he didn't share his body with her. But now he wouldn't even share with her how he got some ruddy scars. It hurt. She refused for him to see how much.

She tried to remove her hand, but he held it firm against him. Lying as she was, she could not move away from him. Her only chance was to go over him to get away.

Robert anticipated her move and he lifted his own leg over hers to anchor her down. He felt Gaira squirm, but he knew he held her firm to his side. It was a small victory and did little to ease the remorse he felt by hurting her. He never meant to hurt her. He was just a man.

No. It was more than that. She was more than that. He would have been able to resist her otherwise. Resist. He was lying here in agony. He could feel every inch of her body.

He had to stop thinking of her body.

'My mother was a young villager in Dent and my father was a nobleman passing through,' he said. He didn't know what possessed him to tell of his childhood. He had never told anyone. Maybe it was because she was trying to leave and he didn't want her to.

'I was told by the village healer, who raised me, that he had forced her. I didn't doubt that. My mother was not well—her mind had been broken since she was a child. She was more a child than a mother. I don't know what happened to her.'

Gaira stopped squirming and eased some of her weight on to his body. He forced himself not to pull her closer. 'I was more fortunate than other bastards and knew the name of my father,' he continued. 'When Edward's court travelled nearby, I sneaked in.'

'How old were you?' she asked.

His heart eased at her curiosity. Perhaps if he revealed some of his past, she would not be so angry with him. No, he was fooling himself. It wouldn't be enough, but it was all his heart was prepared to tell her. He wasn't telling her how he got the scars.

'Young, maybe ten or eleven. In truth, I don't know how old I am.' He shrugged. 'When I got to court, it was easy to find my father. I demanded a sword and training. He never questioned I was his son. I didn't either, once I saw him. We looked too much alike.'

'But you were not the same,' she said, her voice holding the merest hint of a question.

He curtly shook his head. 'I'll never know.'

'He did not take you in?' she asked incredulously, her voice rising. 'He did not train you? How could he! I hope you gave him a kick in the shins or at the very least—'

He pressed his fingers against her lips. It was just like Gaira to champion a child long grown up. 'He did take me in. Said it was his blood giving me courage to travel to court and I could hardly be faulted for my blood.'

She frowned and bit her inner lip. He felt the slight movement of her lips and the sensation meandered down his arm and into his body. He quickly removed his fingers.

'Was he standing alone when you demanded your rights as his child?' she asked.

He glanced at her, surprised she knew. 'He wasn't. There were others around him. I could tell from their expressions they didn't expect him to do it. But when he bragged about our shared blood, they laughed and exchanged knowing glances.'

He breathed in deep, held it. He remembered that day well. 'I should have hated him, but I couldn't. I didn't even know him to have any emotion. I think he kept me as an amusement. But I trained, hard. I didn't want to be an amusement for long. Not at his expense, not at anyone's expense.'

Gaira eased more on to him and he felt the full

weight of her luscious body, the draping of her legs against his. His blood burned at the contact. He needed to finish his tale.

'My drive was noticed by King Edward and he took me to his training lists. I never looked back to my father or talked to him since. He had served his purpose, just as my mother had served his. I would see him occasionally, but he was not a favourite of court and I never encouraged otherwise.'

'Does he live?'

'I haven't thought of it.' He hadn't, not for many years. What he was thinking of was how well matched Gaira's body was to his own. How brave and stubborn her heart was. And how he could never have her.

'We should return to camp,' he said.

He heard the slight cry of distress before he heard the dull thump of a sound he knew. Fists against flesh.

He sprang up. It was still early morning and he had probably only been asleep for a few hours. Gaira, Alec and Maisie were nowhere in sight. Flora and Creighton, however, were still in the spot where they had fallen asleep. But they were not asleep now.

Creighton was half-sitting and his fists were swinging. Flora was alternately covering her head with her arms or trying to grab her brother's arms. She was whispering frantically.

He ran over, grabbed Flora around the middle and dragged her away from Creighton.

'Nae!' she cried. 'He needs me!'

Reaching for her brother, she twisted against him.

'Not like that he doesn't.' He roughly set her away from her brother. She didn't like it, but he didn't care. Gaira wasn't here to intervene.

'You cannot let him hit you!'

Flora's eyes got huge and big dollops of tears welled. He opened his mouth, but nothing came out and Flora started crying in earnest. He splayed his hands out in front of him. 'Stay here.'

He rushed back to Creighton. The boy's arms were no longer swinging, but he was still locked inside his nightmare. His hands were clenched, his body rigid.

Robert put his hand against his hot brow. The boy woke with a violent shake.

Rage flashed out of the boy's blue eyes. In all his years on the battlefield, Robert had never seen such absolute hatred. Just as quickly, however, the rage rolled into awareness and terror. Robert brushed his hand against Creighton's forehead and over the sweat-soaked hair.

Creighton pushed his hand away and scrambled to sit. His eyes found Flora where Robert had set her.

Her hair was tangled, her thick dress scrunched and already large red welts appeared across her cheeks.

Creighton shot him a look and he looked again at Flora. His eyes were wide now. Scared. Worried.

Flora was trying to smile, but her bottom lip bled and she quickly sucked it in to stop the blood from dripping.

Creighton let out a cry. It was half anger and half pain. But it wasn't words.

Creighton knew he had hurt his sister, but Robert had had enough. 'You need to stop your silence! Now. You've hurt her badly—you've hurt Gaira badly. It must stop.'

Creighton scrambled and stood; his expression changed to remorse, to anguish.

Robert couldn't stay angry with the boy, but repairs had to be made. 'Go to the stream and get some cool water for your sister.'

Creighton didn't move and he didn't take his eyes off his sister.

He addressed Flora. 'He can hear me, aye?'

Flora nodded, but she kept her eyes on her brother. 'He can hear.' She sucked in her lip again. 'And he'll go if I ask him.'

Creighton let out a sharp sound and ran towards the direction of the stream.

Robert let out a breath. He didn't know whether to run after Creighton or help Flora. He had no experience with children. He didn't know how to talk to them even in the most peaceful of times. He certainly didn't know how to talk to a nine-year-old boy who suffered from the type of anguish he'd only seen in grown men.

And he didn't know how to get him to talk. Some of his men had been battle-shocked, but they were only silent a day, maybe two. It had never extended to weeks. The boy was purposefully staying mute and he had no idea why. Gaira had never told him and perhaps she didn't know, either.

But he knew Flora understood something. She had taken her brother's beating and said he needed her.

She was standing a bit behind him and staring towards the stream where her brother had run.

'Why doesn't he talk?' he asked.

'He won't tell you,' Flora said. Her voice was so soft, he almost didn't hear her. 'And…I doona think he's returning.' She glanced at him and a speculative light entered her eyes.

He felt he was being sized up and resisted the urge to move away from her. The look was too piercing and too knowing for a child.

'I have some water in a skein. I doubt it is much warmer than the stream.'

Grabbing a spare tunic, he poured the water. It was still icy cold from the night.

She walked in front of him, but her head was

bowed. He suddenly didn't know whether to hand her the tunic or tend her himself. She didn't give him any instructions.

Crouching before her, he gently wiped away the blood before pushing aside her hair and pressing the tunic against her eye.

'This needs to stay there to reduce swelling. You tell me when it gets warm.'

She gave a slight nod and her hands pressed the tunic to her face. ''Tis warm,' she said immediately.

He suspected it felt like fire against her battered face, but she neither cried nor complained. She just kept looking at him. He put more water on the tunic and lifted it to her face. She wasn't blinking and he again felt she was assessing him.

He glanced around the camp. He neither heard nor saw any sign of Gaira or the rest of the children.

'It's my fault he won't speak,' she whispered.

He continued to look over her shoulder, but his focus sharply returned to her. 'Why do you think it's your fault?'

'I lied to Gaira. Will you tell her?' she said more quickly. 'She'd be terribly upset if she knew.'

'I think it'd take a lot more than a lie to upset Gaira.' He should know. He had personal experience with telling her lies. He doubted anything could dampen her spirit.

He waited, but Flora did not continue. He felt

something was in a fragile balance. The whole forest seemed to have become unnaturally quiet. He could barely remember if he had ever been a child, but he did remember what it took to tip the scales. Trust.

'I swear to keep your secret.' He wondered how the words emerged from his memory. But he suddenly remembered how often he had said those words when he was a child.

Her whole demeanour changed and relaxed as if what he said was the password she had been looking for. 'Oh, it's not my secret. Not really.' She started to remove her hands and he took the tunic.

'Gaira thinks we hid in the forest, but that's not true,' she said, her voice no longer tentative. She acted as if they had always been confidantes. 'We were there in the village when it happened.'

Dear God, he had had no idea. He wrung out the warmed water and kept his eyes averted in case he'd scare her away with his sudden emotions. This was a strong secret she held and he had to seem calm for her sake.

'We heard the pounding horses crest the hill and like ants from an anthill they flowed down towards Doonhill.' She pulled in her lip and gently sucked. 'Lit torches waved high above their heads. The fire's light flashed against their pointed swords. Everyone started running towards the lake or into their homes. Papa was one of the men who grabbed an axe and ran towards them. I dinna see what happened to him because Mama was dragging me into the house.'

Robert put more cool water on the tunic and pressed it against her swollen eye. His hands shook. She raised her own hands to press it there with him.

'At first they left the children alone. It was just our parents, but they dinna stop. They dinna stop with my Mama. They dinna stop.' She breathed in. 'Then a man came for me.'

Robert let go of the tunic. He didn't want this secret.

'He dinna get me,' she continued. 'Creighton surprised him. He grabbed Mama's cauldron and hit the man over the head. The man fell on me. I couldn't move. He was heavy.

'Creighton pulled him off me and pushed him into the fire climbing the walls of our home. I watched the man catch fire. I think he was already dead.'

She kept the black fabric against her face and the excess cloth spilled to cover most of her face and body. Still her exposed eye never wavered from him and he was helpless to pull his gaze anywhere else. Even in self-preservation.

'Creighton grabbed my hand and we started running out of the hut. Alec was running and screaming in the street.'

'They were killing all our friends now. I couldn't move. But Creighton grabbed Alec and ran us all up the hill and into the trees.'

She let the fabric fall from her face and he automatically took the tunic. His hands were shaking too badly to pour the water.

'I know why Creighton won't speak. 'Tis because he killed that man.' With the fabric gone, there was nothing there to catch her flowing tears.

His throat dried—his eyes stung.

'He won't talk.' She shook her head. ''Tis as if he's gone somewhere, like Papa and Mama, and I can't reach him.'

Her eyes, the colour and vastness of the sky, framed her bruised face and they looked to him as if he could help.

He couldn't find his voice. So instead he took her bare hand, which felt colder and smaller than before. She didn't flinch as he slowly pulled her slight body closer to his. He felt too large, too clumsy for her little frame, but she seemed to know what he was trying to do. She climbed into his lap and laid her head upon his shoulder. It took all his concentration to force his hesitating arms to lower gently around her.

'This is a great secret you told me, Flora,' he whispered.

He felt her nod on his shoulder.

What he needed to say next would not only affect her life, but his. If he thought he felt clumsy with his comfort, he knew he'd be clumsy with his words.

'I think Gaira needs to know this secret, too. She'll want to know if you suffered any hurt.'

'But he dinna hurt me.'

Oh, aye, he did. Just the thought of it sent anger coursing through Robert. 'It frightened you, though, didn't it?'

She nodded.

'Gaira loves you and she'd want to know about your fright.'

'She'd be mad at me for not telling her.'

'I think she'd understand why you didn't.' He paused. 'Will you tell her?'

He could feel her struggling with the thought. 'I'll try.'

She still didn't want to tell Gaira what had happened to her. Gaira was the one with the loving heart and the soft touch. Gaira would have known what to say to her, how to comfort her. Yet she had told him, a hardened warrior. An *English* soldier.

'Flora, why did you tell me this?'

She pulled away so she could look at him. He could have imagined it, but she looked younger. It was as if, in her telling, she'd become a child again. Her eyes, however, began to hold that speculative gleam again.

'Gaira says you're a soldier,' she said.

'I am.'

'You'd understand why Creighton is the way he is,' she said.

He didn't follow. But she continued.

'I can't reach him. He has gone to some place I've never been, some place Gaira's never been, too. I doona understand it and that's why I never told Gaira, because although she would try to comfort us, I do not think she'd really understand.'

She lowered her eyes and started to pluck at the fabric of her dress that was bunched between them. 'Creighton killed someone. God's probably terribly mad at him. I told him God would understand. That there would be an exception for him going to hell.'

Her reasoning was with a child's innocence. Who was he to tell her there were no exceptions? He was a warrior. He fought and killed because he wanted no exceptions. He wanted to go to hell for what he had become, for what he had done in the past. He didn't want to tell her that. But what could he tell her?

She moved and plucked at his tunic. He didn't know why she did it, but her fingers were near his heart and he felt every pull of the fabric. 'I want my brother back. I think he's punishing himself by not speaking.'

Creighton's anger made sense. He wasn't just

angry at Robert for representing the men who'd killed his family and home. He was mad because he'd been forced to kill. He doubtless thought he was damned for eternity.

He cleared his throat. 'By what you told me, his actions saved you and Alec.'

'I told him that!' she said, relief clear in her voice. 'I even told him it's similar to what you did for us yesterday. You killed that man because he attacked us. Yet you speak. You killed, but you haven't gone somewhere where we can't reach you.' She jerked her head up and scanned his face. 'You're not going away from us, are you?'

He hadn't planned on being here at all. But he was and it was his own feet that had carried him.

He brushed one of her locks away from her face. It was so light and soft he hardly felt it against his calloused fingers.

'I'll talk to Creighton, though I can't promise what will happen. But I'll try.'

She smiled. It wasn't a tentative or gentle smile, but reached from ear to ear and lit up her entire face.

'Then it's as good as done. Because all your trying so far has come true for us, Robert of Dent. I...I believe in you.'

The quick yet gentle stab to his heart took him by surprise and something tight within his chest released.

He nodded once. 'I may as well start now.'

She scrambled out of his lap and was already running in the opposite direction of the water. Her loosened plaits waved like banners behind her. He had never seen her run before.

'Flora?' he called out to her.

She stopped and looked back at him expectantly.

'I'm staying. I'll not be going away from any of you.'

She gave a quick wave and skipped as light as a child and just as accepting of the future.

He was rooted to the spot and didn't think he could lift a foot. He wished he could feel as light as she. The words had come easily to the surface as if they had been there the entire time. The promise he'd be there for them, that he'd care for and protect them, had just skipped out of him before he'd even thought.

It was a promise he vowed never to give again. The last time he'd given it, he'd failed. Since then, filled with pain and regret, he had merely existed.

Yet he'd made the promise again. Already the resolution of it was freezing through his veins and enclosing his heart with the icy heat of determination. For he knew...he *knew*. If he broke it again, he'd make sure he'd die this time.

Chapter Twenty-One

He found Creighton by the stream. He was throwing sticks and watching as they swirled and bumped over rocks.

'You should try rocks.' Robert rooted around and found a flat one. Then, arcing his arm, he let it go. The rock skipped three times.

'I used to do this when I was around your age. I had a friend who could make it skip five times.'

He searched again, found another rock and handed it to Creighton. The boy didn't move, but Robert could see his eyes shift to the rock. He held it out for a while, but Creighton didn't take it.

Flipping the rock up, he threw again. It skipped twice. 'I never could make it skip past three. I went to the water again and again, but I never got past three skips.'

Robert picked up a handful of pebbles and threw them. They dotted the water like fat rain drops.

'But I was better at our sword training. I made sure to be. He had the advantage of being older and having a better upbringing and equipment, but we trained together and I practised. I made sure to get up before my friend and went to sleep after he did.'

He rubbed the back of his neck. 'It was the same to us, the throwing of rocks and the sword practice. It was just games for two boys.'

'Eventually our practice increased and we didn't have time to throw rocks any more. The practice became more serious, but it was a game still. It was a way to compete and laugh in our exuberance. It didn't stay that way for long.'

Robert thought hard about how to phrase politics to a mere nine-year-old. 'There was this young girl whom both England and Wales wanted for their own political reasons,' he continued. 'They fought about her until Edward decided Wales didn't need to be a separate country any longer. Then my friend and I went to war.'

Finding another flat rock, he rolled it between his fingers. 'That was nothing like a game.'

Creighton neither moved nor acknowledged Robert in any way, but he was listening. Robert just hoped what he was saying made sense.

'It was not a huge battle, maybe only a couple of hundred on each side. The day was blue, the field green, I think there were some trees at our backs.'

'Both sides ran to the centre of the field and suddenly a man stood in front of me. Every instinct in me demanded to stay alive and every bit of training demanded I not flee. In order to accomplish both, I extended my sword.'

He stopped rolling the rock and pressed the thin edges of it deep into his palm. 'He sliced his sword towards my chest. I easily blocked it. With a simple wave and thrust at an angle different from training, he was dead. I had no more than the span of a breath to parry from the next man.

'But even in the heat of it, when my senses were crisp, I remember feeling disbelief. As though what was happening couldn't possibly be. How could I do something so easily and men were falling dead around me, as though they had never existed?'

He threw the rock in his hand. It sliced into a wave and was gone. 'I confessed to a priest later that night, drank heavily and woke the next day with a crashing headache, spurs for my boots and a sense I'd never be the same again.'

He breathed in deep. He didn't know what more to say, how much detail to relay. Creighton had seen enough horror at Doonhill and he didn't want to add his own horror to that.

So he stood there, not wanting to throw more rocks. The water rushing its course seemed unnaturally loud in the silence.

'What happened to the girl?' Creighton's voice was higher pitched than what Robert was expecting. But he was only nine. Only a child, who had experienced a man's nightmare.

'She was sailing from France to Wales when Edward captured her ship and held her prisoner.'

'Did she die?'

Robert kept every muscle still. He didn't know what he had done to receive the gift of Creighton speaking and he didn't want to change the circumstances.

'No, he released her and she married and had a child.' He didn't conclude she had died in childbirth.

'I'm unclean.' Creighton's words were rushed.

Robert looked over. Creighton's eyes were fixed fiercely beyond the water to the shore on the other side.

'What do you mean?'

'If I speak, I'll just taint everything around me.'

'You're speaking to me.'

'Aye, but you're unclean, too. I saw what you did to that man. It is all the same. My mama and papa were hacked like reeds. And they fell just as suddenly.'

Robert crouched down, but continued to stare ahead just as the boy did. 'There is a difference in what those men did to your home and what I have done on the battlefield. Your family was innocent and should not have suffered the way they did. They did not ask for this war.'

He continued. 'The men I met on the battlefield were trained to fight. They came to the field knowing they could die. They agreed to the war, the pay and the outcome.'

'But they're still dead,' Creighton argued. 'They're all dead. What's the difference?'

Robert hadn't spoken this much in years and he knew he was bound to fall short at some point. This was one of those moments.

'Sometimes a boy or man cannot avoid making a hard decision. Sometimes there is no other option available, no other person to take on the burden. It just comes down to us and what we're going to do about it.'

'I dinna mean to kill him.' Creighton gave a gasp of breath that cracked. 'I knew he was bad, but I just wanted him to stop.'

'But you were scared and angry and if you didn't hit him hard enough he'd not only hurt Flora, but come after you.'

Creighton nodded and bowed his head.

Robert placed his hand on Creighton's shoulder. The boy met his eyes. His forehead was furrowed, but his eyes were still dry. A world of guilt and regret weighted his slight shoulders.

'It is not for me to forgive you or to make it endurable.' Robert gentled his voice. 'That is between you and God. Sometime in the future, you will understand what you did was very brave and your sister and Alec would be dead if not for the hard choice you made.'

Creighton's face reddened and crumpled an instant before his eyes filled with unshed tears.

Without thought, Robert hugged the boy. He didn't have any more words to help Creighton. He still wanted to convey to the boy that he'd feel safe again, that it was all right to be a child. He had no idea how to do it, so he tightened his hold; the boy's cries increased and it was a long time later when they stopped.

After another pause, Robert cleared his throat and loosened his grip. 'Have you ever skipped rocks?'

The boy pulled away and ran his arm across his face. 'Nae.'

Robert looked around his feet until he found what he was looking for. 'Aye, then.' His voice cracked, he cleared it again. 'The important thing is to find a smooth, flat rock like this here. Can you do it?'

The boy stopped rubbing his face and nodded. Then slowly, he looked around on the ground until he came up with one of his own.

It was probably no more than an hour later when he and Creighton returned to camp. Gaira, Alec and Maisie had returned. Gaira had her lap full of Maisie and Alec was doing a crazy dance with Flora. All the girls were laughing.

Creighton ran up the rest of the hill and stopped eagerly before Flora and Alec. Flora immediately stopped twirling. She gazed worriedly at her brother.

'Doona stop on my account, Flora,' Creighton said.

Robert heard Gaira's cracked gasp even through Creighton's laughter.

'You're funny when you spin!' Creighton grabbed Flora's hands and spun her faster than she was before.

Robert could see Flora's tears flying off her face as she beamed at her twin. Alec was leaping even higher and faster around them.

Gaira was crying and laughing all at the same time. Maisie clapped loudly in her lap. Both of their faces were completely absorbed with happiness. It was the most beautiful sight he had ever seen.

He had never met a woman like her. Brave, determined, but happy with her heart still whole. Over the past few days, she had giggled and made funny noises as if she were one of the children, but then she'd turned to stern mother hen making them wash and go to sleep.

He didn't know how she did it. He knew her heart

wasn't light. Her sister's death and brother's deeds had devastated her.

His words to Creighton came spilling out of him again.

Sometimes a boy or man cannot avoid making a hard decision.

Last night, before he had met her by the stream, he had watched Gaira wrap Maisie snugly against Flora. Flora's face had lit as though she had received a gift and Gaira had smiled tenderly back before bending down and kissing Flora's head.

The moment had seemed too intimate, but he couldn't tear his eyes away. These children were not her own, yet she loved them fiercely. And just as fiercely she fought for their protection.

Sometimes there is no other option available, no other person to take on the burden.

Was she a playful child, rescuer or mother? He was certain he had never met a woman like her. Maybe that was the reason he reacted to her so. He wanted to protect her, laugh with her and make love to her all at the same time.

It was his reaction, his emotions compelling him to make the promise to Flora. To them all.

It just comes down to us and what we're going to do about it.

Over Maisie's head, Gaira's eyes locked with his. He recognised most of her emotions in her expressive eyes. Happiness, gratefulness and something else that made his chest fill and lighten.

Last night he had told Gaira he was leaving. Now he needed to tell her he was staying. He wondered, after what they'd shared, how she'd feel about it.

Happy. She would be happy. Creighton was talking now. She couldn't possibly be angry or hurt with him any more.

'Nae.' She crossed her arms in front of her. 'You won't go with us. We're parting now, just as we agreed last night.'

She was glad she had sent the children off to gather kindling. Robert was not going to see reason.

'I thought you wanted my help,' Robert answered.

Aye. She did. Terribly. But not at the risk of his life. She couldn't believe she had ever demanded his help, but how could she have guessed it would come to this? 'I've changed my mind,' she said. She could not have him go now. Not after last night; not after she'd realised she loved him. The realisation hadn't been a surprise. Her heart had been softening for him ever since he'd churlishly agreed to bury her kin. She loved his churlish behaviour. Just not now.

'I've changed my mind,' she repeated. 'We do not need you any longer. We have our supplies and 'tis not far to the protection of my brother's lands. We were just fine before your arrival and we'll be just fine without you now.'

She hoped he'd listen to her argument. The truth was she still had to go over Clan Buchanan land and she still wasn't sure what her brother would do with her.

'I'll not leave you or the children behind,' he answered. 'I did not expect you or the children, but I cannot change that. But what also cannot be changed is I'm here. Even if you did just fine before my arrival, I'm here now and if I'm to help, I'll start with you.'

Contrary. Stubborn. Why was he arguing with her on this? 'I am not some project for you to protect.'

'But I will.'

She felt her anger in every fibre of her body.

'My brother,' she enunciated, 'is a Scottish laird. He will likely kill you.'

'He could try.'

She added arrogant to her litany of his attributes. 'Ach, do you not know what they'll do to you when you get me there? I'm safe, I'm telling you. I know these hills more than I know my own self.'

'Good, we can get there faster. I'd like to see you protected by your brother's walls before you tell him you're not wed, your betrothed was murdered and you brought home four more mouths to feed.'

'The fact you helped me and the children will nae sway him.'

'My reputation is my concern.' He looked at her speculatively. 'You will be safe within your brother's walls, will you not? He did, after all, marry you off to get rid of you.'

There wasn't anywhere else to go. 'My safety is *my* concern.' She repeated his words as haughtily as she could.

He leaned towards her and her resolve began to weaken.

'It better be safe,' he said. 'I can't take you and the children back to the English camp. It wouldn't be appropriate, even if you weren't Scottish.'

'And what's wrong with my being Scottish, you thrae trump toad?'

A corner of his mouth went up. 'I find not even a freckle wrong with it.'

She blushed from her feet to the roots of her hair. With her colouring, she knew she looked like a tall red stick.

What was worse was Robert looked even more handsome to her than he had just yesterday. The sun's light reflected off his hair, making it that rich brown colour she loved. The dark colour of his tunic made his brown eyes even darker. Although this particular shade of darkness did not hide the devilish light he held in them. She did not find that at all pleasing.

He was enjoying being contrary this morning. Something in him was different. He'd never teased her so before.

She hadn't been long searching for food this morning. But when she returned, her whole world had changed. Creighton was speaking. And this stubborn, contrary, arrogant man had caused that miracle.

Now, Robert wanted to help them. She wondered about the why of that. She bit down on her hopeful heart. It had no place being hopeful. Not when Robert was telling her he was riding to his death.

'We are not your responsibility,' she said.

'That is a matter of opinion. It was merely chance you reached Doonhill before I.'

'Chance! Chance had nothing to do with it. I'm Scots and so are they. I was there by God's will, not by any such randomness. He chose me to take care of them and so I shall!'

'And so you shall, Gaira, but I'll make sure of it.'

She narrowed her eyes. 'Is this about your so-called sense of duty?'

He straightened. 'The children being orphans are my responsibility.'

She knew it. Her anger scattered in different directions. First at the men who were responsible, second at Robert for his misplaced sense of duty. Third, and more important, towards her heart for being hopeful Robert had motivations other than duty. Her heart wanted him with her. She had even shared herself with him, opened herself to him in the vain hope he'd open to her, as well. But he hadn't touched her—he'd denied himself what she so freely wanted to give him. He had held himself apart. Now she wanted him gone to save himself and he chose this moment to say it was his duty!

'You did not kill their parents!' she said. 'You were not there.'

'The men who did were English soldiers, just like myself.'

'It wasn't you. It could never be you.'

'I have killed—'

She waved her hand in front of her. 'Not children, not women, not those who are innocent.'

'How can you be so sure? I am English. Doesn't that, by your Scottish blood, make me evil?'

'Doona be foolish. God does not judge by blood, but by our deeds. You're pig-headed, aye, but not evil.'

Laughter interrupted them. She glanced over her shoulder. Maisie and Alec were running ahead of Flora and Creighton. She'd run out of time to persuade him.

'This discussion is not over,' she hissed.

'I suspect not, but the outcome will be the same.'

'You infuriating succudrus...man!' she whispered furiously. 'Do you not know any better?'

Robert was silent. Not even his eyebrows rose. Nothing she was saying was swaying him.

Clumsy arms grabbed her legs and she stepped forward to keep her balance. Patting Maisie, she gave up. 'Fine, take me to my brother. What's it to me if he chops off your head?'

'Head!' Maisie squealed.

'I'm glad you two are in agreement,' he answered. 'We may need to ride harder than before. I have a feeling we've not much time left.'

Chapter Twenty-Two

Torture. He was torturing himself. It was the damn fog. It covered everything and limited his vision. Every sound was magnified. Black grouse and roe dear were so plentiful he kept stumbling into them. Animals he couldn't see skittered in the mist.

It was also the unfamiliar territory. The terrain was rockier and steeper, soft grass gave way to more low shrubs. Suddenly and without warning, hills gave way to short cliffs.

Anyone could be hiding just beyond the next hill and he wouldn't know it until it was too late. Although he continually scanned the terrain, he felt he was heading into a trap.

'How far do we travel east?' He slowed his horse to move closer to Gaira's. Alec immediately leaned in his seat to pet Gaira's horse. Robert pulled him against him before he fell off.

'Two, maybe three days,' she answered. ''Tis the only way to avoid getting close to Busby's land.'

'Won't we be too deep into Buchanan land? You told me it wasn't safe.'

'I doona think we'll be too deep.' She shifted Maisie in her lap. 'Buchanan land is large. I've never been, but my brothers have done a bit of borrowing.'

'Borrowing?'

'Stealing sheep.'

'Hence the reason you don't get along any more.' He looked to the sky. 'If this damn fog does not end, we'll have to wait on their land to travel. Let's hope they have some understanding if we're caught.'

'We won't be. The fog is good cover and at least the children have been quiet.'

Quiet, but not silent. The twins, who rode their own horse in the middle of their paltry party, hadn't stopped talking since Creighton decided to speak again. Riding together, they kept their voices low, but it wasn't without excited giggles. Alec and Maisie were quiet only because they were separated. He did not expect the quiet to last.

He'd grown accustomed to the children's natural chattering. No, it was more than that. He wasn't just accustomed to them; he'd grown protective of them. His promise aside, since he didn't know how Gaira's brother would react to Gaira returning with four children, he wasn't letting them arrive on their own. It risked their safety.

However, he didn't know how to protect them and not fight her brothers. It was a no-win situation and Gaira would be forced to pick sides. He still could not think of a way to avoid it.

Torture.

Even now Busby's or Gaira's clan could be bearing down on them. He had promised Flora he would not leave them. He wondered if she'd understand he might have no choice. He might soon be dead.

'We'll need to rest,' Gaira whispered.

He did not question it. They had travelled long already this morning and Alec was like a puppy in his lap.

She easily dismounted from the horse, keeping her hand on Maisie until she could get the girl down and away from the horse.

'How is your ankle?' He dismounted and freed Alec to run after Maisie.

She flexed her foot. 'I forgot I hurt it.'

She was still wearing the man's tunic and leggings and her movement shaped and lengthened her leg. So simple and yet his body's immediate response reminded him he was in a dangerous state of need when it came to her.

She straightened and looked around her. The children had gone into the woods. 'You should return to England,' she insisted.

He knew she would not let go of the subject so easily.

'I will not go, Gaira. No matter how many times you ask.'

She brushed her clothes to wipe the dust. 'I do not understand your stubbornness.'

He watched her hands against her covered legs. He'd seen her legs; felt their softness as they lay bared to him. Repeatedly on this endless journey, his body painfully reminded him he'd not got to touch them nearly enough.

'Should be one trait you would understand,' he replied.

'Auntie Gaira, I'm hungry.' Alec emerged from the wood. The long complaint carried in the air.

She quickly stepped to him. 'Shh, we can't have noise.'

'But I'm hungry,' Alec argued.

The rest of the children returned. They were probably all hungry. He breathed deep to release his wayward thoughts. 'We have oatcakes,' Robert whispered.

'I doona want any more oatcakes,' Alec whined.

'Trapping will take too long,' Creighton chipped in, his voice louder than Alec's.

'Sir Robert won't let us starve.' Flora's eyes and

comment bordered on hero worship. Her voice was even louder to be heard over Alec, who was now complaining with multiple sounds.

Gaira looked helplessly over her shoulder at Robert. 'Berries aren't holding them off.'

'I'll see what I can catch.'

He should have purchased more dried meat. They had some, but not enough if they had to wait until the fog lifted. Gaira had blithely informed him it could be a sennight before the fog lifted in this hilly country. Fresh meat would feed them and keep them quiet, but their position would be sacrificed by the fire and smells.

Walking in unfamiliar territory, with rocky terrain, made hunting difficult. It took him over an hour to kill the feral goat.

The flutter of wings to his left froze him. He could not tell how far they were, but something large had startled them. Another animal? Or something more.

A high-pitched squeal was heard to his right. Maisie.

More rocks being scattered to his left. They sounded closer.

He dropped the goat under a shrub, wound side down. If the body was found, maybe who or what was to his left wouldn't look too closely.

More scattering rocks, the snort of a horse.

Robert stopped hesitating; he ran in the direction of the children.

When he cleared the tree line, he saw Gaira's arm waving frantically. Horses coming. He made to the trees just as three riders emerged on the other side of the clearing.

Frantically rubbing dirt along their cheeks, Gaira hunched over Maisie and Alec. Creighton and Flora were behind another tree, their bodies low, their faces already covered in dirt.

The three riders were Scots. Their manner was relaxed as they looked around them, but their horses stepped impatiently. Robert carefully pulled his last arrow out of the quiver.

Suddenly, one of the men pulled his horse away and the other two followed. Robert waited until he no longer saw the swish of a horse's tail before he replaced the arrow in the quiver and walked over to Gaira and the children.

If the three men had been any closer to them or alert to the sounds of other horses, they would have been caught.

'That was close,' Gaira whispered.

'How did you know where to hide?' Robert asked. 'I thought they were on my left!'

'I had to…go into the trees again,' Flora said.

'You saw them?' Robert asked.

Flora nodded.

'Brave lass,' he praised.

'She ran out of those trees so silently, she gave me a fright,' Gaira added. 'They must have been nae more than two men's length away from her. If her eyes weren't so big, I would have given our position away with a scream.'

They could have all been caught.

'They made too much noise. Those men were not hunting game,' he said. 'Is there any chance your brothers would have alerted them to your disappearance?'

'I do not know. I can't imagine them mending relations just to find me.'

Robert would mend relations between God and Satan if it meant he would find Gaira. What kind of brothers did she have that she would have so little knowledge of her worth? 'We can't take any more chances,' he said. 'From now on we won't stay in any clearings. It's too dangerous.'

Chapter Twenty-Three

'How much further?' Robert asked.

The nearer they got to her home, the quieter Gaira became. She was worried. Since the moonlit night, he had tried to ignore her, but watching her had become as important as breathing. It was the way her long limbs moved as she rode the horse, the arch of her back, the curve of neck. And her hair. Since the fog had lifted, he felt blinded by the way it caught the sunlight. She had kept it bound, but the wind kept unravelling it and the various shades of red taunted him.

'Not far.' She strained in her seat. 'Look! 'Tis my tree!'

Robert saw many trees along the horizon.

'Which tree, Auntie Gaira?' Alec scrambled to stand in the saddle. Robert pressed down on his shoulder before he toppled over.

Gaira urged her horse towards a tall lone larch,

heavy with branches and leaves only on one side of its trunk. The wind whipping around them had shaped the branches and the trunk leaned precariously.

'Your tree?' he said. 'Other than the lanky limbs and height, I hardly see the resemblance.'

She laughed. 'Nae!' She dismounted and helped the children to dismount. 'Look at its base!'

He moved his horse closer. The base of the tree was large and knotted and extended past the rest of the trunk. It was some sort of abnormal growth.

She sat on the contorted base. 'See! It's a perching place. For ages, it's been welcoming Colquhouns with a place to sit.'

He dismounted and braced his feet against the wind buffeting against him. His breath left him, not by the wind, but by Gaira.

Her hair, still partially bound in a plait, whipped around her face. Her eyes were squinting from the sun, her cheeks red, her smile large and wide. She'd given her shawl to Flora and her tunic plastered against her body. Even under its thick cover, he could see her body was cold.

To see her nipples peaked made his body burn and his mouth go dry. 'Aye, very welcoming,' he admitted. If her hair taunted him, her outlined breasts mocked his denied body.

Without looking at him, she grabbed a handful of

dirt and held it out to him. 'So, do you want some now?' She offered him Scottish soil again. But this time it was her family's soil. This time, he knew what it felt to be close to her.

But he didn't move until she looked at him. Then he waited until her smile turned to confusion, then turned to comprehension.

Only then did he dare to be close to her again.

'Robert?' she asked, her voice hesitant with the beginning of desire. Her eyes darted behind him, but he knew the children were too far away.

Gaira felt Robert's intent, his eyes on her, then on her legs, then back. A message she understood all too well. He wanted to touch her again and he was asking her permission.

She looked behind him again. The children continued to chase each other.

She had only meant to show him the Colquhoun tree and to share some land. Now, with him looking at her as he did, she didn't know what she wanted to do.

She kept her hand out to him, though, and the dirt slipped through her trembling fingers. Robert moved closer until his legs barely touched her knees.

Such a small touch, knees against legs. In strangers, the touch would have meant nothing. But her body wasn't a stranger to his and it was quickly responding to his touch.

He grabbed the dirt, spilling more than he took. Trying to calm her too-fast heart, she placed her hand in her lap. Rejected by his too-brief touch. Again.

'There now, was that so difficult?' she said, trying to hide her painful awareness of him.

'Aye,' he said. 'It was.' The corners of Gaira's mouth wobbled into a smile, but her whisky-coloured eyes had darkened as he stood before her, telling him of how she really felt. He wanted to step closer, between her legs, to see if her eyes would darken more. At the peak of her desire, her eyes had turned—

Laughter. The children were returning.

Her cheeks flushing, Gaira quickly stood. He didn't stop her when she pushed him out of the way and ran towards the children. Laughter and squeals increased behind him.

He stood staring at the tree, imagining her still there. Imagining that they were alone so he could take a step closer. Could have... Exhaling slowly, he focused only on the tree. She had been jubilant to see it again. The tree was gnarled and ugly, except, through her eyes, he was beginning to see its beauty, too.

He turned to look at the rest of the land she loved. Then he saw them: two riders approaching from the north. They were setting up great swirls of dust as they rode fast. His heart thudding in his chest, Robert ran to his horse.

'Gaira!' he called. Cursing his wandering mind, he freed his long sword. His delay could cost them their lives. 'Take the horses and the children, go south and wait for me on the other side of the stream!'

She didn't answer him.

He turned to see she was gathering the children behind her, but she wasn't heading south. She was walking towards him.

He should have known she'd be stubborn. 'This is no time for your bravery!'

'I'm not going,' she said.

The riders were almost upon them and he could make out the grim looks on their faces. This was not a friendly visit. There needed to be distance between them.

'Dammit, Gaira, move!'

'I think I'll see what my brothers have to say first.'

Her brothers. With grim faces. 'Move so the children don't have to witness this.'

She folded her hands in front of her. 'There'll be nothing to witness if I stay. My brothers are reasonable.'

'It may have taken you some time to know who I am, but I doubt it will take any time at all for your brothers to guess. When they do, reason will have no play in this.'

'I'm staying.' She jutted out her chin. 'My motivations for staying are more powerful than reason.'

He had no time for her riddles.

The two men pulled up their mounts, kicking up small pebbles as they stopped.

One had long dark hair, but the sun's light gave it a hint of red. His grey-green eyes were cold, merciless.

The other, younger, had short dark hair, not a hint of red, with dark-green eyes that were hot with anger. Neither drew their sword. But they had the advantage. There were two of them and both on horseback.

They moved the horses close to him to intimidate him. He knew the procedure. He kept his gaze on the men, not the horses.

These men were not lackwits like Busby. He could see their eyes assess and take measure. Though they were angry, they held their temper.

'What do you do with our sister?'

Not the question he was expecting, but certainly the most pertinent. It was the older one who talked first. He wondered if it was Bram, the laird, but quickly dismissed that thought. Gaira had described the laird as having red hair. This was probably the second son, Caird.

'I am returning her and four children to your care.'

He did not try to talk in their tongue. They would guess he was English.

Caird did not spare his sister or the children a glance. Robert knew he had already taken in the entire assemblage when they rode up.

The younger one brought his horse closer. Robert guessed he was Malcolm, the youngest brother.

'Her care does not belong to us, but to her husband,' Malcolm stated. 'You are not he, Englishman.'

'No, I am not. He is dead.'

Neither of her brothers looked surprised. They were testing him.

'How?' Caird asked.

'By my own hand.'

Malcolm pulled tight on the reins and his horse sidestepped roughly. It forced Robert to move to avoid a hoof crushing his foot.

'Few men could fell Busby of Ayrshire,' Malcolm reported, his voice harsher than his brother's. His anger was not so neatly under control.

'He did not give me the opportunity to know that,' Robert answered, 'as he attacked me from my back.'

They did not seem surprised by that news either. Yet they came from the north and the town was south. The only way they could know what had happened there was either to have travelled to Doonhill or they had messengers.

The two extra days when they travelled through Buchanan land had given her brothers the advantage. He wondered how well informed they were.

'Perhaps you gave him reason for attacking your back,' Malcolm said.

'Nae, he did not, Malcolm, and doona you go accusing him of such!' Gaira walked towards them.

Robert was surprised she had waited this long to speak.

'Gaira, stay put!' Malcolm ordered.

'I will not! My complaint is with Bram, not you, but I demand you stop circling this man as if you intend to hurt him.'

'You defend him overmuch,' Caird said.

'Aye,' Malcolm sneered. 'Interestingly, we doona know who it is you defend. Neither of you have mentioned his name.'

There was no use denying it. Robert flexed his wrist on his sword.

'Robert of Dent.' He waited until they reacted. He did not have to wait long.

With a roar, Caird pulled his horse roughly away, dismounted and drew his sword. Malcolm was right there by his side.

Free of the horses circling, Robert widened his stance and placed his sword low and in front of him. Gaira was in his peripheral vision and much too close should her brothers attack. Robert shifted his feet. He didn't want the swords anywhere near her.

'So the infamous Black Robert is not dead after all,' Malcolm growled.

'Seems we have to remedy that,' Caird joined.

'You will not, Caird!' Gaira said. 'This man has done nothing but help me return here.'

'That's not what we heard,' Malcolm stated. 'You wouldn't need help returning if not for this demon you stand too near. Move away so we can kill him.'

'I'll do nae such thing, you daupit argle-barglous beetle!'

'Gaira, do you know who this man is?' Malcolm demanded. 'Do you know what he has done?'

'Aye, I do and I stand by my word I've been safe and so have these children. Children, I should tell you, who have seen too much violence. I'll not let them see more.'

'My sister's too protective of you.' Caird spat on the ground. 'What have you done, English?'

Robert did not want to fight Gaira's brothers, but he'd defend himself if he had to. He wasn't planning to die today. 'I'm returning your sister. Nothing more.'

'Stand away from him, Gaira.' Malcolm pointed his sword for her to get out of the way.

'Oh, hell, can't you men just use your wanwordy heads for once!'

They didn't hear the lone horse and rider galloping hard, until he was upon them. The horse snorted loudly when he came to a complete stop.

Robert was not going to be distracted. He kept his eyes on Caird and Malcolm, but glanced briefly at the rider. Gaira said she had three brothers. It appeared he was to be graced with the entire Clan Colquhoun before the end of the day.

But it wasn't a Colquhoun. Hugh dismounted and brought his sword up with a flourish. 'Am I late?'

Chapter Twenty-Four

It took his mind far too many seconds to realise who he was seeing. 'Hugh!' Robert shouted. 'What are—?'

Malcolm took advantage of his distraction. Robert blocked the blow right when the tip of Malcolm's sword was an inch from slicing his chest.

The ringing of the two swords ended any peaceable truce and it didn't take long for Hugh and Caird to join in.

Gaira was forced to move away from the swords swinging. The children stood a few feet from her and they watched everything.

It appeared she was the only voice of reason. If she didn't stop this nonsense, the children would either be in danger from the swords or see something they shouldn't.

She winced as she heard Malcolm's sword reverberate against Robert's. He had made a powerful arc towards Robert's head. It was similar to what she saw Busby do. But Robert didn't react as he had with Busby.

She watched more closely. Robert *wasn't* fighting her brother. He defended. Malcolm seemed to realise it, too, and his movements became more aggressive.

She looked at Hugh and Caird. Hugh's intent was clear with each swipe of his sword. He was not trying to defend. He was trying to kill and so was Caird.

She wouldn't have any deaths on her hands. She looked around at her feet and found what she was looking for. Taking a handful of the largest rocks, she aimed at their heads.

She might as well have been doing nothing. Other than a bit of flinching, they continued in their idiotic fighting.

She looked at her feet again. There was no hope for it. She'd have to resort to stronger measures. What did she care for a lost or blackened eye? It was their fault.

Despite the wind, her strategy worked. Pelting multiple small rocks at their eyes forced them to be distracted.

'Halt!' Caird shouted, wiping the sand and grit from his eyes.

She was relieved to see Hugh stopped his fighting and give Caird the courtesy of sight. Apparently this was another Englishman with honour. She wondered if her brothers had noticed.

Malcolm's face was pock-marked with red welts. She had been throwing especially large rocks towards his nose and was quite satisfied it was bleeding profusely. It served him right for starting the attack.

'What in the hell are you doing?' Malcolm shouted.

'Getting you to stop, you idiot!' she shouted equally as loud.

'Bram will not want this man alive.' Malcolm finished wiping his face.

'Aye, maybe so, but that is for Bram to decide as laird of Colquhoun and not the likes of you two!'

Caird hesitated. Robert shifted. Hugh was glancing at Robert, taking measure of his actions.

Good, they were listening, but they hadn't put their swords away. She'd have to use guilt. She didn't want to. Not like this, in front of Robert and Hugh and in the wake of anger. But they were giving her no choice. She knew her sister would understand.

'You cannot fight these men.' She softened her voice. 'Robert helped me bury Irvette.'

Caird visibly shook. Malcolm's sword dropped. She knew she had finally got through to her brothers. She just hoped Robert would keep his sword still.

'Robert?' Hugh asked. It was clear he wanted to know what to do.

'Stand down, Hugh,' Robert answered. 'This is not your fight.'

'So it is true,' Caird said, his voice hoarse.

Gaira felt for him and Malcolm. She did not want them to know this way. She just wanted them to stop fighting. 'Aye.'

Caird regained his colour. 'Did he have a play in it?'

'Nae. He did not,' she said.

Caird lowered his sword and looked at Robert and Hugh. 'My sister is right. We will wait for Bram's judgement.'

Robert did not say anything.

Caird continued. 'You will each give me your swords.'

'No,' Robert said. 'But you have my honour they will not be raised.' He paused. 'Until we hear judgement from your brother.'

Malcolm whispered into Caird's ear and looked levelly at her, a question in his eyes. She nodded to him. Robert could be trusted.

Malcolm placed his hand on Caird's shoulder. 'Come, we'll let the laird do business with the man and his weapons.'

'And your man?' Caird asked, his eyes on Robert.

'Do not question his honour if you expect there to be no fight.' Robert sheathed his sword.

Caird hesitated, but it was Robert's actions, more than his words, that seemed to sway him. He sheathed his own sword.

It took them only a half a day's ride to reach Colquhoun Keep. The keep was not hidden behind trees or rocks and its thick vertical towers stood tall even against the cliffs that surrounded it.

Robert slowed his horse, so that he could get a better view of the land and its inhabitants. He knew his curiosity was an odd emotion to feel at a time like this. Within an hour or so, he most likely would be dead.

The people stopped their work and were openly staring. He knew now what Gaira meant, that a Buchanan would know if he'd caught a Colquhoun. Most everyone around him had varying shades of red hair. None had the brilliant vibrancy of Gaira's hair, but the bright frequent shade coloured the landscape better than any purple heather or yellow broom.

He slowed his horse just a bit more and he heard the rough snort of Malcolm's horse behind him.

Gaira was riding just to his right and staring at the gate opening upon their approach. Her freckles stood out against the paleness of her cheeks and her lips, pinched by her teeth, had lost their normal colour. She was more than worried now. Maisie, slumped and asleep, was clasped tight against her, not out of affection, but because Gaira was terrified she'd be snatched away. Alec seemed to understand Gaira's fear and kept his arms around her back.

Inside the gates, a large man with red hair walked down the keep's steps. Four men flanked him from behind. The laird of Colquhoun had come to greet them.

Malcolm moved his horse slightly to Robert's left to block him from the closing gate. When the gate closed, Scottish soldiers, enough to fell an English army, surrounded them. He had nowhere to go.

He could have told them to save their tactics. He had no intention of leaving until Gaira and the children were safe. He didn't know how he would accomplish that fact, but staying around as long as possible was part of the plan.

Caird dismounted before Bram reached them.

'I see your trip was successful.' Bram's voice boomed in the quiet courtyard. 'But I see also you have brought some…guests.'

Caird indicated with his arm. 'This is Robert of Dent and one of his men, my laird.'

Bram fixed his eyes on Robert. 'So, Black Robert lives,' he said curiously.

Robert threw his sword to the ground and twenty soldiers unsheathed their swords.

Bram did not flinch when Robert slowly dismounted and walked towards him.

The four men around Bram moved, but Bram held up his fist and they stopped. Robert spoke first.

'I have brought your sister and four surviving children from a village my men massacred. A village near Dumfries.'

Oh, God, what did Robert do? Gaira's worry escalated. Bram knew who Robert was. That alone was enough to order him killed. Now Robert had told her brother he was responsible for Doonhill?

Bram's eyebrows lowered and his eyes flickered towards Caird. Bram knew Doonhill was near Dumfries. Gaira could see he didn't want to make the connection.

Caird swiftly leaned in and whispered into Bram's ear. The skin around his eyes and mouth tightened.

Bram had been especially close to Irvette. She had no idea what gave him the strength to still stand, let alone not show the grief he must be feeling.

Maisie squirmed in her lap. Gaira didn't have an oatcake or drink to keep her still.

Bram faced Robert again. 'You will die, English.'

'I have some concessions to ask first,' Robert answered.

'You are in nae position to ask for favours.'

'Your brothers live. Do you think I willingly allowed them to bring me here?'

Caird snarled.

Bram raised his arm and slowly lowered it. 'Even if that is so and I am not willing to agree, what makes you think I'll spare your life?'

'I am not asking you to spare my life.'

Bram pointed to Hugh. 'Your man's life is worth less than yours.'

'That is also not the boon I ask.'

Bram's eyebrows rose.

Gaira could not wait any longer. Maisie was awake and listening. As was Alec, and Flora and Creighton. They had seen and heard too much.

'Stop!' she called. 'Both of you. Robert, I doona know what game you are playing.'

She pointed at Bram. 'As for you, I know you have nae intention of granting any reprieve.'

Bram's colouring deepened. 'I am glad to find you are alive, Gaira. But you have disobeyed your laird and should hold your tongue.'

'Or what? Are you going to banish me?' She swung her leg over her horse. She was careful to keep Maisie and Alec atop until she got her balance. Carefully, she pulled Maisie into her arms and walked to Bram.

'If you banish me, who is to take care of Irvette's daughter or the other children?' She set Maisie on the ground and the child sat atop her feet. 'You may not value Robert's protection of me, but he did protect your niece. For that, I ask you to listen.'

Bram's nostrils flared. 'Ask your favour, Englishman, but know that I will probably not grant it. I am looking forward to killing you.'

'I willingly will not raise my arm against your clan,' Robert said, 'if you take in and care for Gaira and the four children she has brought.'

Gaira's heart lurched, sank and rose in her throat.

Bram laughed. 'You waste your boon, Englishman. I had nae intention of doing otherwise.'

'Is that the word of a laird or of a brother?'

'That is the only insult you'll pay me,' Bram said between his teeth. 'Take them to the cellars.'

The men behind Bram went to stand by Robert. Caird and Malcolm flanked Hugh.

Gaira tried not looking at Robert. 'Bram, we need to talk,' she said.

Hatred filled his eyes. 'What makes you think I would even acknowledge you are my blood? You have sided with a murderer.'

Chapter Twenty-Five

Gaira strode into Bram's private solar and slammed the door behind her.

'You need to hear me.' She wasn't wasting one moment. She knew Robert's life depended on her. Her brother was stubborn and, when it came to her, he was an idiot. But in matters that involved the clan, she knew he could be fair.

He did not acknowledge her. 'You must not kill him,' she urged. 'Robert is not the man you think he is. If you'll just let me—' She stopped. He wasn't listening. Instead he stared out the window. He was not looking at the courtyard below, but beyond the keep to the Clyde.

'How was she?' Bram asked.

She didn't recognise her brother's voice. Grief. She wasn't ready to talk about Irvette.

'Dead,' she whispered.

'I wish…' He bowed his head.

'I wish you could have been there, too,' she said. 'I wish all of us could have been but a few hours earlier.'

'Did she suffer?'

Her sister had been face down in the dirt. Her arms had been splayed, blood pooled around her torso. There was no doubt she had suffered. But she didn't want to give that answer, nor could she avoid the truth.

'She had two stab wounds to her stomach,' she said.

He grabbed the shutters and leaned his full weight on their handles. The shutters held, but she heard the deep creak of the wood giving at the hinges. 'And Aengus?'

She had not known Irvette's husband well, but Irvette had loved him beyond distraction. Had she watched him die? 'Burned,' she said. 'His head was severed.'

He shoved the shutters open and leaned out towards the courtyard. His body was prostrate over the courtyard a full storey below. If the hinges broke, he would have no balance to catch himself. She looked away.

'I found Maisie under a chest,' she said. 'She was unmarked. Until I found her, I had seen nae survivors. I had given up any hope.'

A sound broke from Bram. 'Leave.'

'I will not leave the—'

'This room, Gaira, you ken? Leave me to suffer for Irvette. Leave me to plan exactly how many pieces I'll hack your precious Robert of Dent into.'

She hesitated.

'Now!'

He did not move his body, but he turned his head. It was the pain in his eyes, not his request, that moved her. She closed the door gently behind her.

The cellar was dimly lit and smelled of drying meat and herbs. It was also large enough for Robert to pace from one end to the other. He saw no need to save his energy.

'How did you find me?' he asked.

Hugh sat with his back to a wall. 'You just disappeared. After every battle, your body wasn't found. Did you think that would go unnoticed?'

He had purposefully distanced himself from everybody for years. It was easy to believe no one would think of him.

'Was it the king?' he finally asked.

'Aye, he sent me to search for you. It wasn't easy at first. Every description I'd give of you, someone would say they saw you travelling with a woman and four children. I couldn't believe them.'

'What convinced you?'

'The town square.'

Robert nodded his head. 'The fight with Busby.'

'The villagers told me how you were attacked from the back and you fought a man almost twice your size with a claymore. I knew it was you. It was easy to follow you after that. You weren't exactly travelling light.'

Robert softly smiled. No, not light at all. Even now he felt the precious burden of Gaira and the children. He feared their weight was somewhere near his heart.

'How'd you not catch up with us?' Robert asked.

'Fell into a bit of trouble with three men calling themselves "The Buchanan". Their sport left me a good distance from you.'

'Your skills must have improved since I left.'

'My skills were always fine. You just never saw them because I was protecting your back all this time.'

'I thought it was me protecting you?'

'We made a formidable pair.' Hugh laughed. 'We could make such a pair again. We're not tied and the lock on that door is not a true deterrent.'

'There are two guards pacing above our heads.'

'You can see through solid earth?'

'I can hear them.'

'I'd risk it.'

'It'd be your head out first and too easy a target.'

Hugh arched his eyebrow. 'Don't you want to get out of here?'

Robert stopped his pacing. 'What I need to do here has not been accomplished.'

'You're here on some mission.' Hugh stood. 'Is it for information? To assassinate someone? Did my showing up harm your plan?'

'No—'

Hugh blew out in relief. 'What needs to be done now? The king didn't tell me anything. I can't say I like the idea of being kept in the dark on something of import.'

'I'm not here on any assignment.'

Hugh's eyes narrowed. 'Then why are you here?'

It was a valid question and one Robert didn't have a prepared answer for. 'I am just returning the woman and the children to the clan.'

'You're *helping* them? They're Scots! We're at war against them!'

'The English are at war with the Scottish,' Robert clarified.

Hugh blew out his nose. 'Are you saying there is a difference?'

'Maybe.' It was still unclear to him on how it was different, but it felt different to him.

'I don't understand, Robert.'

Hugh wouldn't understand until he gave him answers. And maybe, just maybe, under the circumstances he owed Hugh those answers.

'I went to Doonhill to see if the claims of destruction were true.'

Hugh crossed his arms. 'And there you found the Scottish woman and children?'

'Aye,' he answered.

'And you felt sorry for them and helped them return to their Scottish clan,' Hugh continued, his voice rising and tightening. 'A clan most likely loyal to Balliol?'

He shrugged.

'So when did you turn traitor?'

And that was a question too many. 'Careful, Hugh. Your anger is justified, but it does not give you permission to question my honour.'

'Anger! Anger is the least of what I feel. If I had not just witnessed it myself, I would have killed anyone for accusing you of disloyalty.'

'If you continue to do the accusing, I'll remind you that my patience is stretched.'

Hugh leaned back against the wall. 'You dare threaten me? I have no worry for your threats. By staying here, we're both going to be killed.'

Not if he could help it, but how could he make Hugh understand something he understood little himself?

'Your actions would kill King Edward if he knew,'

Hugh said, derision lacing his voice. 'Our liege deserves more than you stabbing him in the back!'

Robert raised his hand. 'King Edward means more to me than a liege lord. But that complicates my being here.'

'Aye, I'd say so.' Hugh crossed his arms. 'If you've not turned traitor, you've allowed yourself to be captured. And I'm to believe you've done it for a woman?'

Robert faced him fully. 'Her name is Gaira. And regardless of what you believe, I am here for her and the children. But it is more than that.'

'It better be a damn good more than that!' Hugh pushed himself away from the wall. 'And before you say I have no right to ask, remember I'm in this cellar, too. I have a right to know why and what you plan to do about it.'

The cellar door slammed above them. Robert squinted into the opening as Caird walked down the steps.

He pointed to Hugh. 'The laird wants to see him.'

Robert stepped forward. 'He knows nothing. I am the one who travelled with his sister.'

Caird stared, but didn't repeat himself.

'I'll go.' Hugh faced Robert. With the door open, the light flooded the cellar and allowed him to see the full extent of Hugh's anger.

Fear pricked Robert's spine. Hugh was too angry

to be facing a Scottish laird. Caution and diplomacy were the only way out of the situation for him. He had only meant for himself to be captured, not Hugh as well. Hugh didn't deserve to die because of Robert's mistakes.

'Hugh—' Robert called.

Hugh walked up the steps. 'I'll go,' he repeated. 'Perhaps I'll find more acceptable answers with the enemy.'

Gaira found Malcolm and Caird in the courtyard.

'Where are the children?' she asked, pulling her shawl close about her. She hadn't had time to change and was gathering stares.

'With Oona,' Malcolm said.

'Oona's older than the Colquhoun tree! She wouldn't be able to chase after Alec.'

'You care?' Caird stated.

She couldn't stop the dull flush creeping up her neck. Caird never spoke much, but when he did, his honesty was almost cruel. Still, he was wrong in this. 'You have nae right deciding who and what I care for.'

'You have nae say in what happens to Colquhoun clan,' Malcolm interjected. 'The laird married you to another clan.'

For Malcolm, there was always right or wrong.

There'd be no changing his mind. Still, she couldn't help defending herself. 'I'm here now,' she said.

'Do you think Bram would keep you after he kills Black Robert?' Malcolm asked, his tone soft. 'Do you think he'd want anything to do with you after you sided with the English?'

Harsh words softly given, but she didn't want to listen to her brother's accusations. For now, she worried for the children. 'Where's Oona?' she demanded.

'At the cottage,' Malcolm said. 'Gaira—'

'Doona,' she interrupted. She didn't want to hear any more. They hadn't listened to her before sentencing her to Busby's care.

Malcolm looked to protest, but Caird put his hand on his shoulder and he let her go.

The walk was long. Oona insisted on living apart from the keep and houses and she heard the children before she saw the cottage.

'Oona, 'tis me!' she called out.

'Gaira! You've got to taste something for me, child.'

Gaira smiled. Another thing that did not change— Oona cooking some potion of hers. When she walked into the cottage, she saw Oona bent over a steaming cauldron. The smell coming from the pot was foul.

Alec pulled a wooden spoon out of Maisie's hands. Maisie instantly screamed for all she was worth.

'Where are Creighton and Flora?'

'Out gathering rosemary.' Oona turned around. No longer able to straighten, she stayed bent.

'Did you tell them how much to get?' Gaira grabbed another spoon and handed it to Alec. He quickly released Maisie's, who stopped screaming.

'Now that might have been something I forgot.'

Gaira laughed. 'Oh, you haven't changed!'

'Haven't changed. What a funny expression. You've been gone less than a full moon. It would take more than that blink of time to change ol' Oona.'

So much had changed though. 'Irvette's gone,' she said quietly.

Oona's reed-thin hand patted Gaira's hand. 'Aye, I know.'

Gaira sat on a stool. 'Ah, what I would give to have your sight.'

'With these clouded eyes, ol' Oona has to be open to other ways of seeing. So I know more things than any of you.'

Gaira clenched her hands. 'I need her so.'

'Nae, it seems to Oona you need someone else.'

'The children need me, but Bram may not keep me here.'

'Children always need someone. That is the joy of children, but you know I meant the outsider.'

'Robert?'

'Aye, it's the man who needs you more than the children.'

'What he needs is to return to England, with his head intact. I fear Bram won't see reason.'

Oona turned back to her pot and scooped up some of the liquid. 'That's because reason has nae say in these times.'

Gaira clamped her lips tightly as Oona brought the spoon close to her mouth. There were chopped bits of green floating things she didn't recognise.

'Nae reason for reason, says Oona. Trust your instincts in this. When have I ever done you any harm?'

Gaira opened her mouth and Oona spooned in the mixture.

She gagged and forced herself to swallow the liquid.

Oona gave a short cackle. 'Course there is always a first time, now isn't there?'

'What—?' Gaira coughed. 'What was that?'

'Just something to make everything better.'

'You should be giving that to Bram. He's the one with the power to change everything.'

'Gaira of Clan Colquhoun, when have you ever

thought someone had more authority over your life than yourself?'

Never. But these were not normal times. Her feelings were so confused she didn't know where to start.

'These times are just like all times,' Oona said. 'Time like all time. You think time changes because of what we do?'

Gaira gave a startled laugh. 'Oona. You frighten me sometimes.'

'Good. Maybe you will all leave me to some peace in my old age.'

'Then who would taste your potions?' Gaira sat on the floor with Alec and Maisie.

'The children. They are most willing to try ol' Oona's mixtures.'

'Are they fine here for now? I doona think the keep is the right place to keep them just now. Bram is too angry. They may hear things I doona want them to hear.'

'But Maisie is Irvette's daughter. He will want her at the keep.'

'I doona want to separate them. They have had too much change.' She took Maisie's spoon and pretended to hide it behind her back. The little girl squealed in protest and reached her arms out to take it.

'You sound as though it would be a burden on

Oona to have such young hearts around. It'll be good for me. You'll see. A day or two here and you wouldn't know who is the child and who is Oona.' Oona gave a raspy laugh at her own humour.

Gaira smiled. They would be safe here.

'So you love them and the man,' Oona said.

'I dinna say I loved him.'

'You dinna have to. You argue for him as you do the children. You love the children. You love the man. Now the question is what you'll do about it.'

Chapter Twenty-Six

Gaira found Flora and Creighton in the herb garden, picking rosemary leaves one at a time. 'You two are busy this afternoon.'

'Oona has us picking rosemary for her magical potions,' Flora said.

'Ah, you are lucky. She must trust you very much. If you take care, she may keep you for a few days.'

Creighton stopped working. 'Aren't we staying with you?'

It was hard to hide the truth from them. 'I need you to stay here for a few days.'

'We want to stay with you!' Flora announced.

'It won't be for long. 'Tis just that I need to get your rooms ready and there's four of you, so it'll take some time—'

'We'll help you,' Creighton interrupted. 'And we can stay together.'

'He doesn't want us,' Flora said firmly.

'Doona be silly, Flora, Robert wants us,' Creighton stated.

Flora shook her head slowly. 'Nae, not him. 'Tis Bram, the laird, who doesn't want us.'

Gaira's heart clenched at Flora's sure opinion. 'Nae,' Gaira said. 'Bram wants you. He just doesn't want me.'

Creighton let out a mocking sound. 'He doesn't have a choice about wanting you. You're his sister!'

'Aye, but...' Gaira sighed and told them why she had fled to Doonhill.

Flora stood up. 'I doona want to stay here. He is nothing but ill-faured!'

'I know he seems mean,' Gaira said. 'But this land is the only place safe for you.'

'But not for you,' Creighton said.

'But not for me,' she agreed. 'That's one of the reasons I want you to stay here. So I can discuss with Bram about my staying here.'

'One of the reasons?' Flora asked.

She'd have to be more careful with her tongue around the children. 'Aye, one of the reasons,' she said firmly. She hoped her tone indicated that she wouldn't discuss it any further.

'Must have something to do with Robert being English,' Creighton said to Flora.

Flora nodded with a knowing smile.

No point in discussing it any further. 'So you'll stay here?' she asked.

Flora and Creighton nodded simultaneously. But they weren't looking at her; they were looking at each other.

Gaira returned to the keep. There was either going to be sacrifices or compromises. But more than the river was going to bend if lives were to be saved. The boulders as well would have to find some way to stop being so stubborn. Including herself.

A hand grabbed her arm. Startled, Gaira looked up. Malcolm started pulling her behind the kitchens. 'Where are you going?'

She yanked her arm free. 'I need to speak to Bram again. Explain why—'

'It wouldn't matter,' he said. 'He's cleaning up.'

'Cleaning up? What do you mean?'

Malcolm kicked the dirt with his toe. 'He questioned Hugh about King Edward's and Robert's plans.'

'If he's anything like Robert, he won't tell anything.'

'Aye, well it ended up being a wee bit more than talking.'

She was tired of her brothers. 'What did Hugh or Robert ever do to this clan?'

'He's English. They're soldiers—'

She whirled around in frustration. 'Nae, nae, nae. The men themselves. They have done nothing to us. Robert's helped us. Hugh is his friend.'

'Doesn't matter. There's too much at stake. Hugh will be bargained off to King Balliol.'

If so, Hugh was good as dead. She didn't know him, but he had travelled a great distance to help his friend, to help Robert. And he'd acted honourably when he fought her brothers. He didn't deserve to die.

'And Robert?' she asked.

Malcolm's face closed shut; he wasn't telling her. She turned to leave.

'Gaira?' Malcolm shook his head. 'I knew what Bram planned to do with you, but you were always telling us to do something...'

She was in no mood for this apology. 'I was trying to help this clan. I was taking care of the keep, ensuring food was on the table, you inding weevil. And even if I wasn't, I'm your sister!'

'I know. I'm sorry.'

'Are you? Then you know what I ask of you. Talk to Bram. Robert deserves to live.'

A muscle twitched in Malcolm's cheek. 'He is too hated, too feared.'

'He is a man, nothing else, and he helped me.' She poked him in the chest. '*He* helped me. What did you do when Bram planned to get rid of me?'

Malcolm stayed silent and she poked him again. 'What did you do when he married me to that… troke of a man? Nothing. You did nothing. You won't be doing that again. You owe me this request.'

Malcolm's lips thinned, but he nodded. 'I'll talk to Bram.'

Gaira reached the steps to the keep when Bram appeared at the top.

'Where have you been?' Bram started down the long flight.

'I was checking on the children,' she said when they were within proper speaking distance. 'Remember them? Irvette's daughter?'

Bram stopped in front of her, his countenance less thunderous. Good. He needed to be put into place.

'I need to talk to you.'

'I know.' She stared at him. She wasn't giving him any boon.

'Can we do so now?' he asked.

Ah, a request. 'Aye,' she answered.

They entered his solar in silence. Bram closed the door behind him and she walked to the window. The room wasn't overly big and she needed to look outside.

'How are they?' he asked.

'Staying with Oona for a few days.' She glanced

over her shoulder. 'Aye, it is safe and a might better place to be than here.'

'Will you turn around so we can talk?'

'We're talking just fine the way we are.'

'I wasn't the one in the wrong here.'

She whirled around. 'Like hell you weren't. Your actions started everything!'

'I dinna kill Irvette!'

She snorted. 'Nae, you wouldn't hurt Irvette. Just your other sister.'

'I never hurt you!'

'I think I'm a better judge about that.'

Bram grabbed a cup from the table, smelled it and drowned the contents. 'I doona know whether to curse or thank God for sending you to Doonhill,' he said.

'It wasn't God,' she reminded him. 'It was you.'

'I sent you to Ayrshire.'

'You sent me to hell.'

'That wasn't my intention.'

'The only intention I saw and felt was to get rid of me. For what? Because I ran this keep efficiently.'

'I'm the laird. I have to get married. You were making it impossible. The servants went to you instead of me for any questions or needs. That role should belong to my future wife.'

She started pacing. 'You dinna think to talk to me about it? Just decided to send me off at your convenience? And to Busby! The man was thick as a tree in head and girth. I would never want a husband such as him.'

He set the cup on the table. 'He wasn't your husband.'

'I beg to differ. I was there when you handfasted us.'

'But that's all it was to be.'

She stopped pacing. 'What do you mean?'

He sat on a large padded bench and leaned his weight back. The bench creaked under his weight. 'A handfasting was all it was to be. There would be nae consummation. You would never have been married.'

'I doona understand.'

'I had a bargain with Busby. He would take you for six months. But you were never to be his wife. In return, he could keep the twenty sheep and would have someone to straighten his keep.'

She slammed her foot into his shins. 'You paid to make me a servant!'

He moved his leg out of her way. 'It seemed like a good trade at the time. You like having projects. Busby's home needed your expertise.'

'Why Busby? He was laird of the southern Fergusons and his alliance was weak at best.'

'Nae, I needed you south. Busby had all the earmarks we needed. He wasn't smart, he was desperate and he was the one most easily intimidated. You would have been fine, Gaira.'

Busby had not touched her. But when he had looked at her, she felt as if she'd stepped into a peat bog, covered in filth and sinking to her doom. She doubted she would have been fine. But there was no point arguing that now. Busby was dead. 'You gave me nae choice.'

'I dinna see how you would protest. You like children.'

'But you just said—'

He slapped his thighs. 'They weren't yours, but they sounded as if they needed you all the same.'

'Busby had children! How many?'

'How many should I care?' He shrugged. 'And it matters not. Busby mentioned an older daughter, I'm sure she's caring for them.'

Gaira sat beside him on the bench. 'You dinna tell me.'

'I saw nae need. You would soon be there and could see for yourself what needed to be done.'

'The younger ones, they'll need care.'

'What can be done? You ran away.'

She refused to feel guilt. 'Aye, I did, but you sold me off, manipulated my life and my future.'

'It would not have been for naught. I probably would have been married by now if I hadn't had to worry about where you'd gone off to.'

'Who would have taken you in so short of time?'

'Margaret.'

Gaira snorted. 'That snivelling weak-kneed wisp? She'd never make it here!'

'See! This is why I made the bargain with Busby. You just doona want me married and happy.'

'Ach, I want you happy. Margaret's not going to make you so. Within a month of you not being besotted with her fair golden hair, you'd be tired of her.'

'This is useless to argue. She won't be coming here now you're to stay.'

'If I'm to stay.' She picked up a small dagger on the table. 'I'm with Robert on whether to trust you.'

'Trust? You have just brought an enemy to my home.'

She rolled the dagger in her palm. 'What will you do with him?'

'Kill him.'

She stood and pointed the dagger. 'Bram, he is not the man you think he is. He deserves to live.'

He shrugged. 'He'll have to die.'

'Nae!'

'Irvette's dead because of the English. There is nae chance in hell I'm letting him live.' He put his hands behind his head. 'I'll question him first, though.'

'Question him like you did Hugh? What torture do you have in mind?'

'None, if he co-operates. But much if he does not. Robert was close to the English king. Any information he has will be valuable to us.'

'He'll never give it,' she said.

'I will get some information from him. He could be a spy or an assassin sent up to get close to King Balliol.'

She snorted. 'Not likely. Maisie still wets her drawers. That does not sound like an assassin's agenda.'

'Then he must be in hiding or running from the English.'

'He's not in hiding or running away.' She set the dagger down. 'He came because I asked him to.'

'His reputation would belie otherwise.'

'I knew nothing of his reputation when he arrived at Doonhill,' she said. She told him how Robert arrived and of the journey to Colquhoun land.

'Robert had to know you would kill him, but he did not abandon me,' she concluded.

He stood and took a couple steps away. 'If he did what you say, there is something more to him than his reputation. But I doona know if that changes anything.'

'It has to.'

'If I spared his life, do you think it would prevent

some other Scotsman from chopping off his head? He is too well known.'

'No one on Colquhoun land will go against your word.'

'In most things, aye, but this is unusual and it does not prevent other clans seeking retribution.'

'We will leave, then.' She had not thought about leaving with Robert before.

'How long do you think you'll last?' He widened his legs, crossed his arms. 'Once he is dead, they will not spare you or the children. You would have aligned yourself with him.'

She swallowed. He was asking questions she was afraid to know the answers to. 'I'll leave the children with you.'

'You love them,' he said, his tone baffled.

'Aye, enough to protect them.'

'He still has to die.'

'Why, you stubborn betraying idiot?' She was willing to leave the only home she'd ever known and was willing to tear her heart in two to do it. And still her brother fought her.

'Because by coming here, he has given the laird of Colquhoun nae choice. I can't be just brother in this.'

She wasn't changing his opinion. 'When?'

'If he co-operates, tomorrow. This is not something needing counsel.'

She slammed the door when she left.

Chapter Twenty-Seven

Robert sat against the far wall of the cellar and tried to sleep. It was the darkest and quietest spot, but it was no good. Hugh had not returned and he was worried. They hadn't harmed him, but that didn't mean they wouldn't harm Hugh, especially if Hugh did not keep his head.

Concern was just another feeling he had thought died out of him long ago. He wanted to laugh at himself, but it wasn't funny.

He had thought he was numb to the variances of life, but then Gaira arrived. Her spirit, as bright as her hair, had illuminated how thin his defences were. It had taken nothing more than a curse from her lips, a laugh reaching her eyes, for his walls to shatter.

The cellar door slammed open. He was too surprised to stand as Gaira, her dress trailing behind her, walked down the steps. Someone shut the door behind her.

'What are you doing here?' he asked.

Her head turned, but he knew he was too far in the corner for her to see him.

'I talked to my brother.' The shafts of light from the cracks in the cellar door highlighted the copper of her hair. It was wet and fell heavy with curls.

He stood. 'You know what he did to Hugh.'

'Aye,' she said. 'I couldn't help him. Your friend... There was too much anger between them. I fear he's been hurt.'

'How bad?'

'I doona know. I haven't seen him. But they have plans for him.' She clasped her hands in front of her. 'Bram told me the plans for you, too. Although you dinna ask me that, did you?'

He knew what Bram planned to do with him. Hugh was his concern now. 'What will he do with Hugh?'

'He believes he's enough of a bargaining chip for King Balliol. He will send a messenger to tell the king of his capture.'

He didn't care for himself. But Balliol would not be kind to Hugh, especially because of his friendship with Black Robert.

Another joke on him. He had tried to maintain

distance from Hugh in order to protect him. Now, it didn't matter.

'Do you think Hugh will live long enough to reach Balliol?' he asked.

'Are you accusing my brother of subterfuge?'

'I will not forget how he treated you.'

'Aye, well. He has explained his reasoning to me and we've resolved that issue now.' They'd resolved it, but she hadn't forgiven yet. 'Is there nae chair around here?'

He walked towards her. She never wore her hair loose and he could smell lavender from her bath. To have her so close and yet never touch her. He cursed himself again for that night. She had offered him everything. He thought he was too damned to have taken from her, especially when he could offer her nothing in return. So he had sought to relieve her ache with only the barest of touches, the lightest of kisses, thinking his body wouldn't burn so painfully afterward. But he was wrong. Her response, her taste, the very way she gave herself to him had tortured him ever since. He thought himself hell-bound before, but since that night, he knew he was already in hell. 'Why are you here?' he asked.

She turned to face him. 'I'm asking you to escape.'

Robert fell silent and she breathed in deeply.

'There's nae guard, the hour is late and the torches have not been lit,' she informed him.

He frowned. 'What do you think he'll do to you when he knows you set me free?'

She raised her chin, readying herself for his response. 'Since I'll be with you, he won't be able to do anything.'

She heard him stop breathing.

'What about the children?' His voice was hoarse.

'They will be safe here.' She pulled his arm and felt him tense. 'Let's go. We doona have much time.'

'You cannot mean to leave the children. Why are you doing this?'

She held back her thoughts of the children. If she thought of them at all, she'd change her mind. And she couldn't do that. If she did, Robert would die. 'I realised something when I was talking to my brother. There is nae reasonable explanation why you travelled all the way to Colquhoun lands to deliver me and the children.'

He tugged his arm out of her reach and stepped back. 'I made a promise to keep you safe and your brothers brought me here. There is nothing more to it than that.'

'Liar. I saw you fight Malcolm. You allowed yourself to be captured.' She stepped closer again. 'There must be an unreasonable explanation why you brought me here.'

She stood on tiptoe and placed her lips against his. She felt his body lean into her and her heart soared. She was right. He did feel something for her. But his arms did not go around her and she fell back to her feet.

'You coward!' She didn't think. With a pull of her arm, she slapped him.

The sound reverberated, but he stood there, waiting.

Anger, desperation, frustration and love boiled within her. She pulled back her hand again.

'Cease!' He grabbed her hand. 'Why do you do this? What do you want of me?'

''Tis not reason or my brothers' skills keeping you here.' She wrenched her hand free. 'I want you to admit you feel something for me. I want your heart, Robert of Dent!'

Suddenly pale, he looked as if she had just given him poison. Ice needles flowed into her heart.

He moved roughly away from her. 'I'll admit to nothing. I am English; you are Scots.'

'So your friend arrives and you suddenly remember your country? You made nae such distinction before.'

'Even if I do not make the distinction, our countries do and they'll remind us. Much was happening before I left for Doonhill and I fear much more since we travelled here.'

'Scotland has a king now. The English have nae say here.'

'He is king, but even some Scotsmen doubt his rule.' He shook his head. 'It makes no difference. Your brother knew his responsibilities to Scotland when he made me a prisoner here.'

'You're only a prisoner because you want to be. I can set you free, right now. We can run together and—'

'Why won't you leave me alone!' His eyes flared. 'I'm broken, Gaira. *Broken.*' He slammed his fist across his chest. 'There's nothing here! Why do you keep asking questions—why do you prod me as if I can give you any kindness? I can't. 'Tis not in me any more.'

Robert turned and rubbed the back of his neck.

He hurt her, but it was the risk she took in coming here. The risk she took because before she left her home and her children she had to know how he felt. And now she did.

It wasn't easy loving this man. He wasn't making it easy. But he did love her, even if he couldn't admit it yet.

Walking to him again, she placed her hand on his chest. Relief flooded her as the tempo of his heart increased. He did feel for her. She wasn't apologising for her prodding. There was too much at stake.

'I think there is something here,' she whispered.

Robert froze and became as remote as Ben Lomond in winter. And just as unpassable.

He pushed her hand away. 'Ah, there you are wrong,' he said. 'There is nothing where my heart used to be.'

She did not understand. But it was the ghost of loneliness in his eyes and the rigidity of his shoulders telling her what she didn't want to know.

She clasped her hands fearing what she'd do with them. 'Have you loved before?'

'Aye. I'll not do it again.'

She realised in all her past emotional and physical hurts she had never felt what she felt right now. There was a word, pain, but it did not encompass the cavern of ache in her chest, the lack of strength in her legs, nor the sting behind her eyes.

In the weeks since he had arrived, she had faced almost insurmountable physical and emotional obstacles. She knew she had survived the journey because he had been by her side. Reluctantly, contrary, stubborn, aye, but *there* none the less. Now, she knew he hadn't been there at all. He couldn't have been. Someone else had his heart.

Her humiliation was complete. She was rejected by her family and also by the man she'd given her heart to. There was nothing more to be said. She turned to leave.

'She's dead,' he said. 'Several years now.'

She lowered her foot from the first step.

'An eternity ago,' he whispered. 'She was Welsh and the daughter of a minor prince in north Wales. I saw her first as a child when I fought for Edward during the Welsh Wars.'

She didn't want to hear any more, but she couldn't unlock her knees.

'We had just conquered Brynmor's gates. I and others rushed the keep to make sure there was no one hiding. When I looked up the stairs, there were these two little girls at the top. They were both blonde with blue eyes and so alike I knew they were sisters. The older girl was clasping the hand of the younger sister, whose face was swollen red and black, but her blue eyes were gentle. That was Alinore.'

Robert's voice became muffled. She glanced behind her. He was no longer facing her. His spine was rigid as though a great yoke had been placed on his shoulders.

'It may seem as though fighting is all I've done, but when the wars against Wales were done I settled at Brynmor.'

'Brynmor by that time was under English rule. King Edward would have given it to me. When I arrived that was exactly what I intended. However, less than a sennight later, I knew I could never do it.'

Gaira turned around and tried to loosen her fingers that she clenched painfully in front of her. But they, like her knees, wouldn't unlock.

'The older sister didn't want anything to do with me and I depended on Alinore to show me around.' Robert hadn't turned around, hadn't moved. 'She was older by that point, but still a child. Her father, Urien, beat her. I tried to stop it, but he would find her when I wasn't around…' Anger laced his voice. 'The man was more drunk than sober, I couldn't even fight him fairly. But Alinore still loved him. I didn't understand it…that kind of capacity for forgiveness and kindness…for everyone. She, unlike me, had the capacity to love and forgive.'

Gaira didn't want him to say any more. Each revelation he made struck deep until she was nothing but skin, bone and ache.

'So instead of taking the manor as lord and having her father killed for treason, I took the position of an English governor,' he said. 'Alinore, because I had saved her father's life and allowed him some pride, was free to care for me.'

He sighed. 'I was there for many years. When Alinore was grown, it was inevitable I fell in love with her. Gently, easily, like swimming in a warm spring brook.' He suddenly stopped.

'What happened?' she said. The words were strangled out of her by a need she didn't know she possessed.

His breathed in raggedly. 'Brynmor burned to the ground.' He stopped talking, but he was not silent. She could feel his unrest. 'She died.'

When he turned to her, his eyes were seething black. The dark bottom of the river that was Robert's soul surged angrily to the surface.

'You were right that day, Gaira. You didn't know why, but you were right. It is grief that motivates me. I *am* grief.'

It was too dark for her to see him. But she didn't want to see him. She didn't want any more secrets revealed, any more feelings displayed. His voice, the story he told were enough for her to know. He still loved Alinore. Not her.

It was late. Already the bailey's torches must be lit. Their time for escape was gone.

It didn't matter. All her hope was gone as well.

'You coward! Some warrior you are. You doona even have the bravery to break my heart properly!' The door crashed behind her as she ran across the courtyard.

Chapter Twenty-Eight

Hugh sprang off the bed as two children entered his room. He recognised them as the ones Robert had travelled with.

'I don't need anything,' he told them. They were treating him far too well as a prisoner.

'We're not here to get you anything,' Creighton answered. 'We're here to free you.'

'What happened to your face?' Flora asked.

Hugh stared at the door. 'How did you get in here?'

'There's only one guard outside. We distracted him, but—'

'Only one?' Hugh interrupted. 'How insulting.'

'Aye, sir, but we doona think he'll be gone for very long so we should leave as soon as possible,' Flora said. 'Your arm is bandaged, is it broken?' She turned to Creighton. 'This won't work if he's injured.'

'There's pain is all.' Hugh gestured with his arm. 'How'd you distract him?'

'I dinna think it would work,' Flora whispered.

'And it wouldn't have worked if the guard had seen us hiding beneath the stairs. But it's Alec, you see,' Creighton said. 'He's done it hundreds of times before.'

'Done what?' Hugh asked.

'Yes, but never purposefully,' Flora said. 'It was always in fun before.'

'But I knew morning was best,' Creighton said. 'Everyone is fed, they are starting their chores. Any later in the day and people's eyes will start wandering.'

'Wait!' Hugh raised his hands. 'Do you always finish each other's sentences?'

'We're twins,' they said in union.

Hugh shook his head. 'Who is Alec?'

'He's our cousin,' Creighton said. 'He steals things. He stole the guard's dagger and the guard chased after him.'

'So we could ask you to help Sir Robert,' Flora said.

'Aye, we can't do it alone and we thought since you were his friend, you'd help,' Creighton said.

'You want to help free Robert of Dent? But you're Scottish!' Hugh said.

The children looked at each other.

'Do you know who Sir Robert is?' he asked.

'Aye, sir,' Flora answered. 'He's supposed to be a very bad English man. But he isn't. At least not all bad. My brother and I know what bad men do and Sir Robert would never do those things.'

Hugh sat on the bed. He felt as if his world was about to be turned around again. First by Robert, now by these children.

'Why don't you explain exactly why you are here?' Hugh asked.

Hugh heard the rushed footsteps up the stairs and wasn't surprised when Caird slammed the door against the wall.

Hugh, sitting on the bed, waited for him. He almost laughed as Caird's anger slammed into his disbelief.

Hugh thought he had better help him out. 'I'm still here.'

For support, Caird reach back to the wall. In his other hand, he held his sword. 'Why?'

'It appears, when it comes to the inhabitants and visitors to Clan Colquhoun, countries just don't matter.'

Caird straightened. 'I doona understand.'

'I wouldn't have either until two children intended for me to escape with Robert. But I've decided words might be just as effective.' He waved to the other end of the bed. 'Why don't you sit down so we can talk about your sister and an English soldier? When I'm done, I think you may want to speak to your brother.'

Gaira woke early. She needed the children. And if she was honest with herself, she needed Oona's counsel as well. It was fine to be the authority of your own life, but did that count when your heart was broken?

The wind was chilly as she walked to Oona's cottage. She wrapped her shawl tighter around her, but it did little good since she wore a dress. She missed the leggings and tunic.

'Oona, it's me!'

The door opened. In one hand Oona held a spoon, in the other, Maisie. Maisie's legs dangled almost to the ground. Gaira peered closer at the spoon. There didn't appear to be any green flecks on it.

'She's fine, lass,' Oona said. 'Is there trouble brewing?'

'How'd you know?'

'You're visiting Oona. That's how I know.' She set Maisie on the ground. The girl toddled over and Gaira picked her up.

'I might have been just looking for the children. Doesn't mean that there is trouble.' She looked around again. 'Where are the children?'

'Off running about as children are wont to do.'

Not these children. They stuck close. 'Nobody came by and got them?'

She waved the spoon. 'Did you want someone to come collect them? Your Englishman, perhaps?'

Gaira tried to bury her face in Maisie's neck to hide her reaction.

'Ah, there be the trouble. Oona knows there's trouble.'

Gaira set Maisie down and the girl flopped on the ground.

'Trouble. More than trouble. He's a sneaky, snivelling coward is what he is. Do you know that he's loved someone before?'

Oona nodded, smiled, but didn't say anything.

Gaira paced. 'And he loves her still!'

'Aye,' Oona said. 'What be the trouble, then?'

'That *be* the trouble,' Gaira said in exasperation.

'The man's lived before he met you, he's honourable, steadfast and handsome and you think some lass wouldn't notice?'

'It dinna sound as if it was the lass doing the noticing!'

Oona pealed into laughter. 'Ah, you've lost your heart well and good, Gaira my child. Let's see if what I've got brewing will heal you.'

Gaira grabbed Maisie's hand and followed Oona into the cottage. 'Not more of that green brew?'

'Ah, nae. I've got something different...'

The smells coming from Oona's cauldron smelled delicious. 'Isn't that just porridge?'

'Aye.' Oona spooned some into a bowl, releasing great wafts of steam. 'Even Oona has to eat sometimes.'

'How's that supposed to fix anything?'

'Aren't you hungry?'

'Aye, but—'

'It fixes your empty stomach is what it fixes.' Oona gave her the wooden bowl. 'As to the other, nothing there needs fixing.'

Gaira spooned up the porridge and let the hot grains drip back into the bowl. 'Aye, it's broken beyond repair.'

'Not seeing straight, Gaira. You've not said that he dinna love you.'

'But I heard in his voice that he loved her.'

Oona took her own bowl and spoon. 'A man's heart is good if he can love. And he has. Doesn't mean he doesn't love you.' She blew on her porridge. 'You love him and you love the children, aye?'

Gaira took a heated bite and nodded.

'Then you love two different people at the same time. The heart has nae limitations if it's good. This Robert of Dent is good.'

Gaira scooped another bite and blew on the spoon.

'Did you ask him if he loved you?' Oona took a bite of her own.

Gaira set the spoon back in the bowl.

Because they'd talked of Alinore, she hadn't truly asked Robert if he loved her, too. Because he had loved before, he denied his feelings for her. Contrary man. Nothing about Robert was straight and simple.

But the river did not always run straight. It ebbed and flowed with the seasons. He was stubborn, contrary and hid every damn thing about him. But every once in a while she glimpsed the bottom of the river that was his soul.

He had buried the villagers and helped Creighton talk. He had comforted Flora and played with Alec. He had even asked Bram for her safety. These were not the acts of a man without a heart. He loved her. It didn't matter if he had loved before. No. It did matter.

It mattered to him very much. He was still hurting.

Every contrary, stubborn, reluctance Robert had displayed on this journey made sense now. He had fought her every step of the way, not because of his reputation as Black Robert, but because of Alinore.

Good God. She had made him bury her kin and accused him of having no feelings. She had been angry at him for not caring, when in fact he cared too much.

He had turned himself into Black Robert after Alinore's death. He did that to protect his heart. She knew about being alone and she knew about grief. But she hadn't hidden behind either because she knew there was a more powerful emotion than anguish. Robert didn't know; his childhood hadn't taught him anything else.

She set the bowl in her lap and whipped her multiple plaits behind her shoulder. It wouldn't be easy, but she would show Robert of Dent what it meant to love.

Chapter Twenty-Nine

'I am glad you are co-operating,' Bram said.

Robert followed Bram into the empty hall. The lack of guards was not an error of judgement on Bram's part. As laird, he was purposely showing his strength to an enemy.

'As long as Gaira and the children are safe, there will be no cause to be unco-operative,' Robert replied.

'And nae cause for your friend?' Bram asked.

He did not rise to the bait. 'Hugh can take care of himself,' he said. If they sent Hugh to Balliol, there'd be a chance for him to escape. For now, Robert had to remain calm. Too many people depended on him.

Bram took the steps to the right of the hall. 'Many of my kin doona understand why I am giving you shelter and food. They believe your reputation speaks only of the warrior and not the man. My counsel has suggested I chain you like the animal they think you are and let nature take its course.'

At the top was a long narrow hall with no windows. 'Why didn't you?'

'Because I know your reputation.' Bram pushed open a door at the end of the hall and entered a room. 'My belief is a man as well trained as you is a rational man.'

Robert slowed his pace and assessed the private solar. The door slammed at his back. Caird and Malcolm were standing by the door.

'A man who maybe doesn't realise the seriousness of his situation?' Bram said.

Robert did not acknowledge Caird or Malcolm. 'Maybe I realise it all too well.'

'Ah, then it is knowledge of your danger making you meek and co-operative.'

It was too obvious a challenge. Robert shrugged.

Bram's lips twitched. 'As I was saying, I disagreed with my counsel. I believe your reputation also tells of the man. I saw nae need to be barbaric.'

'A fair decision,' Robert replied. This was the first opportunity Bram had spoken to him and it was the most crucial. He did not expect his own situation to change, but there was a chance for Gaira and the children.

'Do not mistake my civility for fairness.' Bram studied Robert. 'However, my sister says I should be fair to you. Much to my surprise, my two brothers have agreed I should give you a chance. I am still trying to understand why.'

Surprised that Gaira's brothers spoke for him, Robert stayed silent.

'Did you have a play in what happened at Doonhill?' Bram asked.

The question was expected. 'Soldiers under King Edward's command did,' Robert answered.

Bram's eyebrows drew down. 'Under your command?'

Robert shook his head.

'But you wanted me to believe it your fault.' Bram folded his arms across his chest. 'Either you are bold or you think me stupid.'

Robert did not shift his gaze.

Bram's lips twitched again. 'You insult me by flagrantly protecting the English King by blaming yourself. You probably think I would kill you and think justice met, thus, not seeking revenge against your fellow Englishmen.'

Robert didn't answer. He knew it was best to listen to all Bram had to say.

Bram tapped his fingers against his arms. 'You insult me further, by thinking I would judge a man unjustly. Did you think I would kill you just because you are English? Tempting, I must admit, especially since I know the fate of my youngest sister. However, as laird, I cannot be ruled by emotion alone. I know each man, despite what tainted blood runs through his veins, is accountable for his own sins. If you had told me the truth, I would have been fair.'

Robert would say something to that. 'I have no evidence of your fairness on which to judge.'

Robert heard Malcolm and Caird stir at his words, but Bram did not seem surprised.

'You speak of Gaira.' Bram poured himself a drink of ale. 'My sister doesn't seem to know what an abomination you are. But never doubt I know exactly who and what you are. You're probably still loyal to the English.'

'King Edward is a strong leader; do not underestimate him.'

'You say that to my face.' Bram set the pitcher down. 'As long as there is one Scotsman, there will always be a Scotland.'

Robert shrugged.

'So how did you keep it from her?' Bram took a sip. Robert wasn't surprised he wasn't offered a drink. This wasn't a social visit.

'Keep what?' Robert asked.

'The fact you have slaughtered hundreds of our kinsmen.'

'She never asked.'

'I thought she was more aware than our sister Irvette, but it's clear I protected her overmuch.'

'You didn't protect her at all.'

'Insults again. With me at your front and two at your back, you still do not curb your tongue.' Bram shook his head. 'What do you know of how I have treated my sister?'

'You abandoned her to a madman.'

'Busby was nae madman. He was not bright, but he was not crazy.'

'Then we knew two Busby of Ayrshire. The man attacked me from the back.'

'You provoked him by travelling with his betrothed.'

'She was no betrothed of his. And she was terrified of him.'

'My sister's terrified of nae one. Her travelling with you is proof of that.'

'She fled from Busby of Ayrshire.' Robert tried to cool the sudden anger flooding his veins. He knew better than to show any emotions when it came to Gaira, but he couldn't seem to stay rational. 'Fled because she was scared for her life. Or did you forget?'

Bram slammed the empty cup down. It wobbled precariously on the edge of the table. 'I forget *nothing*, you pompous English bastard.'

'Your anger is with yourself, not with me.'

'I will kill you.'

'You can try.'

Bram's eyes lighted and his lips twitched again. Robert did not understand the sudden humour. The man wanted to laugh. Interesting. He saw nothing to laugh about.

But Gaira had that same ease of laughter. She had that kind of open heart. Maybe her brothers had it as well. He didn't understand it, but he envied it.

'God,' Bram said. 'Having you here disturbs me like nothing else. Why are you here?'

'Your sister asked me to help her.'

'I'm to believe that?'

Robert shrugged. 'Since you plan to kill me, it probably matters not.'

'Why did she ask you?'

'You should ask her that yourself.'

'I want to hear it from you.'

He didn't know. He was still baffled that Gaira had asked him. 'I was convenient. There wasn't anyone else.'

'If you dinna have anything to do with Doonhill, why were you there for her convenience?'

Robert did not want to reveal personal reasons, but he would not hide the truth. 'My men should never have killed innocents.'

'Remorse?' Bram tilted his head, a strange gleam in his eyes. 'Black Robert feels remorse. And he helped my sister through Buchanan land.'

Bram walked towards the window. He heard Malcolm or Caird pull a chair across the floor. He did not move. No matter how civil this discussion went, he was still Bram's enemy.

Bram turned. 'Those facts will not change matters. I will still have to kill you.'

'So you keep saying,' Robert answered.

'Even if I show you mercy for what favours you have done my family, every Scotsmen would be at war with my clan.'

'You could just let me go. Say that I escaped,' Robert offered, though he knew Bram would never do so.

'A plan that will solidify my reputation with my fellow Scotsmen,' Bram said wryly.

'Not true, King Balliol would be pleased to know you survived our meeting.'

'Testing my loyalties, Englishman?'

Robert kept his voice level. 'I see you are here instead of...elsewhere.'

'Now goading me for secrets? I know where I belong.' Bram shook his head, the corners of his mouth lifting. 'Your soul really is as black as your name.'

'On that we will agree.'

Bram looked to Caird and Malcolm. 'My sister has pleaded for your life. I understand she has even asked you to escape.'

Robert was not surprised Bram knew. He was intelligent enough to keep some spies.

'Your sister, as you pointed out, is not aware of my deeds or how I have lived my life.'

'Aye, I think she does know,' Bram replied. 'If I am not mistaken, when she told you to run away with her, you told her every black truth of your soul. Why would you do that?'

It galled him to know he was read so easily by this Scotsman. 'Your sister is an unusual woman. Her kindness deserves to know the truth.'

'Kindness? Gaira is a harpy.'

Bram walked in front of Robert. He was close enough to attack and kill before either Malcolm or Caird could protect him, but Robert was not here for himself.

'Again we differ with our judgement of people,' Robert replied.

'You tried to scare her away from you. What is my sister to you?'

'I think she deserves more than to be abandoned.'

Bram took a few steps away. 'We are back to that.'

'It is a fact that deserves clarification.'

'I will not explain my reasons to you. I refuse to be on the defensive to a man such as yourself.'

'So you say.'

Bram put his hands behind his back and rolled on his heels. 'Why am I on the defensive with you?'

'Because you were wrong to do what you did.'

Bram chuckled. 'God, you're not reserved in your thoughts, are you?'

'I see no need.'

'Since it's honesty you're so proud to claim, what facts of King Edward's campaign are you hiding?'

'None,' Robert said. This was an area he need not be reserved about. 'I was his arm, but not his tactician.'

'You were more than that.'

'I knew him well. Aye. But I was never his confidant.'

'Held yourself apart, did you?'

Robert shrugged.

'Damn. I believe you again. You leave me nae reason to keep you alive. You know that?'

'We all die.'

'True, but your time is sooner rather than later.' Bram again looked to Caird and to Malcolm. 'Tomorrow we fight.'

'Kae-witted argle-barglous outwale!' Gaira murmured. 'Succudrus neep-heided man!'

Gaira fisted her hands into her dress as she quickly sidestepped horse dung. It was nighttime, but the courtyard was not empty. She didn't care that her voice carried because there was no use being quiet. There was a use to hurry, however. Malcolm had told her Robert and Bram had talked. He also told her what Robert had said.

Oh, how her heart had wanted to hear those words.

She could not change Bram's mind. He had made his decision as laird. But maybe, with Robert, she had a chance to stop this whole foolish affair.

She crept around the kitchens and hastened her steps till she reached the cellars. The guards immediately opened the door when she approached them.

This was not what she expected, but they were averting their faces. She was glad they closed the cellar doors behind her. She knew now they would not hear anything.

Robert did not wait in the shadows this time, but she felt as though he did. His face was inscrutable, his countenance dark.

She tried to assess his mood by using her other senses. Even among the drying herbs, she could smell the cedar, the leather and the essence that was his alone. She remembered the heat and gentle touch of his hands, the way his mouth felt as it caressed her, opened her, made her want him. She still wanted him. Regardless of his mood, she wasn't leaving without getting an answer.

'I think I know something else motivating you, Robert of Dent,' she said. Her voice seemed unnaturally loud in the silence of the cellar.

'What do you do here, Gaira?'

His expression was shuttered, but she saw a muscle twitch in his cheek. God, he was a handsome man. A private man, but one who reluctantly revealed himself to her. And she wasn't missing this opportunity. She had never shirked a day in her life. She wasn't starting now.

''Tis love that motivates you,' she stated. 'You love me.'

He took a step back, but it was too late to hide the surprise in his eyes when she made her declaration. She knew she was right.

'What do you do here?' he repeated, his voice hoarse.

'I'm here to ask you to escape.'

'Again? I cannot run from this.'

'I think you won't run from this. But I doona think you have to run. I think you already have.' Her fingers loosened in her skirts. 'But you can't run any more, Englishman. You can't hide behind this Black Robert you've made yourself into.'

'It is what I am.'

'It is not who you are. Black Robert wouldn't have helped me or the children.' She took a step closer. 'You are more than your reputation; you are more than your grief.'

'No,' he whispered. 'It is all I have ever been. I hold no illusion to it even if you do.'

His words hurt. But it was hurting her worse not

to help him. She breathed in the scent and warmth from his skin. It gave her strength to fight him. 'Free yourself of grief. Let it go. You can love her still without the pain.'

His breath cracked. 'You want me to love her still?'

He held so much pain. And it hurt her, too, but she knew how to let it go. 'Aye, I do.'

'I don't understand.'

'You loved her. I know if you gave your heart, she was someone worthy of it.'

He took two quick steps away. 'She died. Maybe there was honour in the giving, but there has only been pain since.'

'There is pain only because there is still love.' She took the step needed to place her hand on his heart. 'You need to let the pain go.'

His heart thumped hard against her palm.

'How will I?' He paused. 'How will I be free from this grief?'

She could feel the wet warmth of her tears running down her cheeks, but she didn't try to hide them. She was weeping healing tears.

'By embracing life again,' she said. 'By embracing love again.' She placed her other hand on his chest. 'By embracing me.'

His body stiffened. His face was pale, stricken. She knew the slightest push from her would topple him over. He stood before her and she felt him with her own hands, but his mind was reeling away. What more could she say? Frustration almost had her shoving him away from her.

'You great big gaupie.' She ripped her hands from his chest and put them on her hips. 'Doona you realise you love me?'

Chapter Thirty

'I can't.' He shook his head.

'Aye, you do and it's about time you admit it.'

'You're wrong. I've loved before. I'll not do it again. Don't you realise that my love is a curse? Alinore died. I was supposed to protect her and I failed!'

He rubbed the back of his neck again. She was recognising that endearing sign of his distress. 'So that stops you from loving me? Fear? Excuses?'

'I don't fear—'

'Ha!' She pointed at him. 'You do. You fear your feelings for me. But you've already done so much to conquer that fear. All I'm asking is for a little more.'

The ache in his eyes hurt so much she thought it'd burn a hole in her heart. 'You're so close, Robert,' she pleaded. 'Can't you feel it?'

He dazedly shook his head. Not in answer to her

question, but as if he was denying something internal, something she couldn't see.

She wasn't giving up on him now. 'When I asked you for help, you could have refused. You could have left at any time along the trail to Colquhoun land. You dinna and I know why. Your heart already loved me even if your mind wasn't listening.'

'I can't—' His eyes widened. 'Oh, God. I do.'

Her heart wanted to soar, but the battle for him wasn't over and she braced herself for further argument. 'Good. So forget all this foolishness and call off the fight. We can live together, alone and away from this land.'

His entire body shuddered. It was as if he had released some dark demon holding back his soul. She thought once he realised he loved her he would feel joy, but his stance was one of a man resigned. He showed no joy and, what scared her more, he showed no relief.

He exhaled. 'I won't be able to do that now.'

She wasn't comforted by the look in his eyes. She saw love, but there was also regret. It was as if he had learned a truth too late. But she had come this far, she wasn't giving him any quarter.

'Why can't you?' she demanded. 'Have you thought of another excuse to deny us?'

He caressed her jaw. 'You've tried to give me this land. Now, I think I'll keep it.'

'Now?' She slashed her arms in the air, effectively removing his caress. 'Now you want the land? You can't have it. It doesn't want you! My clan doesn't want you!'

'That's why I must fight your brother.'

Fear swamped anger from her heart. She didn't need his stubbornness. She needed him alive.

'Why are you insisting on this? It doesn't make sense.'

'To remove any doubt, Gaira,' he said.

'There is nothing but doubt! We have to go. Doona you see it's our only chance?'

'But you made me see there could be more than just chance.' He fell to his knees before her. He knelt, but he didn't look humble. He was all male, all powerful. If she was a boulder in the flow of his river, she felt the full assault of his strength.

'I love you, Gaira of Colquhoun. I have since the moment you hit me in the head with the cauldron. Will you forgive me if I didn't recognise my love for you?'

His words made her tremble. She tugged at her hands, but he held them firm.

'There is no comparison,' he continued. 'With Alinore, love was like spring flowers. With you, it's been deep-red roses full of thorns.' He kissed her palms and she felt the heat from her fingertips to her belly. 'But I'd take those roses,' he said, 'hold them in my bare hands until my palms bled if it meant I'd have you in my life.'

He stood. The dark did not hide the wicked light in his eyes. 'But I may know something better for my hands.'

There was no warning; no intentional movement she could have braced herself for. Suddenly, Robert's body was against hers; his lips crushed to hers. She felt every hard plane of him and her body froze.

She pressed her hands against his shoulders. Her fingers splayed, curled, splayed again. He held firm and her frozen body melted. Then simmered.

His fingers tightened into the sides of her dress. Was he stopping again? She moaned her protest and his laugh was a deep rumble against her breasts.

'Oh, I'm not stopping,' he whispered against her mouth. 'I couldn't.' In one savage pull, her dress was off. 'Can't.' Her thin chemise was no barrier and he shoved it off her shoulders where it pooled at her feet. 'Won't.'

She was not embarrassed at her nakedness. She was surprised. It was all so fast, her frustration turning into need. Her worry turning into desire.

He left her little time to catch up to her emotions when he grasped one tender breast in his rough hand. Her body burned at his touch. Then his fingers moved, calluses scraped, fingers tightened. Fire seared away the last of her worries and frustration. She gasped.

He inhaled and released his hand. 'I knew I couldn't be gentle.'

She covered her hand over his and reached for his other hand. Raising them to both her breasts, she tightened her hands until he cupped her again, until the searing heat pooled through her. His breathing was harsh, but he held still. 'You should have gentleness,' he said fiercely.

'I want you.' She tugged at his hands, wishing them to move. 'I wouldn't know the difference.'

'But I would know the difference. I know what you deserve.'

'I want you.' She released her hands, grateful his stayed where she placed them. 'If this is the way it needs to be—'

'It doesn't need to be— No, I'd be lying. 'Tis what it's to be. Need. Want. Desire. I cannot give you gentleness.'

Despite his words, his hands softened. His fingers caressed in circles. Her breasts became full, heavy. His hands cupped, weighed. Her nipples ached.

Reaching for him, she tugged and pulled at the material still covering him.

'Do you know how I've dreamed of seeing you like this? That windy day beneath your tree, your breasts outlined by the tunic. My God, I thought you'd beggar me then.'

She remembered, remembered him standing before her asking permission to touch her.

'Next time,' she whispered, desperate for his hands to keep moving. 'Next time ask permission.'

He yanked off his tunic. 'Next time,' he repeated the words reverently. 'Not now.'

He slid both his hands to her sides and jerked her towards him. 'God, not now.'

His lips took hers, demanding a response. She gave it. With a sound, her lips parted, giving him the access he needed. He murmured his approval as the kiss changed. His lips now softening against hers; his tongue now tracing, tasting, enticing. He held back, asking her a question she didn't know the answer to.

But she wanted to know as she touched his jaw, encouraging more.

Instead, he tilted his head, trailed his kisses along her jaw, running his teeth and tongue against the cords in her neck, nipping and tasting along her collarbone.

All the while his hands brushed feverishly along her sides, warming her, heating her.

His mouth gentle, his hands rough, Gaira felt her body spiral, tighten.

When his mouth reached her breasts, she couldn't

help the murmurs of need that came from deep within her. As if eager to taste all of her, he gave tiny licks and kisses until his tongue curled around her nipples, peaking and inflaming them.

Allowing her weight to be supported by his wide palms at her sides, she arced her body towards his mouth. His eyes narrowed on her. She saw the heat of them. There was no anger, no control. No Robert she recognised.

She didn't understand any of his emotions. Her own feelings were just as foreign. But she knew one thing. He might have released her body from her clothes, but he had left one part of her confined. And she wanted to be free of it as well.

'My hair,' she said. 'Unbind my hair.'

One hand caressed her side as he straightened to gaze at her bound hair. 'Your hair,' he whispered, slowly stroking her plait from the base of her neck to the wrapped tip. 'Your hair is like fire to me.'

Robert gave a gentle tug to the leather strap and dropped it. 'Once I saw it, the sun's rays held no heat for me.'

His hands cupped the back of her neck before his fingers threaded from the base of her head to the tip of her hair. 'It was torture watching you brush it, touch it, plait it.' His fingers were sure, reverent. She felt every caress on every strand. 'You touched it so easily, while I yearned to be burned by its flames.'

He repeated the motion till her hair fell loose. Then he arranged each coil. She felt the tips of his fingers along her collarbone, the brush of his knuckles against her breasts.

Watching her, he threw off his shoes, his belt, his hose and his braies. Again, there was no warning. She barely comprehended the bared maleness of his body and her own emotional response, before his arms were around her, pulling them down to their clothes at their feet.

His body was hot broad planes of flesh and muscle. He supported his body beside her, but she felt pinned beneath him as his hand roughly rubbed from her hip, down her leg and back up again. It was not a caress, but an imprinting on her body. Having once denied touching her, he touched her everywhere. And everywhere his hand touched pursuits of heat raced through her body. She felt as if it was something other than her own blood pumping through her veins. And it was. Desire was hotter, sharper.

But his mouth was hotter yet as it followed behind his hands. Greed fed desire, became lust, want, need. She felt her skin indenting under his fingers. His breath prickling her skin under the wet heat of his tongue.

On her shoulders, on her arms, on her breasts and lower still, his hands and mouth coaxed and pulled at something deep inside her. And then he stopped before raising himself.

She wasn't giving him a chance to ask. She widened her legs.

She watched the change in him. Watched his control slip before he gathered himself.

'Touch me,' he said hoarsely.

Touch him, when her body demanded more. Touch him, when she knew his body demanded release.

He was letting her body adjust to his. But it couldn't, didn't adjust. Not when emotion after emotion sped across his face and great muscles across his chest and arms glistened with a fine sheen of sweat. She felt as if she was swimming in a rapid river: frightened and exhilarated at the same time.

Compelled, she flattened her palms against the parts of him she could reach. The curves of his shoulders, the rough hairs of his arms, the ridges of his abdomen. He trembled with every stroke. And she did it again. Her fingers curved, pressed, traced. When her hand went against his thigh, he grabbed her wrist.

'Not yet. Not while I need to be closer to your flame,' he said hoarsely. 'Need to be inside you.'

He released her wrist and moved between her legs. His hand went to her centre and stroked the wetness she knew he found there. Gently, carefully, frustratingly. She wanted more.

She grabbed his hand and linked her fingers with his. Joining with him in the only way she knew how. She felt the rapid pulse in his wrist. Knew the effort it cost him to wait. Her body readied even more. She untwined her fingers, moved his hand to stroke her more.

He clenched his eyes, his features sharpening. 'Is it enough?' he asked. 'Are you ready enough?'

'Aye, I am ready, Robert. Aye.'

Sliding his hands underneath her thighs, he lifted her pelvis towards him. The position pressed her closer. It was not enough. Without the direct contact from his fingers, she tried to use his body. She retracted her legs, pulling his body closer. His control slipped.

'God!' He moved. She felt the sharp entrance; the sweep of fire searing her. The pain was too much. She grasped his shoulders, her fingernails dug in, but he did not stop.

He was lost in the feelings consuming them both. Hunger. Desire. Need. And she gave herself.

For him.

'Closer,' he said. He released her legs; his hand braced at her sides. 'Your heat burning.' His hips bucked harder and she pressed back. No longer pain, but fire and pleasure.

With each thrust he moved her, her dress and chemise bunched beneath her shoulders. She lost her grip on his shoulders and grasped his wrists, trying to hold on.

He had said closer. And they were. She felt him, every bit of him. But it still wasn't enough. She wrapped her legs tightly across his thighs and pulled tighter. Closer. She tightened against him.

'Robert!' She broke, her body releasing in contractions.

Her slackened limbs could no longer follow his movements. When she didn't think he could go any deeper, he tensed. A surge of wetness joined her own. She was held suspended before he rolled to his back.

She felt the loss of his weight, but not the heat. His hand and fingers trailed along her side. The meandering caress matched the way her body felt. Replete...joyful.

She turned her head to look at him. Even in the dim light, she could see he did not feel as she did. There were grooves by his lips and his brow was furrowed. She turned to her side and tried to flatten the creases with her fingers. He grabbed her hand and placed it by her side.

'Nothing, but...' she began.

He laid a finger against her lips. 'Peace, Gaira. I'll have peace now.'

She didn't want peace. She wanted to talk, to argue

away his frowns. 'Are you regretting already?' she asked, her tone sharper than she intended.

'I regret many things. Not this.'

She laid her palm against his chest, feeling his pounding heart.

His mouth curved slightly. 'I'm savouring, Gaira. Savouring how your body felt against mine. It has been a long time for me, too long for any man. I could not be gentle with you, but I'm trying now.'

He closed his eyes, but she kept hers wide open. The moonlight cast bright rays throughout the cellar. There was no doubt why she gave her heart to him. English or not, he was a braw man.

She traced the white scars from his cheek down the side of his neck to his chest. The scars were worse across his chest and on the insides of his arms. They were broader, but they were not sword cuts; they were too flat and there were too many. She knew what these were.

'These burns were from the fire, weren't they?' she asked.

He tensed under her. 'Aye,' he replied.

She flattened her hand and caressed his chest until his body relaxed. Then she moved to his arms. On the inside of both his arms, the scars were almost symmetrical. Her hands stilled, then trembled.

He opened his eyes and looked at her. He did not

say anything. It was as if he was waiting for her to say it.

'You carried her from the fire, dinna you?'

He looked away from her. 'The fire started in the room next to hers,' he stated, no emotion in his voice. 'I found her on her bed. Too still. Her gown was on fire. Her hair...' He breathed in raggedly. 'Her golden hair was turning black. Brynmor was burning to the ground. The stairs were already gone. By the time I got her outside to the courtyard, fire and people were everywhere. There was no safe place to roll her, to stop her from burning.'

He looked far into the blackness of the cellar. 'Outside the gates, I stopped every last ember flaming on her body, but I couldn't stop the fact she breathed her death into her. There was so much smoke. She never woke.'

Gaira's tears hit her hand resting on Robert's arm. She imagined how he fought against fate, God and himself to rescue Alinore. She imagined the agony of his failure. It wasn't hard...she knew the destruction of fire.

Leaning over him, she followed the fall of her tears with her mouth. She kissed every spot where they landed. When his arms crushed her body to his own, she wrapped her own around him.

She knew that physically, his body could be inside her. Yet, she felt closer to him than that. She didn't feel any distance between them. It felt as though he was holding her, closer, deeper, than was physically possible. As though he was holding his very soul against hers.

When he cupped her face and kissed her again, she tried to convey every piercing emotion she felt. She wanted to love and heal him. When he deepened the kiss, all she wanted was him.

They must have slept. Dim light streamed in from the cellar door, giving Robert an ample view of Gaira's long limbs draped against him. Her head was tucked in the crook of his arm, her breasts curved into his side. She slept, but desire was already sweeping away the contentment of holding her.

He had not had enough of her. He glanced at her lips, knowing their natural colour would be darkened red by his rough kisses. She was so giving in her response to him. Perhaps this time he could be gentle. He eased away from her and pushed himself up. Her hair wrapped around his arm and his body quickened.

No, not gentle. He wanted her too selfishly again. Wanted to see her in the light as he took her again, see her wake as she— Dammit. It was morning.

Their time together was over. But if his plan worked, he could hold her forever.

It was hard to stop what his body wanted to do and even more difficult to stop his heart's demand to hold her longer.

They had to separate and fast. He stroked her hair away from her face. Her eyes slowly opened. The joy shining from them was brighter than any sunshine.

'It is morning, my love,' he whispered.

Her brow furrowed and her eyes darkened.

'You are not escaping,' she said, tension in her voice.

He shook his head. 'You have to go now. If we are caught, your brother won't give me a sword to fight him.'

She stood and grabbed her chemise. 'I doona know why you are doing this.' Shoving her arms and head in, she warned, 'Do you think I'll love you still if you kill my brother?'

'Aye.'

Glaring at him, she grabbed her dress and pulled it over her head.

'You won't do it easily,' he said, 'but when you love, Gaira, you love for life. Just as I love you.'

Damn the man for going soft on her.

He smiled and stood. Naked, every finely defined muscle was displayed before her: the carved mounds of his chest, the ridges of his stomach, the bulge of his thighs. He was a feast for her female eyes. She didn't want one more scar on his body. But what did he care? And damn him for being right.

If he killed Bram, she *would* still love him. Even if Bram got past Robert's defences, she could no more stop her heart for her brother than for Robert. Rage and helplessness poured through her. She hated feeling helpless.

'Oh, I wish the lot of you to hell!' she raged.

Chapter Thirty-One

The sun's heat made the air thick with the morning's light rain. Robert's clothes were damp and confining. He tore off his tunic.

He was aware of the crowd gathering, just as he was aware of the earth under his feet and the slight wind pulling at his body. They were all part of the terrain and might be of some use in the fight to come.

What he wasn't aware of was Gaira. He couldn't see her anywhere. It was just as well. He could ignore the crowd; he didn't know if he could ignore her.

Even now, he tried to release his body from the feel of her. But she was coiled with each fibre of his body. When he breathed, he still smelled her scent. He even felt the rise and fall of her chest resting against his own. He held his sword, but it wasn't steel, cold and flat, he felt. It was her flesh, hot and supple.

It would be foolish to fight today as he used to: empty, but for his training. Gaira was with him now. Just as he fought for her, he would fight *with* her now, as part of him. He was no longer empty. She had filled his heart.

If only the last night with her had not ended with thorns. But the thorns were part of their love as well. And because of that love, he had to fight her brother.

It was more than his promise to protect. Her brother needed to know the conviction of his feelings for Gaira. It was their only hope. He had committed too many crimes against the Scottish people.

He must prove his love for her. If it was through death, then so be it. He had run out of ideas of how else to prove it. He'd also run out of time.

His sword glinting, Bram walked into the circle. Malcolm and Caird followed behind him. Their voices were low, but the conversation heated. Bram raised his hand and both brothers walked away.

Bram began to speak to the crowd. Robert assumed he was reciting the crimes against him. He didn't listen. He knew what he was.

Gaira stood on the steps of the keep and listened to every word Bram announced. She didn't have a choice. Her feet wouldn't move.

Using every word she knew, she began to curse.

When she didn't have any more, she made some up. The words didn't bring her satisfaction. 'More the wanwordy I. They'll break my heart as surely as cold porridge sticking.'

But she wouldn't worry any more. She was going to do something about it. It took a long time to reach Caird and Malcolm through the thick crowd blocking her view of the fight. But each ring of metal felt like a knife prick on her heart.

When she finally reached Malcolm she hit him on the side of the head. She took some satisfaction in his wincing.

'A fat good you two are.' She nudged between them. Malcolm and Caird were in front and she could see Robert and Bram circling.

Malcolm gave her a rueful glare, but Caird spoke. 'He is laird.'

'I'm supposed to think that's the law? What good will the law be when our brother is dead?'

'Bram's never lost,' Malcolm boasted.

'Robert beat you both.'

Malcolm shifted. 'It was a draw.'

There was another ring of metal as Bram and Robert's swords met above their heads. She could see the sweat glisten on Robert's brow and his arms rocking with the effort to break the pressure. Bram's frown deepened. He did not look angry, but frustrated. She didn't have time to wonder why.

'I thought you would speak to Bram?' she demanded.

'We did,' Caird said.

Gaira rolled her eyes and looked at Malcolm. She didn't expect Caird to elaborate.

Malcolm obliged. 'We did. Apparently, the children—'

'The children!' Gaira interrupted. 'What did they do?'

Malcolm raised his hand. 'They're fine, but they talked to Hugh, who talked to Caird. We felt…compelled then to talk to Bram about…you know.'

'About what?' Gaira gestured helplessly. 'I doona understand. I see nae difference. They still fight!'

'Aye, but,' Malcolm continued, 'there's nae hiding Robert's still English. Some sort of punishment must be done. We are at war.'

'Aye, he's English, but not necessarily Black Robert,' Caird added.

Gaira's jaw dropped. Caird hadn't freely offered information in years. It took her a minute to realise she didn't understand what he said.

Malcolm's face looked just as blank. Then his eyes lit and he flashed a quick grin. 'The clever bastard.'

Caird arched his brow.

Gaira felt far from clever. There was a gasp from

the crowd and her eyes flew to Robert. His right arm was cut, blood slid down his bare skin in rivulets.

'If you doona tell me what you mean, I swear I'll march straight into the middle of the circle and be damned to the consequences.'

Caird glanced at Malcolm. Malcolm grinned wider, clearly relishing withholding the information. Gaira curled her fist.

'Bram never said Robert was Black Robert,' Malcolm said.

She didn't release her fist. Robert bled. She had no time for stupidity. 'I was standing outside when Bram made his announcement.'

'Aye and you were probably too busy thinking of ways to stop the fight than truly listening.'

She couldn't argue with that.

'He said Robert was English and, *like* Black Robert, he needed to be punished.'

'I doona understand.' She blamed the roaring in her ears. The fact that Robert bled. The fact that he fought for his life. For their life together.

'He dinna tell the clan he's Black Robert,' Malcolm continued. 'He just said Robert's an English soldier. Bram's leaving options.'

She released her fists. 'Why does it matter if he's Black Robert or an English soldier? They point swords at each other! What options are there, other than injury or death?'

'If Bram wins, then he could announce his true identity and release him to King Balliol. If Bram loses, then the entire clan won't necessarily ask for Robert's head.' Malcolm shook his head. 'I should have guessed at it. If Bram had wanted to treat him like Black Robert, then he would have already summoned our king. But he fights him fair and gives him honour. A chance for the clan to accept him.'

Gaira felt a buzzing in her head. One truth making itself clear, over and over: not Black Robert. Bram announced to the clan that Robert was English, but not the most hated of all English.

She tried to remember the rest of Bram's words and couldn't. Could it be true he had given Robert a chance to live?

But just as her heart released some of its fear, it froze. One fact could not be ignored. Bram and Robert fought. Someone she loved was still going to die.

They fought too long. Hours had gone by and lessened any chances of victory. Robert's muscles were past exhaustion; his body past the pain. He was weakening. But Bram still stood. Robert's plan for the fight was failing.

When the fight started, Robert had been confident Bram would fight like his brothers. And if so, it would take perhaps an hour to tire him out. Exhausted, but unhurt, Bram would call off the fight. Gaira wouldn't lose her brother. And he would keep at least one promise in his miserable, lonely life: to stay.

But tiring Bram wasn't working. Robert shuffled across the dirt. Both his shoulders sagged. His fingers were numb from holding on to the sword—its weight pulled like a hundred men.

Bram raised his sword awkwardly. Robert didn't know if Bram had the strength to lift it higher, but it didn't matter. He had moved too close to Bram. He hadn't the space to deflect even a half-raised sword.

But that didn't mean he was prepared to die. Keeping his sword hanging at his side and hoping he could knock Bram over, Robert fell against him. Their shoulders locked and both dropped their swords to push.

Robert knew how to knock a man to the ground just by the manoeuvre of his body and a swipe of his feet. Too late to realise, he didn't have enough strength in his feet. Dammit, they must look like two men embracing in welcome.

He felt anything but welcoming. What he did feel was anger, frustration, and a desire to end the hellish quagmire he had sunk in. His heart pumped harder and rage finally flowed again. It gave him the strength to speak.

'You ragabash loun. Why don't you fall?'

Bram stiffened against him and Robert had his advantage of balance, but the sound emitting from Bram stopped him from making the last push.

Bram was laughing. *Laughing.*

Stunned, Robert didn't stop Bram as he straightened himself and waved to Malcolm and Caird, who immediately appeared by their sides. Both looked as confused as Robert felt.

What the hell was happening?

Malcolm whispered in Bram's ear, Robert caught only a few of the words, but Bram shook his head. He moved away from Robert and faced the crowd. Caird came closer to Robert and Robert took the support.

Bram wiped his eyes. 'The fight is over.' His voice boomed over the crowd.

In laird fashion, he waved his hand to emphasise his decree, but he stumbled over his feet. Malcolm reached to help him, but Bram again shook his head.

'Clean him, feed him and return him to a vacant room in the keep for sleep.' Bram kept his voice low. 'After I do the same, I'll need to talk to our sister.'

Robert didn't protest when Malcolm picked up his sword. Bewilderment rocked him and he could barely keep to his feet.

He was alive and so was Bram. He searched the crowd for Gaira, but she was nowhere to be seen.

* * *

It was hours later when Gaira was summoned to Bram's chamber. Her heart refused to work properly. It skipped and stuttered, but it felt as light and bright as a ray of sunshine across yellow broom.

Bram sat on the large bench. His hair was clean, but dishevelled as if he slept when it was still wet. Bags hung below his eyes and his cheeks were drawn from exhaustion. But her brother was alive.

She flew to him and hugged him as close as the bench would allow.

Bram chuckled. 'You still love me.'

Gaira pulled away from him. 'How could you ever doubt it?'

'I tried to kill the man you love.'

She sat heavily next to him and leaned her head against his shoulder. 'I'd have loved you even if you had killed him.'

She heard his swallow and she felt a lump in her own throat.

'Gaira,' he spoke hesitantly, 'do you know what it means to love him?'

She knew he wasn't asking what love was. He asked if she knew the man.

She nodded.

'He has killed hundreds of men.'

'I know what he has done.'

'How can you have any kind of feeling towards him at all, let alone love him?'

'I know him. I know his anger and his kindness. He was meant to meet me. He was meant for me.'

He sighed. 'I doona understand it.'

''Tis not your heart to understand. 'Tis my own and I understand it all too well.'

He was silent and she was too content to interrupt the silence. It had been a long time since her brother had held her and comforted her.

'You did not ask me why I dinna kill him,' he finally said. 'Where is my curious sister?'

'Too happy to question the results.'

Bram chuckled. 'He cursed me for not falling.'

'Stopped by a few words?' she teased.

'Nae, it was what he cursed. He called me a ragabash loun. You've only ever called your brothers good-for-nothing scoundrels.'

She laughed. 'So you assumed that particular insult was a form of affection? And when Robert used it on you—'

'I knew the curse came from you,' he cut in, 'and that you loved him.'

'But I told you I loved him.'

She waited for him to answer. When he didn't she pulled away. 'You dinna believe me! What did you think I was doing? Lying?'

'Nae! 'Tis just you had spent an inappropriate

time with him and I dinna know the man. You could have been motivated by gratefulness or fear.' He rubbed his face. 'I was worried for you.'

His reasoning was for her safety, but she wasn't completely satisfied. 'That's twice now you've tried to manage my life. I'll not have you doing it again. I pick my own man. Not you.' She snorted. 'And Busby of all the men to pick!'

She was glad he had the decency to turn red. 'Going to remind me of that?' he asked.

'For the rest of your life.'

Bram laughed and Gaira laughed with him. The laughter released her fear and anxiety and she suddenly fell apart. She had almost lost her brother and Robert. Hysteric giggles turned to great gasps of air. She started crying in earnest.

Bram's pats on her back stung, but she stayed there until she could talk again.

'I thought...' she breathed in raggedly '...you were going to kill him.'

'That was my intention, but I think...I doona think he was going to let me.' He gave a rueful smile. 'In fact, I doona think he was trying to kill me.'

She wiped her cheeks. 'When did you finally realise?'

'Not long. I was frustrated how the battle started and in my haste, I hit his sword too high. He could have turned his wrist and I wouldn't have had a sword. He knew it, too, but instead he stepped back and released our swords. It was as though we were in training and his only goal was to wear me down.'

'He's a fine braw man and I have seen him fight. I have nae doubt he would have achieved his goal.'

Bram gave her an imperious look. 'A Colquhoun lass speaks against her brother and laird?'

'You may be laird and my brother, but he is Black Robert.'

Bram's smiled faded and she immediately regretted her reminder.

'What do you plan for him now?' she whispered.

'I have an idea.' He shrugged. 'I will nae have much trouble if he doesn't cause me any.'

'Nae, much trouble? You'll have plenty of trouble raising Busby's children.' His look of incredulousness was something she would never forget. She laughed, but she was very serious. 'Aye, Busby's children are now yours. Your responsibility. They wouldn't be orphans if you dinna force me into marriage.'

'That's ridiculous!' he spluttered.

'Ridiculous!' She stood. He stood along with her and used his height to intimidate. It didn't work. 'Nae, it's not and if you weren't such a coward about it, you'd own up to it, too.'

'But what am I to do with children? I'm not even married!'

'You should have thought of that before you got yourself into this mess.'

He walked agitatedly to the window and looked out at the courtyard below. He was quiet a long time, but she didn't push him any further.

He turned to her. 'Aye. I'll take them.'

She peered at him closely. His face was resigned, but not defeated. She was instantly suspicious. 'What are you up to?'

He smiled gently. 'As much as I am loathe admitting you're right, it *is* my fault the children were involved in my plans. They are my responsibility.'

She crossed her arms. 'Aye, then—'

'But not all messes were made by me. You made a few of your own. Some you'll have to take responsibility for.'

'I've already paid for any responsibility. You've already made me suffer enough.'

The corner of his mouth twitched. 'I have a plan, Sister, or did you forget? There is more required of you.'

He opened the door and called out. Bram did not close the door again until Caird and Robert entered the room.

Joy made her legs feel like water as she watched

Robert. He was unharmed and whole and she loved him so very much.

His hair was wet from his bath. Bram had had the graciousness to give him his personal belongings back. His tunic and hose, still black, were clean. But unlike his previous clothes, these were well ornamented. A border of black silk rimmed the cuffs and hem. Thick elaborate embroidery, all in black, blazed across the chest and both his sleeves. At his waist was the fine jewelled dagger she had once held. They were elegant clothes for grand banquets or court presences before kings.

Bram had said Robert was King Edward's right hand. She might have found him in the middle of her precious Scotland, but dressed as he was, it was a reluctant reminder he had not come from her Scotland. He came from England; he came from power and wealth.

Foolishly, she'd begun to imagine a life with him and the children. But she did not know if that was what Robert wanted. He had lost Alinore. What if he couldn't or didn't want to make the same commitment to her she was wanting with him?

She barely registered Bram's nod to Caird, but she did register Caird forcefully taking her arm. She yanked her arm and his fingers dug in, until they hurt. She moved to stomp his foot. He anticipated her move. She glowered at him, but her wrath was with Bram.

'What do you think you are doing?' she demanded.

'As I said, there are more requirements for you.'

'Is this necessary?' Robert growled.

'Maybe not the means,' Bram stated, 'but I am unprepared for any delays. I can see how she bites her lip and confusion mars her brow as she looks at you. I will not have any indecision now I've decided what course there is to take.'

'But there is no question on my part—'

'I do not appreciate being talked about as if I am not in the room,' Gaira interjected.

Robert shot Caird a glance and Gaira felt the imperceptible loosening of his fingers. But he did not let go.

'When she is—' Robert stated.

Bram held up his hand. 'I will not transgress more than a laird or a brother is allowed. But I will have co-operation.'

Gaira was tired of their exchange. Mostly, she was tired of being manipulated.

She turned her attention to Bram. 'I thought you weren't dictating my life any more!'

He scoffed. 'As if I'll stop dictating a woman's place.'

Gaira held back a few words. 'What are you planning to do with me now?'

'What you most want,' he answered. He waved to Caird. 'See that she is prepared.'

'Bram, so help me…'

'It will be fine, Gaira. Trust me,' Robert stated.

The gentleness of Robert's request soothed her as no explanation could. She didn't want to be dismissed or manipulated. But although it would take her a long time to trust her brother again, she did trust Robert.

She nodded just a bit to him before she glared at Bram. Caird sensed her compliance and loosened his grip. With as much pride as she could muster, she walked out of the room.

'When she is mine, you will never treat her that way again,' Robert stated vehemently when the door closed behind Gaira.

'What makes you think she is to be yours?'

Robert plucked at the fine sleeve of his tunic. 'You asked for her to be prepared, but it seems you prepared me as well.'

'You think I care what you wear?'

'You let me live. Marrying us is the most logical choice for loyalty.' He folded his arms. 'Why did you not simply tell her?'

'She is too headstrong. I could not trust her to make the right decision.'

'Your sister is intelligent and strong. She does not need you dictating to her how to live her life. And neither do I.'

'As laird, I make it my right and you will marry her.'

Robert chuckled. 'I cannot wait till you meet the woman you want. And even better for me if she's repulsed by your leadership and arrogance.'

Bram looked stunned, then chuckled wryly. 'As if a woman wouldn't want someone to lead them!' Bram poured them drinks. 'You defend my sister well.'

'She is worth defending, even if it comes from me.'

Bram pulled his glass away from his lips. 'You love her.'

'Aye. But that does not change who I am.'

All amusement disappeared from Bram's face. 'Aye, it does. Because I doona think you know who you are.'

'I am Black Robert. I have killed hundreds of Scotsmen. I am King Edward's right-hand man.'

'Nae, you're not.'

Robert raised his brow.

'You are those things nae longer. From this day you will not be known as Black Robert. That man was killed by my brothers days ago. You are a survivor of Doonhill.'

Robert slammed his cup on the nearest table. 'You dress me and dress her, but there may still be repercussions. Someone may recognise me.'

'Nae one will recognise you.' Bram put his glass down and leaned forward. 'What I'm to say is treasonous. Do you understand? I will speak now and not speak about this again.'

Robert waited. Bram wasn't asking for a response.

'I believe you doona know the English machinations, but I will tell you the latest messages,' Bram continued. 'What happened at Doonhill has happened elsewhere. I will not rest till my sister is avenged. Scotland will not rest till their deaths are avenged. I may be here, but this clan is already involved. You cannot be seen.'

From the Welsh Wars to these borderlands, Robert had fought his entire life. He'd known nothing else. But now he was gifted with a family and a home of his own. If he was recognised, not only his life, but theirs as well would be forfeit. Could he do it? Easily.

'I will stay my hand unless I'm to defend Gaira or those she loves.'

Bram's mouth quirked. 'She loves her brothers.'

'An unfortunate problem,' Robert replied. 'Yet, I will stay close to defend those who need my arm.'

'A compromise, then.' Bram nodded. 'Nae one can know who you once were or that you are alive.'

'One does,' Robert reminded him. 'What will you do with Hugh?'

'We will release him,' Bram answered, 'and my clan has orders not to raise their swords to him if he honours our understanding for his silence.'

Bram grabbed his cup and settled back in his seat. 'I doubt it will come to anything. You do not resemble what the legends say. Once we get you out of those clothes, I do not think anyone will know you.'

'I shaved my beard and cut my hair to—'

'Protect my sister,' Bram interrupted.

Robert shrugged.

'Ach, you can protect my sister for the rest of your life. This night I marry you.' He poured more ale into his cup. 'Are you saying you doona want my sister as your wife?'

He did, but on his terms and because she wanted to. Not because of a political agenda.

'Aye, you know damn well I do. But I doona want you to believe your manipulation had any play in this.'

Bram gave a wolfish determined grin. 'Speaking like a Scots? I'll have you loyal to me in nae time.'

Robert sought Gaira in her chambers.

She lay on the bed, her face turned away from

him. Her gown, crumpled around her, was the finest of yellow wools. The colour was vibrant against the red of her hair, which was brushed to a sheen. Two tiny plaits swept her hair off her face, leaving the back lush and free.

She did not move when he entered the room because she had not heard him. Her weeping was not quiet.

'Those had better be tears of happiness,' he stated, resting his hand on her shoulder.

She gasped and he pulled her into his arms. Her warmth and sweet scent engulfed him. Everything was so right until she cried harder.

Robert rubbed her back and pulled her tighter into his embrace. He was all strength and comfort. Gaira clung to him, relishing the way his arms felt around her.

'I dinna mean to do this to you,' she said. 'I hadn't thought of the consequences, it was just my own selfish feelings and now I've made such a terrible mess and I—'

'Shh, there is no mess,' he interrupted. 'We are alive. We are together and now, with the blessings of your brother, I can be part of your family.'

She sniffed. She didn't want him forced to marry her.

Robert lifted her chin and kissed her eyelids, each side of her cheeks, her mouth. 'Open your eyes, my love. Am I in such a state, that you do not want to see me?'

'Nae, I doona want you seeing me,' she whispered. It was her last defence against his feather-like kisses melting her worries and starting other feelings at the same time.

He chuckled and she opened her eyes. What she saw in his eyes warmed her more than the sight of Colquhoun tree.

'I want to marry you, Gaira of Clan Colquhoun,' he stated. 'Even with puffy eyes, red cheeks and paleness under those freckles of yours. I want to marry you, not because your brother demands I do so, but because if I did not have you in my life, I would have no life. So I will take these thorns in our marriage vows just as I take your love. I want to marry you if you'll have my love in return.'

'How could I now accept? I see your clothes, the pouch of coins you had strapped to the horse, that dagger. If these are things you merely carry, what do you leave behind?'

'I leave nothing behind. Nothing. My home is here; my family is here. I am nothing but Robert of Dent. The man who loves you.'

She wanted him here, with her, with the children, all so desperately. With his words, she believed he needed to be here, too.

Pulling slightly away from him, she wiped her

eyes. '"Nothing but" is not how I'd describe you,' she teased.

'Just how would you describe me?'

She rested her hand on the side of his cheek. She felt her heart splinter into tiny parts, then collect and grow even bigger. 'I'd describe you as the man I love.'

He was going to kiss her and she was more than ready.

Chapter Thirty-Two

'They would allow you to return with me,' Hugh stated, adjusting his horse for travel. No sooner had Bram married Robert to Gaira than he announced Hugh's release to return to England.

Hugh wanted to leave immediately, despite the sun setting.

Robert had not talked to Hugh for days. Everything had changed since the cellar. If he was honest, everything had changed when Gaira had hit him with the cauldron.

It hadn't been his love for Alinore that made him empty, it was the guilt of her death.

He would never forget Alinore, but he would no longer mourn her. He knew the difference in his feelings for Alinore and his feelings for Gaira. Alinore had died, but he had lived. Crippled, aye, but his heart still beat and he could still draw breath. If Gaira died, he knew his heart would simply stop.

'I won't be going back,' Robert said.

'But the king—' Hugh interrupted.

'They need me here,' Robert said, 'and I need them.'

Hugh nodded. 'So what the children came to tell me was true. It matters not if you're English and they're Scottish. I can hardly believe this marriage is real.' Hugh gestured towards Robert's chest. 'Someone breached that wall around you after all?'

'Aye.' Robert reached into his pouch. The gold-and-ruby ring that King Edward had given him glowed dully in the dying light. 'Take this to him. Tell him I'm dead. This ring will prove the worth of your words.'

'But you're not dead, Robert. I cannot lie to the king; he has need of you.'

''Tis the truth. The Robert King Edward knew is dead.'

'But what about his campaign? It's what you've been fighting for all these years.'

'I respect the King greatly, but I did not fight those battles for him. I fought them for myself, *with* myself.'

Hugh took a step back, his brow furrowed. 'That is why you never let yourself forget each battle.'

'I know what I'm asking you is great. But Black Robert and everything I was must be gone if I am to continue living here. I will not jeopardise their lives. I must be dead.'

'But I'll know you're alive. I'll know it's a lie.'

It was a risk he'd have to live with. King Edward probably would not accept Robert's death easily. Everything depended on Hugh being believed.

'Aye, you will know the truth,' Robert said. 'I can live with that. Can you?'

Hugh's smile was uneven, the responsibility already weighing on his normally easy grin. 'You're asking for my trust,' Hugh said. 'You'll always have that.'

Robert nodded his head towards the four guardsmen seated on their mounts. 'They're waiting for you.'

Hugh's gaze narrowed on the guards. Robert smiled, understanding Hugh's ire. He'd take annoyance over any more deaths. With the mistrust between England and Scotland escalating, he had readily agreed with Bram's order.

'They'll only travel with you through Buchanan lands,' he stated. 'Think of them as part of the scenery.'

'I'd rather not think of them at all,' Hugh replied.

Robert placed his hand on Hugh's shoulder. 'I will never be able to thank you for the life you are giving me.'

Hugh straightened fully. 'We share that sentiment. Without you, I wouldn't be returning to England.'

'I wouldn't want your death, my friend,' Robert replied.

Hugh mounted his horse and pulled the horse's head towards the entrance. 'Nor would I ever wish for yours,' Hugh replied.

Robert watched until Hugh was through the gates. Hugh was his last connection to his former life and he was gone. It was as it had to be. He did not regret the decision, but he did regret he wouldn't have Hugh's friendship. He just realised how valuable it was and how much trust he placed in it. If Hugh confessed willingly or not, Robert knew his life would be forfeit.

The fact was a slight darkness, but it did not mar the bright beauty of his future; a future with a fiery-tongued woman.

He found them in the garden. Gaira twirled Flora and Maisie, her multiple plaits swinging wild around her. Alec was racing around them, trying to get into the fray. In the distance, Creighton wrestled with his soldiers.

One moment he hadn't known Gaira and the children existed. The next, he couldn't imagine existing without them. Gaira stopped twirling when he grabbed her waist. Maisie and Flora collapsed at her feet.

He leaned in, his lips just under her ear. The smell of wild heather and Gaira was too tempting. He kissed her neck.

'You know I plan on having more of them?' he whispered against her warmed skin.

She blushed. 'Ach, I hope so.'

Alec gave a big roar and dived on to Flora and Maisie. The girls squealed, arms and legs going every direction. The adults were forgotten and Robert spied his opportunity.

'Shall we get started?' he said.

* * * * *

MILLS & BOON®

Why shop at millsandboon.co.uk?

Each year, thousands of romance readers find their perfect read at millsandboon.co.uk. That's because we're passionate about bringing you the very best romantic fiction. Here are some of the advantages of shopping at www.millsandboon.co.uk:

* **Get new books first**—you'll be able to buy your favourite books one month before they hit the shops

* **Get exclusive discounts**—you'll also be able to buy our specially created monthly collections, with up to 50% off the RRP

* **Find your favourite authors**—latest news, interviews and new releases for all your favourite authors and series on our website, plus ideas for what to try next

* **Join in**—once you've bought your favourite books, don't forget to register with us to rate, review and join in the discussions

Visit **www.millsandboon.co.uk**
for all this and more today!

Ex